i

II

Iris and Mo

Marilyn K Blair

KID SPIT PUBLISHING

Life is hard, but God is Good.

Acknowledgments

Cover Design

Holly Blair, Brittnie Blanchard

Thank you to

Anne Morris

Kelly Barr

Tessa Ftorek

Michael Allen Bigelow, *Lieutenant Commander, Chaplain Corps, retired*

Jesus Christ, *the Author, and Finisher of my faith*

Dedication

To Jim, Holly, and Kimberly

Table of Contents

"Surely the Lord is in this place, and I did not know it."

Genesis 28:16

CHAPTER 0

Prologue

2005

He introduced himself to Iris one sweltering summer day in Hannibal, MO, as she tended the garden in her front yard. He approached her, looked her up and down, then wove himself in and out of her legs. Iris looked down at him.

"You know I hate cats, right?"

The cat ignored her, as cats are wont to do, and he continued weaving. Iris tried to ignore him, and attempted to go back to her weeding, but the feisty feline persisted in interrupting her day. He walked up the steps to her front door and from there, he leaned over, and smacked her shoulders. He "talked" to her, trying to gain her attention. When she sat down on the ground to give her back a break, he crawled up on her lap and refused to leave, as cats are wont to do. Despite Iris's pleas, and even a little light pushing and shoving, the cat stayed put. He decided. Iris was his person and she had nothing to say about it.

Eventually, Iris gave up, stood up, and went inside. It took some doing, but she made sure the cat did not accompany her. Undaunted, he perched himself on the sill of her front picture window and he watched her every move. Iris tried to pretend he wasn't there, but she could feel his iridescent green eyes fixed upon her, as if they were a laser tracking device. At one point, she drew the curtains shut, in the hope that doing so would dissuade him, but she didn't know this cat. He made his way round to the rear of the house to the kitchen windowsill, and positioned himself there, giving Iris a start when she went to make herself dinner. This little game of cat-and-mouse continued for the next hour. Each time the cat found a new way to spy on Iris. At last, Iris surrendered.

"Okay, you win." She opened the back door.

Mr. Cat turned his head away from her as if to say, "*I shan't enter now. Thou hast offended me.*"

Iris rubbed her face with her hands. "This is one of the many reasons why I hate cats, just so you know." She started to close the door, and the cat jumped from his perch on the windowsill, landed at her feet, weaved his way between her legs, then sauntered inside.

"Now, let's get a few things straight, Bub," Iris said to the cat while he examined her kitchen. "First of all, if you're going to stay here, it's temporary. Don't get used to it. I enjoy having a pet-free zone, especially a cat-free one, so don't get comfy."

Iris turned to lock the back door and switch off the lights. As she did this, the cat made his way to the living room. Iris followed him and watched as he spotted her rocking chair, then leapt upon it. He pawed at the throw blanket tossed on the side, pulled it onto the seat, and made himself a cozy nest. He circled his creation once, then lay down, and curled up into a ball, as if to remove himself from all the world's worries and cares.

"Go ahead and make yourself at home, why don't ya? Seriously, are you not listening to me, cat?" The cat stayed put in his contented ball. "Well, you're going to hear this. If you're staying here even one night, *you* are getting a bath, mister."

Mr. Cat heard that. His ears twitched at the word "bath", and his eyes narrowed into slits, scrutinizing Iris.

"Trying to see if I'm serious, are you?"

The cat confirmed Iris's suspicions with a roll of his shoulders as if to say, *"You wouldn't dare."*

Iris smiled a devilish smile and nodded at him. "I'll be back." She continued to smile and nod as she left the room.

Iris returned after she prepared for what she was sure would be more of a battle than a bath. She wore the sturdiest pair of rubber gloves she owned, approached the cat with caution, slid her arm under him and with one swift motion removed him from the rocker. He was quite perturbed at being separated from his newly claimed comfy spot and told Iris so with language she was happy she didn't understand. She held him tight against her body and ignored his protestations as she walked back to her kitchen.

Two inches of warm water filled the sink, and a stack of towels and washcloths were standing by. "Okay, here we go." She lowered the cat into the water. He didn't put up a fight and seemed suspiciously resigned.

"Well, that's a surprise. All of a sudden we're quiet. I guess I've insulted you. Too bad. Don't think you can lull me into a false sense of security. I don't trust cats.

"I don't have any cat shampoo, but I do have Dawn and since it's good enough for ducks covered in goo, I'm sure it'll be good enough for you." Iris poured a dab of dish soap into her hands, lathered it up, then shampooed the cat's hair being sure to avoid his face.

Head up, chin out, the cat sat as if he were the Egyptian god Bastet. While he allowed Iris to shampoo him, his look of contempt did not go unnoticed. Iris rinsed him off without delay, then with a washcloth, she attempted to clean his face. The cat would have none of it, turning his head every which way to avoid the cloth.

Iris glared at him. "All right, listen cat, this is the last thing. If you want to stay here tonight, you'll let me do this. Otherwise, you're out on your keister." The cat went back to his Egyptian god stance and allowed Iris to complete the distasteful task.

"Thank you." She looked side-eyed at the cat.

Did you understand me? Hmmm.

The cat allowed Iris to finish without any additional fuss. "All done. That wasn't so bad, was it? Let's get you dried off." She swaddled him in a towel and carried him into the living room.

No sooner had she sat down on her rocker with the cat on her lap then he escaped and dashed throughout the house. He leapt on furniture, on counter tops, on top of cabinets, and bookshelves. He flung off anything impeding his progress. He was a one-cat wrecking crew on a demolition mission.

"I'm too old for this, cat!" Iris said, as she tried to chase him. She followed behind him, as fast as her almost fifty-year-old knees would allow, into the dining room, through the kitchen, through the hallway and into her bedroom, back through the hallway and over to the guest room, then once more through the hallway and into the den. Iris felt like she was playing a new game called "Catch or Replace" as she tried to catch as many things the cat flung as she could before they hit the floor and shattered.

The cat came to a halt, having taken the self-guided tour of the house, and air-drying his coat along the way. He surveyed the damage, then sashayed back to the living room. He sat down on the floor, licked his front paw several times, raised his royal head, and stared at the rocker.

"Are you quite finished?" Iris asked, with her hands on her hips. He looked up, nonplussed, then walked over to her and rubbed his head again her legs.

"Oh no, no, no, no, not after that escapade. Don't try to be friends now." The cat responded with a purr as he nuzzled her. "Seriously?" Iris ignored him and sat down on her rocker, exhausted from the entire ordeal. As soon as she relaxed, the cat jumped onto her lap and pawed at her hands until she petted him. He settled in, purring sweet nothings to her. Iris shook her head and muttered, "I hate cats."

Following their introduction, Iris made a valiant attempt to find the cat's owner. The cat was so tame she was sure he was not feral, and he seemed well cared for. She thought surely, he must belong to someone. Despite posts on social media, a notice placed on the local vet's bulletin board, and posters put up around Hannibal, no one claimed him. According to the vet, the cat was in perfect health, seemed to be about two years old and he showed no signs of disease or what Iris feared most—fleas. The vet's best guess was poor Mr. Cat had been abandoned.

Iris had to admit, he was a beautiful cat. A black coat of fur enrobed a chest of white hair and white paws, giving him a formal tuxedo-wearing look. He had the palest pink nose, and the long white whiskers on his forehead acted as arrows pointing to his piercing green eyes. He, like most cats, was very sure of himself, and had a mind of his own, but when Iris put her foot down, he would obey, much to her surprise. Even though she hated cats as a matter of principle, she couldn't imagine how anyone could leave a pet behind, especially one as handsome and, at times, as charming as this cat. He was making himself very much at home with her, so she accepted the inevitable and allowed him to stay. It was then Iris decided to call him *Mo*.

CHAPTER 1

Iris & Mo

2015

That looks like about ten miles of bad road. Let's take it!" Iris said, turning to Mo. He looked up, yawned, then went back to sleep. "Well, I like the idea." Iris folded up her map and turned off the GPS. She adjusted her review mirror, rolled up the windows to bar the dust, and turned down the gravel road. Mo wasn't much of a traveling companion, but he's all Iris had. Despite his being with her for ten years, Iris still maintained she hated cats. She had an understanding with Mo though—he annoyed her, and she put up with him.

The road certainly was bad, and there was a bit more than ten miles of it, but the scenery surrounding them was beautiful. Lush forest with the distinctive scent of pine, and the occasional pond or lake delighted Iris. Even so, her body tensed every time she heard a stone clank off the undercarriage of her SUV.

"Ugh. Another one. Are you hearing this? I hope any damage is only cosmetic." Mo turned on his side.

Five miles down the rough and tumble thoroughfare, Iris turned on the radio.

"Nothing but static. Why did this seem like a good idea, Mo?"

Mo raised his head a notch and gave her a look that said, *"Why ask me? You do this kind of thing all the time."*

She gripped the wheel tighter. "I should have listened to the GPS."

At mile twelve, the road changed from gravel to dirt. "These ruts feel like we're in a Conestoga wagon instead of a comfy SUV. Still, no clanking is an improvement. Well, at least it's not raining."

Mo stood up in the front seat and arched his back.

"I know, I know. I shouldn't have said that out loud." As soon as she had finished her sentence, the April spring sky stepped aside, nudged out of place by dark clouds. Within moments, the rain came, first as a soft shower then a deluge transforming the dirt road into a Maine mud wallow.

"How nice, Mother Nature is giving the SUV a mud

facial. Just what it needed."

Iris raised her shoulders with each whack of mud flung on the front, sides, and back of her vehicle. Her shoulders raised even higher as the rear of the SUV fishtailed and strained to maintain its forward progress. Driving through five inches of gelatinous sludge now, she kept her eyes trained on the road, and her hands gripped even tighter on the wheel.

Keep your speed constant, Iris. You've got this. Slow and steady wins the race.

"If we have to put on the brakes, Mo, we're doomed. I should have paid more attention to how you shift this thing into four-wheel drive."

Mo circled in the front seat, hopped to the back seat, paced for a few moments, then returned to the front seat.

Iris watched the miles tick off on the odometer.

Another mile down. I hope there's not too many more to go.

"What's that? Oh no, not now."

About a half mile ahead, in the middle of the road stood a full-grown, massive bull moose.

"I would love to see you any time but now. Can you go away? Can you? Please, Mr. Moose? Can you please go away?" She kept her foot on the gas. The moose gave no indication he was inclined to go away, or that he even noticed her approaching.

"Moooo, moose, move!" Iris yelled through her closed window. "God, I know you own the cattle on a thousand hills, and this thing might not be cattle, but can you round it up or something? Please?"

She tapped her horn. "I need you to move, moose. Just don't move in the wrong direction." Still, he remained still, his head down as if he were dining on some succulent morsel of vegetation in the middle of the road.

She rolled down the window and poked her head out. The cold rain stung her face. "Move, Mr. Moose! I mean it, if you don't want to end up on the wall over somebody's fireplace, you've gotta move. Now!"

When she was a mere fifty yards away, the moose raised his head, then lumbered up the embankment and into the safety of the adjoining field.

"Thanks for the heart attack." A slight shade of pink returned to her knuckles. "That was close, Mo." She rolled up the window, wiped her face with her sleeve, and kept her foot on the gas. Crisis averted, Mo curled up into a ball and went back to sleep.

Another mile down the road, she came to a crossroads and left the mud behind. "Ah, civilization!" She turned her GPS back on and made a left onto the macadam. "I think we're almost there. Remind me not to do that again." Mo yawned and Iris could have sworn he rolled his eyes at her. "We are definitely going to need a car wash."

Forty minutes and a car wash later, Iris arrived at her destination, Eastport, Maine. She made a left at Raye's Mustard Mill and Museum, then followed her GPS instructions to proceed down Washington Street. She made a right onto Water Street, went past the park, and a massive statue of a fisherman cradling a sizable fish. She passed by the Tides Institute and Museum of Art, and the WaCo Diner.

"Do you think it's pronounced *Way-co* or *Whack-co*, Mo? Surely, it's *Way-co*."

Iris drove a few more blocks, then made a left into the parking lot of the Sunrise Inn. "Stay here. I'll be right back."

Mo shifted his position, yawned, then decided it wasn't worth the effort to stand, so he turned on his side to dream of goldfish, and minnows, and moose.

CHAPTER 2

Emma

Iris walked toward the entrance of the Sunrise Inn and smiled at the slogan on the sign: "The Easternmost Inn in the United States". As she entered the inn, she surveyed her surroundings.

Looks like a movie set from *White Christmas*. Exactly how a New England inn should look. Spacious lobby, welcoming, warm.

She looked to her left at a few small tables with upholstered chairs tucked beneath them. She walked toward one table and touched the petals of a pink hydrangea centerpiece.

Hydrangeas are so pretty. And this pink gives the place just the right pop of color.

The wood-burning fireplace caught her eye. She ran her hand across the back of an overstuffed chair placed nearby.

Perfect spot for a conversation with a friend.

She turned to her right. At the opposite end of the lobby, two steps led up to the landing of an impressive wooden staircase with a sweeping turn that wound its way to the second floor.

Incredible craftmanship. Great for wedding photos, I'm sure. And a big chair for Santa would be perfect in the elbow of that turn.

Facing her, an immense front desk with a warm mahogany top welcomed weary travelers. She walked the length of the desk and noticed an oversized book on the corner.

What's this? Ah, guest book.

She opened it and glanced at the pages.

Vermont, Pennsylvania, California. *New Zealand?* They get the prize for long distance. Nice that so many people say the staff is helpful, and they enjoyed their time in Eastport. Hope I can say the same.

She closed the book and made her way to the center of the front desk. She waited a few moments, then tapped the service bell.

"Be right there!" a voice called from the office behind the desk.

A moment later, a woman appeared, wearing a black

tailored skirt, light pink sweater, and a friendly smile.

"Welcome to the Sunrise Inn. How may I help you?" the woman asked as she made her way to the desk.

"I'd like to check in. I have a reservation. The name's Iris Hornbeam, like the tree."

"There's a tree named 'Iris Hornbeam'?" the woman asked with a raise of her eyebrows.

Iris laughed. "No, just 'hornbeam'. It's a tree that mostly grows along swamps, so I guess it's not too popular around here."

"I should say," the woman said with a smile. She went to her computer and looked for Iris's reservation. "Here we are, Hornbeam, Iris. Says you have a cat?"

"Yes, that would be Mo. He's in the car."

"Cats are welcome. Just a reminder—he must be in a carrier when you bring him in or out. When you leave your room, please put the 'Do Not Disturb' hanger on your door so housekeeping doesn't let him out by accident."

"Will do. Mo's a pretty experienced traveler. We know the routine."

"Great. Well, here's your room key." The woman handed the key to Iris. Then, reaching into a jar on the counter, she smiled and said, "And a treat for Mo. You're in Room 210, second floor, down the hall from the elevators. My name's Emma. Give me a holler if you need anything.

Breakfast is from 6:00-10:00am in the Morning Room around the corner and to your left." Emma pointed the directions like a flight attendant.

"Thanks, Emma." Iris tucked the key and the treat into her pocket, then left to retrieve Mo and her suitcases.

Once she settled into her room, she fed Mo, ate the remainder of her sandwich from lunch, then took a shower. Afterward, she opened her curtains to take in the view. The afternoon shadows hung low over Passamaquoddy Bay as trawlers and lobster boats returned to the nearby docks with their catch of the day.

Mo hopped up on the bed and stood, staring at her. "Good idea." Iris stretched out next to Mo, and he nuzzled into her, purring an evening song.

"What do you think? It's a pretty town. Do you think we could be happy here?" She looked down at Mo. He was sound asleep. Moments later, she joined him.

The next morning, Iris rose early. She caught the image of herself in the mirror, stared for a moment, and sighed. "Iris Hornbeam, what is that bird's nest upon your head? That's what you get for taking a shower at night and going to bed with wet hair. No curly locks for you today. A messy bun is what's called for."

Having experienced the bird's nest coiffure more than once in her life, she wrapped her hair into a messy bun with a few quick motions. Adding a light touch of make-up, she pronounced herself ready to face the day.

She looked after Mo, then put the "Do Not Disturb" hanger on the door handle and made sure the door was secure as she left. She walked down the curved staircase, then stepped outside to breathe in the fresh air.

"Good morning, Eastport!" She took a little walk around the inn and greeted the bay from the back patio. "Good morning, bay. This is the day the Lord has made. Let us rejoice and be glad in it! Thanks for a beautiful morning, Lord. Looking forward to a great day."

Iris turned back inside the inn and found her way to the Morning Room. Emma was there, making a fresh pot of coffee.

"Emma, do you live here?" Iris said with a laugh as she walked into the room.

"Actually, I do. This is my inn." Emma smiled. "I don't usually handle breakfast, but one of my girls is out, so I'm filling in."

Iris watched as Emma went about her work with delicate grace.

Such a pretty dress, love the pale blue on her. Brings

out the color of her eyes. Her chestnut brown hair is a great shade with her skin tone. How does she get that braided bun to look so neat? I always have hair sticking out somewhere when I try.

Emma greeted a guest and the little girl with her. The girl showed Emma a picture she'd been coloring and Emma showered the artist with sincere complements.

How sweet. If first impressions count for anything, I'm sure Emma's a gentle soul with a kind heart.

Emma looked over at Iris. "It's a beautiful day, isn't it? Are you doing okay? Need anything?"

"No, I'm good, thanks," Iris said, going to the breakfast bar. "The inn is beautiful, Emma. It reminds me of a movie set."

"*White Christmas*, right?"

"Right! That's exactly what I thought when I walked in yesterday."

"Everyone says that. I think it's the front desk. It looks a lot like the one in the movie. The inn was built in 1948, a few years before they made *White Christmas*. I like to think they used it as inspiration for their set, but I have no proof the producers were ever in Maine. It's a nice thought, though."

"So, are you a life-time Mainer?" Iris poured herself a cup of coffee.

"The proper term here would be 'Downeaster', but no, I'm not. I'm originally from Kansas."

"Kansas?" She raised her eyebrows. "I bet you had a lot to adjust to moving here."

"Sure did, but it was worth it." Emma looked around at the Morning Room and the guests inside.

"That's good to hear." Iris finished making her coffee, then turned to Emma. "So, I've been trying to figure this one out. What exactly is a *Downeaster*?"

Emma laughed. "Yes, that took me a minute, too. A Downeaster is anyone from Maine, but it's mostly used for people who live along the coast."

"But why Downeaster? Makes no sense. I get the 'east'-er part, but Maine is not down, it's up."

"You're right." Emma paused, then said, "And I have no idea. I moved here in 1982 with my husband for his work, and I've been here ever since, but I never thought to ask that question."

"Wow, you've been here a while. Really set your roots in." Iris picked up a banana, placed it on a tray, then made herself a bowl of oatmeal.

"Yes, we loved it here. We bought this place in 1985 and spent the next several years renovating it from top to bottom. We're celebrating our thirtieth anniversary this year."

"Well, you did a magnificent job. Congratulations. You and your husband should be very proud." She gave Emma a nod, then sprinkled raisins on her oatmeal.

"Thanks, we are . . . were. My husband passed away about five years ago."

"Oh, I'm so sorry."

"No need to apologize. He would have been pleased to hear how much you like the place," Emma smiled and finished wiping down the coffee counter. She picked up the empty coffeepot. "Well, enjoy your breakfast and let me know if you need anything."

"Actually, you may be able to help me with something." Iris took a seat at a table. "I'm house hunting. I'm looking for a small rental house that would accept cats."

"Just for the summer season?"

You think I'm the usual flatlander. Understandable. I may not be from Maine, but I'm not a tourist either.

"No, I'm not sure how long, but for at least a year. I'm semi-retired and I'm looking for a place to call home before the big day. I've been working my way up the east coast and so far, Maine is a winner."

"You haven't been here for winter yet," Emma said with a tilt of her head. "But if you're prepared, it's not so bad, especially here on the coast."

"I'll be sure to be prepared then."

"Other than accepting cats, is there anything else you're looking for?" Emma set the empty coffeepot on a nearby table.

"I'm flexible. I'd like something small and affordable. I wouldn't mind if there was a yard where I could have a little garden, but that's not a must."

Emma nodded. "Well, normally things go quickly around here, but I do know of one house that's been on the market for a while. Seems the owner's been having trouble getting it rented."

"Why is that? Do you know?"

"My guess it's because the owner is . . . how shall I put this? He's not the friendly sort. And he lives next door." Emma made a face.

"I see. Well, I'm a military brat, so I'm used to the 'not so friendly sorts'. Do you know the address? I'll take a drive over and check it out." Iris peeled one side of her banana.

"No need. Go out the front entrance, turn left, walk down about four houses and you'll find it. It's the little gray cottage. The owner lives in the next house, the white Victorian. His name is Frank Happy."

"Frank *Happy*? You're not serious."

Is this a set up for a prank? You seemed so nice.

"Yep, that's his name. I know." Emma laughed. "And

believe me, his name does not reflect his personality."

"Forewarned is forearmed." Iris raised her cup of coffee toward Emma. "Thanks, Emma."

Perhaps you're trustworthy after all. We shall see.

Emma smiled. "You're welcome. Good luck." She picked up the empty coffeepot and left to continue her morning routine.

Iris finished her breakfast, gave herself a nod for confidence, headed out the front door of the inn, and turned left.

CHAPTER 3

Frank

L ooks like it belongs on the cover of a fairy tale book." Iris stopped in front of the cottage and studied the house and its surroundings.

The quaint Cape Cod cottage with gray cedar shake siding nestled itself between two white pine trees. Slate blue trim outlined the windows and the matching front door. To the right of the door, flower boxes hung under the picture window with ferns and flowers beginning to poke their noses out of the soil. A three-foot-high riverstone wall sheltered the small front yard from the public sidewalk.

Looks well cared for. So far, this has potential.

She glanced at the house next door. There stood an immaculate, two-story white Victorian house with a wrap-around porch. It practically screamed *New England*.

House is charming. Lawn and grounds, impeccable,

even this early in the season. Owner must be fastidious. Could be a good thing. Or not.

The house shared the same window box and stone wall features as the smaller Cape along with a few white pines lining the outer side edge of the property. Iris walked onto the porch of the Victorian and rapped on the front door. Moments later, a man opened it. He didn't greet her, he merely stared.

Iris took a moment to assess her opponent.

Tall, but not too tall, about six feet, I'd guess. Lean, his skin looks weather worn, must work outside a lot. Nice angular jaw. That nose has been in a fight or two. Full head of gray hair, lucky man. Fascinating crystal blue eyes. Looks to be about my age, perhaps a year or two older. His facial hair could use a trim. What's with men and scruffy beards? Still, he could be considered somewhat handsome, depending on his temperament.

"Good morning," Iris said with a smile. "My name is Iris Hornbeam and—"

"Like the tree?" the man interrupted.

"Excuse me?" She blinked.

"Hornbeam, like the tree," the man said gruffly.

"Yes, exactly. You know it?"

"Swamp dweller."

"Yes, you know it," Iris mumbled.

He would pick that feature. So much for his temperament . . . and his handsomeness.

She pointed to the Cape Cod. "I'm here because of the cottage next door. I understand it's available for rent?"

"Meb-be. Who wants to know?" the man replied flatly.

"I do, Iris Hornbeam, like the tree," she said just as flatly. "I'm looking for a small home and so far, it seems to fit the bill. Is it available?"

"Meb-be."

You're not gonna make this easy, are you. No worries, I know your type.

She kept her eyes planted on the man. "May I see the inside? If this isn't a good time, I can come back. I'm staying up the street at the Sunrise Inn."

"Hmph," was all the man said, and he closed the door.

Iris stood for a moment and looked at the door. She looked to her left, then to her right, then back at the closed door.

What just happened?

As she was about to turn and walk away, the man opened the door and stepped out. "This way."

He passed by Iris, went down the steps and onto the sidewalk. Iris turned and fell in behind him.

Pepper spray, where's my pepper spray?

The man turned toward the cottage as Iris fumbled in her jacket pocket.

There it is. He's probably harmless, but I'm keeping my hand on the spray, just in case.

Without a word, the man opened the cottage door and allowed her to enter first. She took several steps forward, then a step backward.

Wow. This place is beautiful. Looks as perfect on the inside as on the outside.

To her right was a well-equipped L-shaped kitchen with granite countertops, and a breakfast bar, complete with three upholstered bar stools.

Great kitchen. I could do some damage here.

The kitchen opened to the dining area, furnished with a live-edge elm table and six ebony stained chairs, with room for two more. She ran her fingertips along the smooth surface of the table.

Gorgeous. Imagine, something this beautiful in a rental.

The dining area folded into the living room which held a floor-to-ceiling fireplace, constructed with the same riverstone as the outside wall.

Stunning.

She walked toward the fireplace.

My rocker here, the wingback over there. And look at that sunlight. She glanced up at an oversized double-door on the back wall. Natural sunlight—the best.

She took a few steps into the hallway on her left, then followed it to the master bedroom and bath located toward the back of the house.

Generously sized. That nook would be a perfect space for a workstation, even has a window.

Back to the main living area, and up a flight of stairs, Iris discovered another spacious bedroom to the right and a storage room to the left, the two being separated by a full bath in the middle.

The rooms of the home were painted in a coastal palette of light blues, greens, grays, and whites.

I can't imagine he picked these colors himself. They're so calm. Unlike Mr. Talkative, this place feels very welcoming. Hard to believe it's so perfect. Hope I can afford it.

She walked through the dining area and living room, then went out the double doors to the back porch. The covered porch spanned the length of the house, and two bent-hickory rocking chairs with a small table set between them waited to be occupied.

A glass of iced tea, and a book. That's all that's needed here.

She turned her attention to the scenery beyond the house, and it took her breath away. About a hundred feet from her, the land gave way to a cliff which opened itself to Passamaquoddy Bay and within the bay, sitting regally, just over the Canadian border—Campobello Island.

Mesmerized, she watched as a trawler put out toward the ocean, causing a nearby buoy bell to clang a melodic wish for fair winds and following seas. A gentle ocean breeze brought with it the sweet scent of salt water and gave her the slightest chill.

I'd love to walk the length of this and get a good look at the bay, but better not. Grumpy Puss might not like it.

The man joined Iris on the porch. She smiled at him and said, "This is quite the view."

He nodded. "Ayuh."

"You've created a beautiful home. Would you consider renting it to me? Before you answer, what's your name?"

The man looked at her for a moment. "Name's Frank. Frank Happy."

Iris smiled. Emma wasn't kidding.

"You knew that already, though."

"Yes. I wanted to see if you'd own up to it."

"Why wouldn't I?" Frank stared into her emerald-green eyes.

"No reason I can tell." Iris stared back. "So, would you consider renting to me?"

"Meb-be. You're from away?"

"If you mean I'm not from around here, that's true. Lately, I'm from New York, not the city, the state."

"Lately?"

Iris kept her eyes in direct contact with Frank's. "I'm the proverbial stone that gathers no moss. I was born in California and my dad was in the military. We moved every three or four years. When I graduated college, I married a Navy man, and continued to move. Kept it up ever since."

"I see. What are you doing now?"

"I'm a writer. I'm semi-retired."

"Look awfully young to be retired, even semi." Frank gave her a quick scan.

"Thanks, but I'm not that young, just well-preserved. Good moisturizer," she whispered with a wink and a smile. Frank remained expressionless.

Hmph. No sense of humor. What a surprise.

"I've saved my pennies, nickels, and dimes so I could retire early, and I think the time is almost here. I've been looking for a place I want to call home. I've narrowed the field to the East, and I've been making my way up the coast." She released her gaze to look out at the bay. "I have to say, I'm falling in love with New England."

"You haven't been here in winter yet."

"True enough, but I've heard it's not so bad if you're prepared, and I intend to be."

I'd put up with a little winter for this view.

"What else would you like to know?"

"Will your husband want to see the place, too?"

"No. My husband passed away. It'll just be me and Mo."

"Moe? You have a boyfriend?"

Iris laughed. "No, absolutely not. Mo is my cat. You allow animals, right?"

"Meb-be. Is he an indoor or outdoor cat?"

"That's hard to say. Mo has a mind of his own. Mostly, he shadows me. Wherever I am, he is."

"Well, I hate cats and I won't have a cat digging in my garden."

"I hate cats too, and I don't think Mo will bother with your garden. He doesn't have much interest in dirt, and he's usually too busy pestering me."

"You hate cats and yet you have one as a pet?"

"Oh, Mo is no pet. He showed up at my house one day and adopted me. He thinks I'm *his* pet."

Is that a smile I see hiding in the corners of your mouth? Maybe there's a beating heart in there after all.

"Rent's $1026 a month, due on the first, no

exceptions. Comes furnished as you see it. Two months security due if you take it."

"So, you're saying I can have it? Great! When can I sign the lease?"

Frank held out his hand.

Ah, old school. I respect that.

Iris looked him straight in the eye and gave him a firm handshake.

Frank returned her look. "I'll need the rest of the week to get it ready. You can move in any time after that."

"Thanks, Frank. I'll plan accordingly."

"Ayuh." Frank gave Iris a nod and walked away.

34

CHAPTER 4

Ben

Iris took her time returning to the inn, admiring other homes in the area along the way. When she was a little over a block away, she stopped, startled to see a truck poised at the exit of the inn's parking lot with her SUV in tow.

Oh, no, what's he doing?

She rushed down the street and arrived at the inn as the tow truck pulled away. She ran inside. A small woman sat behind the desk, entering information into a computer. She stopped typing, and peered at Iris over her reading glasses, not moving a finger away from the keyboard. "Can I help you?"

Out of breath, Iris managed to say, "My car. It's. . . towed."

"Your car's a toad?" The woman raised an eyebrow,

her fingers still hovering over the keyboard.

"What? No, my car—a truck is hauling it away as we speak." She pointed toward the parking lot of the inn.

"Oh, it's being towed. Why didn't ya say so? Wait here." The woman hopped off her stool and came out from behind the desk. No more than five-feet tall, with an indiscriminate color of hair pulled back in a fist of a bun, the woman walked with shoulders hunched and steps that were tiny and quick.

Elf in disguise. I'm sure of it. A hundred if she's a day.

The woman exited the inn and returned in a few moments. She walked over to Iris and looked up at her. "Silver SUV? Got some mud on the flaps?"

"That's the one. You stopped him?"

Please say yes.

"Nah, Chip's already down the road a piece. Tried to flag him, but he didn't see me."

No wonder.

"Wait here." The woman pointed to the spot where Iris stood.

"Like I have a choice," she muttered. She drummed her fingers on the front desk.

The woman disappeared into the office behind the desk. A moment later, she returned with Emma.

"Emma, a tow truck just made off with my car. You know anything about that?"

"Oh, I am so sorry. We'll get this straightened out." Emma paused for a moment, tapping her finger to her lips. "Did you fill in your car's information when you made your reservation? Chip comes by every day and checks the parking lot. I give him a printout of all the cars registered here and any car not on the printout, he tows."

"You're Hornbeam, right? See, here," the little woman had gone behind the front desk and flipped the computer screen around. "That section's blank. You musta missed it."

"Great. Good job, Iris." She shook her head. "Well, how do I get it back?"

"I'm sorry this happened, Ms. Hornbeam." Emma gestured to the little woman. "This is Mary. She's my assistant. Mary, would you give Chip a call?"

"Already did. Called him when I saw him going down the street."

"Good, thanks. He'll bring it back, Ms. Hornbeam."

"Any idea how long it will take?"

Mary made a tsk-tsk sound through her teeth. "Hard tellin' not knowin'. Ol' Chipper doesn't answer the phone while he's driving, and he's coming from north of Perry. Depends on how many more stops he has to make."

"We'll be sure he gets back here as soon as he can." The worry lines on Emma's forehead became more pronounced.

"It's okay, Emma. It's fine."

Smile, Iris. It's not her fault.

She pasted on a smile. "I think I'll take a walk around town in the meantime. Get my bearings."

"Good idee," Mary said as she typed away on her computer.

"Really, Ms. Hornbeam, I apologize."

"Call me Iris, please. And don't worry, it's fine. I can manage. Besides, it's my fault for not providing all the information I was supposed to. Sometimes I wonder about me." Iris started to leave, then turned and said, "Oh, and thanks for the tip about the house. I've rented it. I'll need to stay here until next Saturday, but then it's mine. Would you adjust the date of my departure, please?"

"Sure, and that's terrific! Congratulations! We'll be neighbors. If you need anything, just let me know. I'd be happy to help."

"Well, for now, all I need is my car back." Iris gave Emma a genuine smile and thanked Mary for calling Chip. She left the inn, this time turning right.

She took a few steps down the street and stopped. A group of people were gathered on the sidewalk underneath a large poplar tree growing at the corner of the inn. They were all looking up, as if inspecting the branches.

What's all the hubbub about?

She looked up at the tree.

Nothing but leaves that I can see.

She walked a little closer, and as she did, a local police cruiser pulled up, lights flashing.

"All right, all right, what's going on here?" the officer said as he stepped out of the cruiser.

"Up in the tree, Sheriff. I swear I saw it, right up there." A young man pointed to a spot in the branches.

Cute kid. About fifteen, I'd guess. What's he looking at?

"What did you see up in the tree, Eddie?" the sheriff asked.

"I saw a black panther. I swear." Eddie pointed again to the spot.

"Black panther? Got it." The sheriff gave Eddie a doubtful nod.

Iris chuckled to herself. Black panther? You're kidding.

She took a few steps closer.

The sheriff stood under the poplar tree and looked up. After a few moments, he said, "Eddie, that's no panther. That's a cat. You need to get those eyes checked, boy. All right, let's clear the sidewalk. Nothing to see here, move along. Just a cat in a tree. I'm sure it'll come down on its own soon."

"Sorry, Sheriff. Could've sworn it was a panther." Eddie looked down at the sidewalk and shook his head.

Pretty funny, cat in a tree. Cat in a tree!

She hurried to the tree and looked up. "Mo, what are you doing? Get down from there."

"You know this cat?" the sheriff asked.

"Yes, sorry, he's mine. I left him in my room at the inn. Seems he escaped somehow. He's pretty good at that, annoying bugger." Iris stared up at Mo. "Mo, come down."

"Well, you need to keep a better eye on him. Can't have wild panthers out and about terrorizing the neighborhood." The sheriff grinned.

"I'll do my best." Iris smiled, then looked up at Mo again. "Mo, seriously, you need to come down from there. You're going to get me arrested."

Mo inched his way down the tree. He stepped onto a small, aging branch and it broke off, hitting Iris on the head. Mo jumped to another branch, then into her arms.

"Ow!" Iris grimaced. Mo squirmed in her arms. She clamped a tight grip on him.

"You all right? Let me have a look," the sheriff said. She bent her head down and the sheriff examined her wound while Mo wiggled and wriggled his way out of her arms, trying to climb over her shoulder.

"Ah-ah-ah, we'll have none of that." She regained her grip on Mo and looked at the sheriff.

"You have a cut, not too deep. Doesn't look like you'll need stitches, but you'll want to get some ice on it. You're going to have a wicked lump in a few minutes."

"Terrific. What a morning this is turning out to be." She scrunched her face and held her temple.

"You feel okay? Nauseous or anything?"

"No. I think I'm fine. It just stings. And I have a pain in the neck." She narrowed her eyes at Mo. He flicked his tail in her face in response.

"Let's get you back to the inn. I'm sure Emma has something that will help." The sheriff picked up the branch and moved it to the side, then he put his hand on Iris's back to be sure she was steady.

"Thanks." She winced as she moved her head to look at Mo. The cat continued to twist and turn, but she held him close as the sheriff walked her back to the inn.

"Sheriff." Mary sneered over her glasses at the sheriff as he walked into the lobby.

"Mary," the sheriff said in a low voice, squinting his eyes at the little woman behind the front desk.

"Office." Mary fixed her eyes on the sheriff, her upper lip curling. Iris watched the interaction between Mary and the sheriff.

What's all that about?

The sheriff kept his squinted eyes on Mary, then called out toward the office behind the desk, "Emma?"

"Be right there!" A moment later, Emma greeted the sheriff. "I see you're keeping the town safe, Ben. You arresting this here woman?"

The sheriff gave one last squinted look to Mary, then turned his attention away and smiled at Emma. "No arrest. This was a rescue mission." He pointed at Mo. "This varmint escaped his room and was up in the poplar tree. Eddie thought he was a black panther."

"Eddie needs to get those eyes checked," Mary muttered with her own eyes focused on the computer as she typed away.

The sheriff gave her a side-eyed glance, then looked back at Emma. "Speaking of checked, could you check out Miss—, I'm sorry, I didn't get your name."

"Iris," she said with one eye closed.

"Could you check Ms. Iris's head, Emma? A branch fell from the tree and gave her a good whack."

"Got it. I'll take care of her." Emma came out from behind the front desk and stood beside Iris.

"All right, you're in good hands. You take it easy now and see if you can figure out how Mr. Panther escaped his room."

"Will do. Thanks, Sheriff." Iris made her best attempt at a smile.

The sheriff smiled back, and with a tip of his hat, he said, "Ladies." Then he removed his smile and squinted at Mary. "Mary."

Mary squinted back, not saying a word, and tracked the sheriff's movements until he exited the inn.

"Have a seat, Iris, while I get the first aid kit." Emma patted Iris on the arm. As she turned to get the kit, there stood Mary, kit in hand.

"Thanks, Mary." Emma nodded and took the kit from her.

"Hmph," Mary grunted.

"Follow me." Emma led Iris over to a seat in the conversation area. Iris sat and as a sign of his resignation to captivity, Mo used Iris as a chaise lounge and sprawled himself over her lap then promptly fell asleep.

"Well, you're having an interesting day," Emma said.

"True enough." Iris looked down at Mo and shook

her head at her indolent cat. "Sometimes, Mo…"

Emma parted Iris's hair and inspected her injury. "You've got a good cut, but it's not too deep."

"It's only a flesh wound," Iris said with an English accent and a laugh. Emma chuckled as she applied ointment to Iris's injury.

"I'll get you an ice pack. You should keep that on your head for a bit. I'll get you some ibuprofen as well." Emma turned and there stood Mary with ice pack, pain reliever, and a water bottle in hand.

"Thank you, Mary. You're quite efficient today."

"Hmph." Mary turned and went back to the front desk.

"Thanks for your help, Emma. Much appreciated." Iris took the ibuprofen. Mo woke and watched, as if wondering when *his* treat would arrive.

"You're welcome. Glad to assist. Maybe you should take a rest now." Emma gave Mo a pet and a rub behind the ears, eliciting a melodic purr.

"Good idee," Iris said with a grin. "And you," she said with a scowl at Mo. "Don't go thinking you can get away with bad behavior just by purring." Mo continued his love song to Emma.

Holding the ice pack on her head with one hand and securing Mo close to her body with the other, Iris walked toward the stairs to return to her room. "Thank you, Mary," Iris said as she passed the front desk.

"Hmph," Mary grunted over the tap-tap-tapping of her computer entries.

Iris spotted Mo's point of exit as soon as she walked into the room—the window. "Guess it wasn't a good idea to leave it open, but I love fresh air."

She went to the window and examined it. "Ah, here's the problem. The screen is loose. Mo, what did you do? Must have pushed against it and squeezed through. As old as you are, it's hard to believe you can do that anymore." She poked her head out of the window. "I see. You took a walk on the window ledge, hopped to the roof, then you had a clear path to the poplar tree. You are reckless, cat."

Iris pulled the screen back into place, then reprimanded Mo. "No more of that, please." Mo ignored her and played with a shadow on the floor instead. Iris shook her head at him, then winced in pain.

Around noon, still waiting for her absconded car to return, Iris took a walk to check out the Eastport dining scene. Emma recommended she try the nearby WaCo Diner for lunch and let her know the correct pronunciation of the diner's name was 'whack-o' after all, which Iris found highly amusing.

She meandered her way down Water Street, window

shopping as she went. She passed several galleries along the way to the diner.

Nice town if you're an artist. Lots of inspiration.

A seascape in a window display caught her eye.

Definitely have to check the galleries out later, but for now, I think I'd prefer to enjoy the sunshine and take a stroll along the water walk.

The water walk is a paved pathway behind the shops and galleries which follows the course of the bay. Iris entered the walk behind the WaCo Diner. She walked by The Commons and came to the fisherman statue with his prized catch held fast in his hands. She read the plaque on the statue's base. "This statue was built in 2001 for Fox Television's filming of its reality mini-series, *Murder in Small town X*. Restored in 2005 with donated funds and services, the statue is now a tribute to Angél Juarbe, Jr., the New York City fireman who won the $250,000 grand prize in the mini-series and soon after lost his life as one of the first responders to the World Trade Center attack on September 11, 2001."

Terrible day. Statue's a little quirky, but I like quirky. And it's a wonderful tribute.

She patted the statue's base then continued down the pathway. She came to a bronze mermaid statue perched on a rock overlooking the harbor.

"Beautiful."

She followed the mermaid's gaze into the bay and watched as a sailboat drifted by.

She walked farther past a park and an amphitheater, more galleries and finally to the docks just as a whale watching tour returned from an earlier run. As the passengers disembarked, she could hear their excitement as they relived the experience of seeing whales, porpoises, and seals.

Add that to my "things to do" list.

She turned back to the path and made her way to the diner. When she arrived, she stopped inside the entrance to admire a large mural of a map of Eastport and the surrounding islands. The map displayed several points of interest: Deer Island, Campobello Island with the Roosevelt Cottage, Old Sow—the largest whirlpool in the western hemisphere, and highlighted in red, the WaCo Diner. She smiled, then entered the diner.

A waitress waved to her. "Sit wherever you'd like. Someone will be with you in a minute."

She nodded and took a seat at a booth by the windows and made herself comfortable. As she waited for the waitress, she looked over the interior of the restaurant. WaCo was a typical small-town diner with booths set up by the windows on the left as you enter, counter service on the right, additional dining space in a room off the back, and even more seating outside on a deck overlooking the bay.

She pulled a menu from the holder on the side of the table and read a little history about the restaurant. *Established in 1924, the WaCo diner is the oldest operating diner in the state of Maine. It derived its name from the two co-owners, Watts and Colwell, who built the building on the spot that was once the original "diner", a parked lunch wagon, circa 1919. The current diner sits on the waterfront, and from the outside seating area, patrons can enjoy a view of Passamaquoddy Bay and the docks on Sullivan Street.*

So that's where 'WaCo' came from. Makes sense now, but I still think it's amusing.

Her waitress, Judy, came, welcomed Iris, and took her order. As she walked back toward the kitchen, the sheriff came through the door.

"Hey, Sheriff," Judy said.

"Judy," the sheriff replied with a nod. He looked toward the booths, spotted Iris, and tipped his hat.

"Hello, again," Iris said.

"Afternoon. How's the head?" The sheriff smiled as he walked toward her.

"It's fine. Nothing a couple ibuprofens and an ice pack couldn't fix." Iris resisted the urge to touch her wounded noggin.

"And the panther? Is he well secured?"

"That he is. Turns out the window screen was loose. I put it back in place, so he should be thwarted in any future escape attempts."

"Excellent detective work."

"May I buy you a cup of coffee as a thank you for your help today?"

Sheriff Ben pointed over toward Judy with his thumb and said, "I was stopping in to pick up some lunch, but—"

"Well, if that's the case, lunch is on me," Iris interrupted, and pointed with an open hand to the seat across from her.

"Can't have you do that, at least while I'm on duty."

"I see."

Sounds like a note of regret. Am I blushing? I can feel I'm blushing. How embarrassing.

"Coffee's fine, though, and I have a minute."

"Terrific, well, have a seat."

Sheriff Ben sat across from her and took off his hat.

"Coffee, sheriff?" Judy called over.

"Yes, thanks, Judy. And could you pack me up the usual sandwich to go?"

Iris watched Judy make the sheriff's coffee to order.

"So, is this the type of town where everyone knows everyone?"

"Pretty much. One of the things I like best about the place." Sheriff Ben looked around at the patrons and acknowledged a few with a nod or a wave.

"You grow up here?" Iris asked.

"No, I'm a transplant. Originally from Boston, probably couldn't tell that from my accent," the sheriff said with a laugh, poking fun at the lack of "r"s in his speech. The waitress set a cup of coffee in front of him and placed one in front of Iris as well.

"Thanks, Judy," the sheriff said.

"Okay, Sheriff Ben, maybe you can answer a question for me." Iris picked up a packet of sugar, shook it, then tore off the top and poured it into her coffee.

"Sure. What would you like to know?" The sheriff sat back in the booth.

"Why are Downeasters called *Downeasters*?"

The sheriff laughed, and as he was about to answer, a woman's voice interrupted him.

"Sheriff Hudson," the voice called over his police radio.

The sheriff unclipped the microphone from his shoulder strap. "Hudson here. What is it, Betty?"

"We got a 9-11 about a panther on the loose by the

Sunrise Inn."

"Already took care of that about three hours ago," Sheriff Ben said with a smile and a nod toward Iris.

"This is a new one."

Iris groaned and rubbed her temples. "Mo."

"I'm on it." Sheriff Ben clipped the microphone back onto his strap. "Judy, can you make this coffee to go? And bag up Ms. Iris's lunch, too?"

Iris shook her head. "I hate cats."

With coffees and bagged sandwiches in hand, Sheriff Ben and Iris left the diner. They walked back to the inn and found Eddie standing underneath the poplar tree, staring up at the branches.

"Eddie? What's up?" Sheriff Ben asked.

"I know you said it was a cat before, but I swear Sheriff, it's a panther this time. I saw it. Black with scary green eyes. I didn't want to move. Looked like it wanted to pounce, so I've been making myself look really big. They say it won't attack if you do that." Eddie kept his position under the tree, standing tall.

"Duly noted. I've got this now, Eddie. Maybe you'd better clear out. Don't want anyone getting hurt," Sheriff Ben said with a serious look to Eddie and a wink to Iris.

"That's okay, Sheriff. I got your back. I'm not afraid."

"Good man." Sheriff Ben motioned with an open

hand to Iris. "Ms. Iris?"

Iris nodded, handed her coffee and bagged lunch to the sheriff, then looked up at her wayward cat. "Mo, come down this instant." Mo turned his head away from her. "Mo, unless you want to take a bath every night for the rest of your life or if you ever want to have catnip again, you will come down. *Now*."

Mo flicked his tail in the air, as if giving a royal wave, then he wended his way down, making the most of being the center of attention. This time, Iris kept an eye out for any falling branches. When he was within a safe distance, Mo did not jump into her arms as she expected. Instead, he touched down on the sidewalk, then wove his way between the sheriff's legs.

"Interesting," Iris said, staring at Mo.

"What's that?" Sheriff Ben asked.

"I've never seen him do that with anyone else." She shifted her attention to the sheriff.

Open face, great smile. Friendly. *Very* tall. Powerfully built, obviously keeps himself in shape. A little gray in the temple gives him an air of distinction. Chocolate brown eyes, very warm. A few creases in his forehead and around his eyes. No longer a young man, but he's got miles to go before he could be considered an old one. Sheriff Ben, you are a handsome man.

She smiled at him, then stooped, and picked up Mo. She turned to Eddie. "Eddie, right?"

"Yes, ma'am." Eddie nodded, his eyes wide and focused on Mo.

"Hi, I'm Iris. I'm new here and this is Mo. He's not a panther. He's just a big cat. A big *old* cat who should not be climbing trees. Sorry he scared you today."

"Oh, I wasn't scared, Miss Iris. I was worried for the town. You know there's little kids around here. I didn't want anybody getting hurt. That's why I hung out until Sheriff Ben got here."

"Well, that was very thoughtful of you, and very brave." Iris patted Eddie's arm. "Looks like I picked a safe town to stay in." Eddie smiled and stood straighter.

"All right, Eddie, I think everything's under control now. You can be on your way," Sheriff Ben said with a nod.

Eddie gave a nod back to the sheriff and said, "Okay, thanks, Sheriff." Sheriff Ben shook Eddie's hand, then watched him walk away.

"Sorry Eddie interrupted your lunch." Sheriff Ben handed Iris back her coffee and sandwich.

"That's okay. He seems to be a good kid." She joined Sheriff Ben in watching Eddie walk down the street.

"Great kid. He's on the autism spectrum, if you know what that means." Iris nodded her understanding. "He's high functioning, but every so often, he gets fixated on something. You've gotta be patient with him. He means well."

"I'm sure he does. It's nice he has your support."

"Everybody loves Eddie. He's easy to support."

"Sorry Mo has been such a public nuisance." She looked down at Mo and made sure she had a firm hold on him. "I guess I'm going to have to leave him crated when I go out. At least it's only for a few more days."

"You leaving town after that?"

"No, I'm staying. I've rented the cottage down the street from the inn." She nodded toward the Cape Cod.

"Frank's place?"

"That's the one. I'll be moving in next weekend."

"Next weekend, huh? Do you need a hand? I'd be happy to help." Sheriff Ben gave Mo a pet.

"Well, thank you, that's very kind."

Wasn't expecting that.

"I must admit, I could use a hand or two. I was going to check with Emma about hiring some help."

"Not necessary. I'm at your service." Sheriff Ben touched the brim of his hat.

"There's not much furniture to move, but I have quite a few boxes being shipped up. You sure you don't mind?"

"Not at all. Tell you what, I'll check in with you before Saturday and you can let me know when you'd like me to show up. If you need more help than me, Eddie's a good worker. He's strong and very conscientious. If you don't mind paying him, he's always looking for ways to earn a few dollars. I can bring him along."

"I wouldn't mind at all. That's a terrific idea!"

"All right, well, back to keeping the town safe from panthers for me. You have a good day with whatever you're doing." Sheriff Ben grinned, then walked away.

"Thanks, Sheriff."

"Ah, you can call me Ben," he said, turning and walking backward. "Welcome to Eastport, Iris."

She watched Ben turn and walk back to the diner and his patrol car. She gave Mo a squeeze, then returned to the inn.

CHAPTER 5

Moving Day

Ready for the big day?" Ben greeted Iris as he got out of his truck with Eddie.

"I think so," Iris said. "The movers should arrive any minute. Emma's here, and the panther is tucked away in his crate. Hopefully, the day will go smoothly."

"I'm sure it will. And here we go." Ben pointed to the moving van pulling down the street. "Eddie, my man, you good to go?"

"Yes, sir. We'll get you moved in in no time, Miss Iris."

"I'm sure you will. Thanks for helping out today, Eddie. I appreciate it."

Eddie gave Iris a nod, then followed her and Ben into the house.

The next few hours were a beehive of activity in the little grey cottage. Ben and Eddie dealt with getting the furniture into its proper place and sorting the boxes into the proper rooms. Emma took on the job of unpacking the kitchen. Iris kept busy answering questions, pointing to where things should go, and helping wherever she could. Mo even cooperated by staying in his crate without complaint.

Throughout the day, Iris noticed Frank keeping watch over the move-in event. As she stood next to the moving van, she glanced Frank's way.

You're keeping yourself busy today. Still hoeing, weeding, and pruning, I see. Hmmm. More than the promise of a bumper crop of roses is keeping your attention, I bet.

"Hello!" Iris smiled and waved as she passed by Frank. He tipped his chin at her with a frown.

Too enthralled with getting rid of that Creeping Charlie to say hello? Go ahead, be cantankerous. You're not going to ruin my day. I'll just keep smiling and waving at you, you old coot.

Several neighbors stopped by throughout the unloading process to welcome Iris to Eastport, and a few stayed to pitch in and help. Her neighbors from across the street, Wayne and Laurie McNamara, brought Iris a casserole. Before they went back home, Wayne helped Eddie put Iris's bed together while Laurie helped Emma finish unpacking the kitchen. Eric and Linda Westheimer, from next door, took over the breaking down of empty boxes from Ben. As the day progressed, it seemed to Iris that as the house was being filled with her belongings, it was being filled with laughter and friendship as well.

After Eric and Linda took care of most of the boxes, Linda found Iris in the storage room upstairs. "Iris, we're going to head home. I left my phone number on the breakfast bar. Please call me if you need anything. And don't forget you're coming over for dinner on Monday."

"I won't forget. Thanks for all you did today, and I will call if I need you. I appreciate the offer." Iris walked Linda and Eric to the front door, thanking them once again.

Glad all those warnings I heard about New England standoffishness weren't true, at least in Eastport.

"Will you all stay for dinner?" Iris asked Ben, Eddie, and Emma.

"Thanks, Miss Iris, but I have to get home. My parents are on their way over."

"Okay, sorry you can't stay, but I'd like to meet your parents. And you two, can you stick around?"

"Love to," Emma said.

"I'm in," Ben said with a smile.

When Eddie's parents arrived, Iris had a quick chat with them. Kevin and Charlotte Barnes were an amiable couple, and Iris mentally added them to her list of new acquaintances.

Iris warmed the casserole the McNamaras had brought by, then uncorked a bottle of wine as Emma and Ben took their seats around the dining table. "I've been saving this wine for a special occasion. It's called 'Simplicissimus' and it's from a vineyard in Michigan, of all places. I discovered it when I lived there. Hard to pronounce, but it's a good wine."

She filled Emma's and Ben's glasses, then joined them at the table. "I'm finding it hard to believe I'm going to live in such a beautiful space." She looked around at her new home. "I have to say, Frank has excellent taste. I wonder what *his* home is like on the inside."

"This place is beautiful, Iris. I'd forgotten what it was like. I've lived down the street from Frank for well over thirty years and I've been in this house a few times, but I've never been in his home. And I must admit, he's only been in mine once and that was a while ago. It has to be at least six or seven years since he visited the inn."

"Really? He paid you a visit?"

Emma nodded. "He stopped by to make some arrangements when his wife was sick."

"His wife? Frank is married?" Iris sat back in her chair.

"Was," Ben said. "To a wonderful woman named Claire. It's been seven years since she passed away. She was a real sweetheart, never had a bad word for anybody. Still can't figure out how Frank nabbed her."

"And she married Frank?" Iris pointed her fork toward Frank's house. "Frank Happy, my landlord, the guy who lives next door and can barely grunt a hello when he sees me?"

"Yep, same one," Emma said.

"Well, that's a shocker and a half. Guess it's true what my grandma used to say, there *is* a lid for every pot." She shook her head. "Well, Ben, what about you? You have a secret past no one knows about?"

"Wish my life was that interesting."

"In your line of work, I'm sure you've got plenty of hair-raising stories to tell." Iris narrowed her eyes at him.

"You're right about that, but you don't want to hear any of them over dinner, believe me."

Iris stood to go into the kitchen. "Coffee?"

"Yes, thanks," Ben said. Emma nodded.

"Have you been in law enforcement your whole life?" She poured Ben a cup.

"Seems like it. My granddad was a cop, my dad was

a cop, as were two uncles and my older brother. Even my older sister got into the act. She was one of the first patrolwomen in Boston. Seemed like destiny I should be a cop, too."

"You have quite a family legacy. Did you start your career in Boston?" Iris set the cup in front of Ben, then went back to the kitchen to pour a cup for herself and for Emma.

"Yep. Went to UMass and got my B.S. in Criminal Justice, then it was on to the Boston Police Academy. Once I graduated from there, I went straight into a beat job. I started on the streets of Back Bay, and eventually, I worked my way up to a patrol car with a partner."

Iris set a cup in front of Emma, then sat herself down. "How'd you end up in Eastport?"

"Every summer when we were kids, my parents would bring us up here. They loved the small-town feel of Eastport. I did too. The area was beautiful, and I made some good friends here. As an adult, I kept coming. When I saw the opening for sheriff, I knew I had to apply."

"And it seems you're a very popular sheriff."

"Everybody loves Sheriff Ben, especially the kids," Emma said, with a nod toward Ben. "Eddie idolizes him."

Ben smiled and swirled his coffee.

Modest guy. He's clearly uncomfortable with praise.

He took a sip, then asked, "What about you, Iris?

What did you do before you retired?"

"I was a writer. Still am. I'm only semi-retired."

"Interesting!" Emma said. "What do you write? Love stories, mysteries, thrillers?"

"No, nothing like that. I'm a technical writer. I write manuals, handbooks, research summaries, that sort of thing. You may have heard of some of my work: *Global 3200 Combine Operators Manual*?" Iris looked at Emma and Ben with a smile. "No?"

Emma and Ben shook their heads.

"How about *Personal Lines Insurance Adjusting: Orientation, Policy, and Procedures*?"

Emma and Ben shook their heads again.

"Or one of my favorites, *Summary Effects of Precipitation, Erosion, and Deposition on Landforms*? I won an award for that one." Iris laughed.

"You enjoyed that?" Ben asked.

"I did. I mean I do. There's something to be said for taking an unclear or confusing topic and presenting it in a way that makes sense. I'm learning new things all the time. I think that's been my favorite part of the work. I get to meet a lot of interesting people, too."

"Meeting people, that's what I like best about the inn." Emma stood and walked into the kitchen. She refilled her water glass. "Well, since you're almost retired, Iris, maybe you should think about writing something else. You've traveled. I'm sure you've seen things, done things. Why not write something personal?"

"Oh, I don't know. I'm not sure I'm prepared for that. That kind of writing, you have to access parts of yourself I'm not sure I'm ready to access." Then she lowered her voice and said to Ben, "Some things are better left undisturbed."

"Now you have me curious," Ben whispered, leaning toward her.

"Well, that's good writing for you," she said, with a tilt of her head.

Emma and Ben stayed for a second cup of coffee, then said their goodnights. Iris walked them to the door. "Thanks so much for your help today. Really, I couldn't have done this without you—both of you. And now that I'm moved in, I hope you won't be strangers. I think I owe you another dinner, at least."

"Glad to help," Emma said.

"Ah, it was nothing," Ben said. He lingered for a moment by the door. "I hope you'll like it here in Eastport, Iris. It may be small, but it has a lot to offer."

"I can see that. Thanks again."

"You're welcome. G'night." He smiled, then turned and caught up with Emma to escort her home.

CHAPTER 6

Garden Spot

The next few weeks breezed by for Iris. As she unboxed and organized her new space, she found herself falling in love with small town life, especially in this tiny city on the archipelago. Most mornings she'd take a brisk walk through the back streets of town, acquainting herself with the area, and on her way home, she'd stop by the Sunrise Inn to share a cup of coffee or tea with Emma.

"What are you smiling at?" Emma asked Iris one morning as she spied her coming into the inn.

"Oh, just another thing to love about Eastport. I noticed this morning on my way over here that it seems like every home has its own patch of paradise. There are gardens everywhere – huge ones that look like they need a team to take care of them, and smaller ones, like a wine barrel cut in half. I even saw a tiny one today made from repurposed lobster traps. Very creative."

"Yes, Eastporters are very proud of their gardens."

"Is there something going on today? Looks like someone's putting up a banner downtown."

"We're heading into festival season. You'll see a lot of those over the next few months. Eastport may be known as the easternmost city in the United States, and we may be the least populated city in the state, but we're also the festival capital of Maine."

"Really? I didn't know that was a thing."

"It's not. I just made it up, but we do have a lot of festivals. I should contact the governor's office and start a petition for that slogan." Emma said with a laugh.

"I'll be the first to sign."

As the spring rains subsided, and the temperatures warmed, Iris watched as all of Eastport came into bloom. Sleeping garden beds awakened, unveiling their spring colors, textures, and fragrances. Daffodils, hyacinths, and spring roses perfumed the air while other blooms waited in the wings for their turn in the spotlight. Inspired, Iris hoped to get her hands dirty in her own garden.

One morning, she caught Frank outside in his yard. "Frank, would it be all right if I plant a vegetable garden in the backyard?"

He nodded. "Ayuh. You be sure you don't stove up the fence."

I have no idea what that means.

She smiled. "Thanks."

I think.

When Emma let her know "stove up" meant "to damage", Iris went to work making a plan to ensure the safety of the fence while researching what plants would do well in this new-to-her climate. She was anxious to put her spade in the soil and was thankful to have her own bit of earth.

A five-foot high privacy fence separated Iris's yard from Frank's. Iris's side of the fence acted as a backdrop for several sea rose bushes, and between the bushes, Iris spotted tulips and hostas being coaxed out of the soil by the sun. She even found the beginnings of a small patch of her favorite flower, Lily of the Valley. If she wasn't convinced she'd found the right home before, seeing those flowers added more evidence to persuade her. Toward the end of the fence, Iris found space she planned to use for her vegetable garden, and she began working the soil, getting it ready for what she hoped would be a plentiful crop of tomatoes, peppers, onions, and herbs. She called it her 'salsa garden'.

As she worked on her side of the fence, she couldn't help but notice the tops of plants on Frank's side. What she could see of his garden intrigued her.

I bet that's dwarf hydrangea. Looks a lot like the oak leaf variety I had in Missouri. That's azalea for sure. Is that a lilac bush? What else is hidden behind this fence? Maybe someday Frank will be human and invite me over.

She laughed at the thought.

Someday came on a beautiful afternoon in late-May. Iris was on her knees, weeding her newly planted garden with Mo stretched out beside her lazing in the sun. A clatter came from the other side of the fence. She stood up and found Frank directly across from her.

"Well, good morning, Frank."

"Didn't see you there. Did I scare you?" Frank said with his usual gruffness.

"Takes more than that to scare me. Just doing some weeding. How about you?"

"Same."

"Frank, your garden is gorgeous, at least what I can see of it. You must have been working on it for a very long time."

"Ayuh, going on thirty years." Frank leaned on his hoe.

She nodded.

Today's the day, Frank. You *will* speak to me in complete sentences.

"May I see it?"

Frank looked down at the garden, then back at Iris. He stared at her for a moment, then went to the gate of the fence separating them and unlatched it. Iris smiled, then looked at Mo. "I'll be back. Do not get into trouble." She turned and walked with a bounce into Frank's yard.

Iris stood by the gate, and held on to it, letting out an audible gasp. She shook her head as she looked over Frank's yard.

Oh my, *The Secret Garden* has come to life. Right here in Eastport.

Frank's garden started with a simple grass pathway leading from the lawn behind his house to the gate where Iris stood. A few feet prior to the gate, the pathway split, and that branch of the path wove its way down the length of the property toward the bay, twisting and turning on itself so that one could not see the end of the garden path when standing at the beginning.

"You know anything about flowers?" Frank asked, startling Iris out of her silent admiration.

"A little, but not nearly enough. Frank, this is stunning, simply stunning. You've done all this yourself?"

"Ayuh."

Frank turned and walked the pathway between the garden beds as Iris followed behind. He pointed out various plants on his right and left, naming them, and explaining why he planted them where he did—this one needs more sun, this one more shade, this one needs a companion, this one is the companion.

Trumpet honeysuckle tumbled its way throughout the garden, and Iris smiled each time she caught its sweet scent. She spotted many familiar plants like foxglove, hollyhock, lavender, and bee balm, but there were others Frank identified Iris knew she'd never seen before like foam flowers, turtlehead, and blue indigo.

"What are these, Frank?" Iris pointed to a patch of red blossoms. "They look like tiny dancers, with their skirts billowing as they twirl. Reminds me of ballet class."

"That's wild red columbine." Frank moved along the path, and Iris hurried to catch up, leaving the delicate dancers behind.

Statues and fountains and rough-hewn benches waiting to welcome friends were scattered about in the beds in what seemed to be a random pattern, but even knowing Frank as little as she did, Iris could tell he placed each one with purpose.

She thought Frank had an unexpected sense of whimsy with some of his choices of sculpture and art, her favorite being a small steel sculpture of three pixies dancing on the bent stem of a dandelion.

Farther along the path, Frank pointed out which plants attracted butterflies and particular birds and which ones served no function at all other than supplying beauty.

You are an interesting fellow, Frank. Much more interesting than you allow people to see or believe.

As the two reached the end of the garden path, Iris pointed to a greenhouse at the edge of his property. "You have a greenhouse too?"

"Can't have a proper garden without one, especially in Eastport."

"May I see it?"

Frank narrowed his eyes at her. "You are the curious sort."

"True. I promise I won't touch a thing." Iris paused and raised her eyebrows. "Please?"

Frank stared at Iris for a moment, shook his head, then walked toward the greenhouse and, as before, Iris fell in behind, this time almost shaking with delight. Frank opened the door and went in first. Iris followed, then froze in the doorway.

"Come inside, close the door," Frank said in a hushed tone.

She did as she was told, then stood still, feeling as if she'd entered a most solemn and holy place. She turned her head ever so slightly to look about the room and found herself surrounded by the most beautiful collection of orchids she'd ever seen.

No words.

She rotated in a slow circle and everywhere she looked, another variety of orchid unveiled itself. Orchids in pots, orchids perched on the walls, orchids seeming to grow from small branches, and orchids cascading down from the ceiling.

"You know, you'll catch flies that way."

Iris looked at Frank, then realized she'd been standing with her mouth open. She closed her mouth, then opened it again to say, "Frank, this is, this is . . ."

"Ayuh." Frank said with a nod.

"How were you able to do all this? How do you know *how* to do this? You must have done a lot of research. Where'd you get them all? I've never seen so many different kinds. How long have you been at this? It must have taken forever. You're a very patient man. What made you get started?"

"You ask a lot of questions."

"Sorry. Occupational hazard." She took another visual turn around the room. "This is incredible. I have seen orchids in my day, but I've never seen anything quite like this."

She walked around the greenhouse, studying the room inch-by-inch, trying to absorb every nook and cranny. There were orchids with blooms bigger than her entire hand, and orchids so tiny they made the perfect hiding spot for fairies. There were orchids that announced their presence with vivid colors, and others who chose to speak in whitewashed tones. Iris felt a pull toward one orchid concealed in the greenhouse's corner.

"Look at you, hiding. I know, your brothers and sisters can be pretty flamboyant. I'm sure you feel safer here." She held her hand next to it. Its bloom was a tad smaller than her palm, with its outer petals painted a deep purple.

Reminds me of sunsets in the west. And that blue in your center? Morning sky.

Iris bent down to the blossom and whispered, "And there was evening, and there was morning, the first day. And God said it was good." She wiped a quick tear from her eye, and still admiring the flower, she said, "Frank, how do you have the time to take care of them all? How are there enough hours in the day?"

"Funny thing about orchids, they're one of the easiest plants to have around." Frank scanned his collection. "The trick is you have to ignore them. Give them too much attention and they wither away. I give them one ice cube on Sundays, and then I pay them no mind the rest of the week. Leave them alone and they bloom like this. They know what they want, what they need. They don't need interference from me."

Iris realized her mouth was open again as she exhaled.

That's the most you've spoken to me since we met.

She nodded at him, then followed him out of the greenhouse. When they rounded the last corner of the garden path, they found Mo digging in one of Frank's garden beds.

"Mo! No!" She and Frank ran toward the cat. Mo took one look at Frank and Iris and hopped the fence.

"Frank, I am so sorry. Mo has never done anything like this before. Maybe he was after a mole or something." Frank knelt and began to patch up the damage. "Here, let me." Iris stooped to help put the dirt and mulch back in the bed.

"No, I've got it." Frank snapped. Iris jumped up. Frank stared at the garden bed. She could see the muscles twitching in his face as he clenched his jaw.

"I am so sorry, Frank. It won't happen again. Thank you for showing me the greenhouse and your garden. They're beautiful." She hustled to her side of the fence, picked up Mo, and took him inside.

CHAPTER 7

First Date

Sheriff Ben became a frequent visitor to Iris's home. He stopped by to make sure all her smoke detectors were operating as they should, that she had motion sensor lights on her entryways, and any other excuse he could come up with to see her again. When at last he ran out of excuses, he worked up the courage to ask Iris out to dinner, and she accepted.

"Emma?" Iris called her new friend on the phone. "Could I ask a favor? Would you mind giving me a hand choosing an outfit for my date tomorrow? I want to be sure I'm getting things right."

"I'd love to! How 'bout I stop by tonight. We can have dinner together and then you can put on a fashion show."

"I'm not sure about the fashion show part, but

dinner sounds like fun."

Later that day, Emma arrived at Iris's and the two women sat down to a meal together. While they chatted, Mo wound himself in and out of their legs and soon made his way to Emma's lap.

"So, I've been meaning to ask about your children, Emma. I saw a beautiful photo of them behind the front desk the other day. Looks like a wonderful bunch."

"They are. I have four children, my double-stuffed Oreo, one set of twin girls sandwiched between two boys. Harry and I started our family right away and the kids are all grown now. They've given me three grandchildren, so far."

"Three? Wow. I used to think there was nothing better than being a mom, but being a grandmom. . . I'm looking forward to that someday. Do any of your kids live nearby?"

"No, the closest one is Christopher. He's my eldest and he lives in Portland with his wife, Sarah. They have two of my grandchildren. The twins, Meghan and Allison, stayed in New Hampshire where they went to college. And you won't believe this, but my twins married a set of twins!"

"You're kidding. How's something like that happen?"

"I know, it's crazy. Meghan met her eventual

husband, Matt, at a basketball game. He was a friend of a friend. They hit it off that night, and when they realized they were both twins, Matt insisted they all get together and that was the end of that. Allison met Greg, and we had a double wedding here at the inn after they all graduated. It was quite the to do."

"I bet. Wish I could have seen that. And your youngest, is he married?"

"Yes, just. He married a lovely girl, Amy, and they live in California."

"Ah, my home state. A far cry from Eastport though."

"Yes, I miss them. But," Emma tapped on the table. "That's not why I'm here. Let's get this fashion show on the road. You go get changed, and I'll clean up."

"Yes, ma'am." Iris smiled and left for her bedroom while Emma cleared the dishes.

"Okay, here's outfit number one," Iris said, emerging from her bedroom with her first choice: a loose-fitting white silk blouse with puffed sleeves tucked into a gray herringbone pencil skirt. Around her waist was a black patent leather belt and black patent leather pumps finished the outfit. Standing five-foot seven inches tall with a slender build, this combination suited her well. She did a little spin, then looked to Emma.

Emma blinked several times, then backed up in her chair and said, "It's a beautiful outfit and it looks great on you." Iris gave her a pleased smile. "But did you say you were going out to dinner or to a business meeting?"

Iris made a face and said, "Got it." She went back to her bedroom for outfit number two.

"All right, here we go again." Iris emerged a second time. She was wearing black dress pants with the same black patent pumps and a sophisticated, yellow floral high-neck blouse with a small, ruffled collar. Emma folded her arms and flattened her lips as Iris modeled.

"Okay, what's wrong with this one?"

"Well, what's right is it shows off your figure and your long neck."

"But . . ."

"But you look like you're going out to dinner in New York City, not Eastport. Do you have something more casual?"

"Yes, but I wanted to look like I at least made an effort."

Emma sat up straight in her chair and said, "Iris, you're an attractive woman, but what's more is you're an interesting woman. Don't let what you're wearing get in the way of that. Go back in your closet, pull out a pair of jeans, nice ones, and a light-weight sweater. I'm sure you have something that will highlight that auburn hair of yours. Put that on. Eastport is a casual town. We dress for comfort and practicality, not to impress. You haven't been on a date for a while, so wear something you're going to feel comfortable in. When you're comfortable, you'll relax, and you'll enjoy yourself. I know Ben. He's going to be nervous too and if you're relaxed, he'll be relaxed. Trust me on this." Iris nodded and went back to her bedroom a third time.

A few minutes later, she returned, this time not saying a word. She changed into dark indigo jeans, brown glove-leather ankle boots, and a forest green boat neck sweater with a gold lariat necklace. Emma smiled. Iris raised her eyebrows and cocked her head at Emma, waiting for a response.

"Bravo, well done." Emma gave Iris a small clap of approval. "It's perfect. I never noticed how green your eyes were before. You should wear that color more often."

"The red hair and green eyes are from my mom's Scottish roots, but I have to admit, *my* roots get a little help from L'Oréal," Iris said with a laugh.

Emma laughed with her, then stood up, went to Iris, and took her hands. "You are going to have a fantastic time tomorrow. I can't wait to hear all about it."

"Thanks, Emma. It's a relief to have the Great Clothing Dilemma solved."

"That's what friends are for." Emma gave her new friend a hug. "Oh, one last thing—wear your hair down. We may be casual here, but no messy buns on a date." Iris pulled her thick hair out of its bun, shook out the curls, and looked at Emma for approval. Emma smiled and said, "Perfection."

The next night, the evening of their first date, Iris paced around the cottage and checked herself in the mirror several times. "Why am I so nervous? I guess I have an excuse. What's it been, five years since I've been on a date? Yes, a little nervousness should be expected. I'm gonna be fine. Right, Mo? I'm gonna be fine." Mo looked up from the sofa, then stretched his paws, kneading the pillow in front of him. "You're right. Just keep breathing. I'm gonna be fine." She clenched and unclenched her hands, a habit she developed as a child whenever she was stressed.

Ben arrived at Iris's home at five o'clock sharp. When she answered the door, he raised his eyebrows and stared at her, not saying a word. Iris smiled and said, "Hi, Ben, come on in."

Ben, still staring, followed Iris inside. He coughed and found his voice. "Sorry, I, uh, I never noticed how you had eyes before. I mean, I know you have eyes, of course you do. I never noticed how green your eyes were before and they look great. I mean, they look great in that color. Sorry, I mean you look great in that color. All of you, not just your eyes. I mean—"

Iris held her hand over her mouth, trying not to laugh.

Ben closed his eyes and shook his head, then said, "I mean . . . Hi, Iris, glad we could do this tonight. You look beautiful."

"Thanks," she said with a blush in her cheeks. "And I'm glad too. I'm almost ready. I have to feed Mo, then we can go."

Iris turned and smiled to herself as she placed Mo's food out for him and made sure he had fresh water.

Emma was right. I need to thank her in the morning.

Ben walked Iris to his truck, opened the door for her, then jogged his way to the driver's seat. "I thought we could go to one of my favorite restaurants on the mainland. It's in Perry. Have you spent any time there yet?"

"No, not yet."

"Well, this should be a nice introduction for you." The two chatted during the rest of the ride, sharing what they'd been up to the past week.

Once seated in the restaurant, and their orders

placed, Ben pulled his phone from his pocket. "I'm sorry to have to do this." He put the phone on silent then placed it on the table. "Hopefully, there won't be any emergency calls, but it's the nature of the business."

"Understood. I'll keep my fingers crossed."

When their meals arrived, Ben shared stories of growing up in Boston and his early days as a beat cop in Back Bay and South End.

"All right, just one hair-raising tale, Ben. I know you have many. Tell me one, please."

"You sure you want to hear that?"

"Absolutely, fire away."

"Okay. Well, there was this one incident where a pretty prominent man in town got in an argument with his wife over some burnt baked ziti."

"Burnt ziti? And this turned into a crime scene?"

"Hard to believe, I know. Things went south quickly and let's just say it didn't end well for either of them. He's still in prison, and she–You know, I don't think this makes for great dinner conversation. Why don't you tell me more about what it was like being from a military family instead. I'm sure that's more pleasant."

"All right. I was born in California, and we lived there till I was four. After that, we moved from one military base to another, my dad was a marine. We lived overseas for a while, that was interesting. I was in middle school at the time. But we came back to the states in time for me to go to high school."

"I've never been overseas. What was that like? Where did you live?"

"We were in several countries. I think my favorite was Australia. My dad was on a special assignment there for about a year. It's an amazing place. The wildlife is something to see. Koalas are the cutest things, but the kangaroos. . . Everybody thinks they're cuddly like the Kanga and Roo from Winnie the Pooh, but those things can be aggressive. They call them "vegetarian gladiators" over there."

"Interesting. A hopping gladiator." Ben laughed.

As they wrapped up their meal, Ben leaned over to Iris and whispered, "I hope you don't mind me asking something personal, but how do you feel about–ice cream?"

Iris laughed. "One of my favorite things, as a matter of fact."

"Well, I know just the place for us to have a little dessert then." Ben settled the bill, then escorted Iris to his truck. They drove to Polar Treat, a popular ice cream stand in Perry.

With cones of moose tracks and maple-walnut, Ben

and Iris found a spot at a picnic table. "What a nice way to top off a meal. This reminds me of a place my husband and I used to frequent when we lived in Pennsylvania. They have some wonderful ice cream in one of the farmer's markets in Philadelphia."

"So, mind telling me a little about your husband?"

"No, I don't mind. His name was Danny. He was my high school sweetheart. We married after we completed college, and then he enlisted in the Navy. He died while in the service."

"I'm sorry. That must have been difficult for you."

"It was a hard season of life. But Danny was a wonderful man. I was blessed to be his wife. We had a son together. He's in the Navy too. He's an aviator."

"Well, that's something we have in common. My father was in the Navy. The stories he tells. He's got this one about being on KP and peeling a load of potatoes to win a bet. He can be a character, my dad, but he's a good man."

Iris smiled.

He's a pleasant man. Family guy. That's nice. Polite to everyone, doesn't seem to be demanding in any way. Considering what he does for a living, I'm surprised how relaxed he is, even with keeping one eye on the phone. I should be more like that.

After finishing their dessert, Ben brought Iris back

to her home, and she invited him in for a cup of tea. While she put the kettle on, Ben made a roaring fire and then the two settled in on the sofa for more conversation. Mo settled in as well by sandwiching himself between the couple.

"So, you're a cat person?" Ben asked, petting Mo.

"Not really. Mo is kind of a happy accident. He showed up at my house one day and claimed me. We've been together ever since."

"How long ago was that?"

"About ten years. Can't believe it. Some days it feels like I've known Mo forever and I can't imagine life without him. Other days, I remember why I hate cats." Iris laughed.

"Well, I know it hasn't been that long, but have you gotten to explore much since you've been here? The surrounding areas, I mean."

"No, but I intend to. There's one place I must visit— the Bay of Fundy. Ever since I was a child, I've heard stories of the Bay of Fundy tides, mostly from my dad. He'd tell me how twice each day the Bay fills and empties with more than a billion tons of water—more than the flow of all the world's freshwater rivers combined!

"I'm going to get to there someday. I'm aching to see how dramatic those tidal changes can be with all that water coming and going. It's hard to imagine. Definitely a bucket list trip, and now that I live closer to it, I'm sure I'll get there. Just a matter of time."

"I'm sure you'll get there too," Ben said with a smile. "So, how are you liking Eastport so far?"

"So far? I love it. The people I've met have been very kind," she said with a nod toward Ben. "And this house is perfect. I love the layout, and having a back porch, and a little bit of earth. It's fantastic. *And* I love being this close to the water. The view is sensational. If I go to the back of the property, I can see seals in the water! Seals. Sunning themselves on rocks. In the water. Amazing."

"Yes, and you should be able to see whales too, usually minkes, but a few years back, there was an orca. That was something to see. If you'd like, I can come over sometime and give you some tips on how to spot them."

"Really? Whales? That would be terrific. With a view like that, I may never leave this place."

Ben put his arm around her and said, "That'd be fine by me." He leaned over to kiss her, but Mo stood, arched his back, and hissed at Ben. Ben sat back. "I see you have a bodyguard."

"Looks like it, sorry." Iris's cheeks turned pink. "Mo has never been around anyone I've dated. He's not used to sharing me. Guess he's a little out of sorts." She put Mo on her lap and petted him to calm him down. "Truth be told, it's been a while since I've been a date. I'm feeling a little out of sorts myself."

"It's been a while for me too." Ben smiled. "I think I should quit while I'm ahead and get going, but I would like to give Mo a chance to get used to me. Maybe we could do this again, soon? He may see I'm not so bad once he gets to know me."

He's talking about me, not Mo. He is a nice guy.

She grinned and nodded. "I'm sure he'll find that out. Thanks for understanding, Ben."

The two stood up and Iris walked Ben to the door. Gazing at Iris, Ben took her hand and kissed it. While still holding her hand, he turned toward Mo, who had been sitting at attention on the sofa, not taking his eyes off Ben, but not making a sound either. Ben smiled and nodded at Iris and said, "Progress already."

Iris smiled. "Goodnight. Thanks for a great evening."

Iris watched as Ben drove off, then went back to the sofa with Mo. "Thanks for looking out for me, but he seems like a good man. I think we'll be seeing more of him." Mo nudged Iris's hand with his head, curled up on her lap, and proceeded to go to sleep.

CHAPTER 8

Housewarming

Iris took the last book out of the last moving box and placed it on her bookshelf. "And that's that! The downstairs is officially unpacked, Mo." Iris stood back and admired her handiwork. "I think it's time to celebrate. Let's have a party and warm this house up."

Mo crawled into a space on the bottom shelf and watched Iris as she paced about the room. "Let's see, who to invite. . . Emma, Ben, Eddie and his parents. Oh, and the McNamaras and the Westheimers." She stopped pacing. "Frank." She made a face and shook her head. "I have to think about that one."

Mo meowed.

"Don't you give me any stuff. It's your fault he's mad at us."

Mo flicked his tail.

Iris narrowed her eyes at him. "Fine, I'll do it. Hope I don't regret this."

Iris kept watch for the perfect moment to approach Frank. The two had spoken little since Mo's garden invasion. She waited for a sunny day when Frank was outside working.

There he is. Okay, friendly smile, cheery voice, you've got this, Iris.

"Good morning, Frank."

Frank looked up. "Ayuh."

"Garden's looking great." She forced a smile.

"What do you want, Iris?" Frank said in a tone that told her she wasn't fooling anyone.

"Seriously, Frank?"

This man is so irritating.

Frank stopped what he was doing, leaned on his hoe, and stared at Iris.

She exhaled. "Okay, fine. I'm having a little barbecue next Saturday, kind of a housewarming, and I was hoping you'd come."

"No."

"That's it? Just 'no'?"

Is he being rude or just being—Frank.

"Ayuh. No."

Iris sucked in her lips and stared at Frank for a

moment. "All right. Well, that's too bad. You're going to miss out on some good food. Emma's bringing her special potato salad, which I understand is very ... special, but have it your way."

Iris turned and walked away. She stopped.

Be nice, Iris. He can't help it if he's a bad-tempered buzzard with no social graces.

She turned back and softened her tone. "Let me know if you change your mind. You'd be welcome."

Frank tipped his chin, then returned to his hoeing.

The following Saturday, the weather chose to be kind and cooperated for the housewarming. Emma lent Iris some folding tables and chairs so the party could be held outdoors. Ben helped string Edison bulbs between the trees and was available for any heavy lifting.

Iris noticed Frank working in his yard throughout the day, and every so often, she'd catch him looking her way. An hour or so before the party began, she approached him once more. She leaned over the fence gate. "Frank, won't you come to the party? I'd appreciate it if you would."

Frank stared at Iris.

Is he changing his mind? Could he actually be

sociable?

He looked down and said, "I don't think so."

Iris gave a nod of disappointment and turned away.

"But thank you, Iris," Frank said in a kind tone, one she hadn't heard from him before.

Iris turned back toward him. "You're welcome." She gave him a little smile.

The party went well, and Iris was happy to get to know everyone better. Early in the evening, she found out her neighbors from across the street, Wayne and Laurie McNamara, have lived in Eastport all their lives.

"Iris, Wayne was born in a house just two blocks from here," Laurie said.

"Really? That's amazing," Iris said, fascinated that someone could live in one place their entire life.

"It's true. My family's been in Eastport for generations," Wayne said.

"So was your family involved in the fishing industry?"

"Some were. I have a couple uncles who were lobster men, others were fishermen, and we had a lot of family who worked in the sardine factories or the canning factory."

"Canning factory?"

"Ayuh. You know the building on Sea Street?"

"Oh, that beautiful old building? Yes. I've wondered

about that."

"Used to be a big employer here in Eastport, the American Can Company. They made roll key opening cans for sardines. I even worked there when I was a teen. Right before it closed, I left the factory and started my own business as a handyman."

"And how's business?"

"I'm busier than a one-armed paper hanger!" Wayne laughed.

Her neighbors from next door, Eric and Linda Westheimer, were both retired professors. He a mathematics professor and she a professor of literature. Their son is on the way to his own professorship at the University of Maine, and their daughter is a nurse at Down East Community Hospital in Machias. The Westheimers love to travel, and Iris enjoyed comparing notes with them about places they've each visited.

"I'm starting a book club this summer. Why don't you join us?" Linda asked.

"Sounds right up my alley. I'd love to. Thanks."

"Do you have any children, Iris?"

"Yes, I have one, a son. I'm hoping he'll be able to visit around Christmas this year."

Laurie pulled out her phone and showed Iris a photo. "I'm looking forward to Christmas this year too. It'll be the first one with a grandchild. This is Marie. She's all of two months old now."

"What a cutie."

"Is your son married?" Laurie asked.

"No, not yet. Someday, I hope."

"And what are you ladies discussing?" Ben said, coming beside Iris.

"Grandchildren . . . and children. Laurie just asked if my son was married, which he's not. What about you, Ben? I'm sure I should know this already, but have you ever been married?"

"No, never married. I came close once, but that was a long time ago." He looked off to the side. "I think I'll get a drink. Would you like something?"

"No, I'm fine, thanks." She watched Ben walk away.

Hmmm. There's a story. . .

The sun slipped below the horizon and the moon took its place, bathing the party with a silver luminescent glow. Ben built a crackling bonfire for everyone to enjoy, then he brought out a guitar he'd stashed away earlier in the day. He made Iris laugh when he encouraged everyone to join in singing, "Yellow Submarine", which they all did mightily.

The evening ended with hugs and well wishes for the hostess and many thank-yous for a good evening. Promises were made for return invitations as couples and families started to leave. After all the guests had gone, Emma joined Iris in the kitchen, and they chatted away doing dishes while Ben folded tables and chairs and put them in his truck to return them to the inn.

"This was a great party, Iris. Good food, good company, lots of laughs. I give it an A plus," Emma said as she folded her drying towel.

"Well, thank you, Emma. I appreciate all your help in making this happen. I hope you'll let me know if there's anything I can do for you."

Emma leaned back against the counter. "Be careful what you offer. I may take you up on that. Seems I'm always running short-handed at the inn these days."

"I'd love to help. Not sure I'd be good at cleaning rooms, but I know how to make coffee and stock a breakfast bar."

"If you're serious, I could use some help now and then."

"You say the word and I'll be there." Iris gave Emma a nod.

"Will do. Thank you." Emma put down her towel. "Well, time for me to head home."

She and Iris went outside, and Emma turned toward Ben, who was stacking the last of the chairs in his truck.

"Ben, I'm leaving for home now. You can drop off the tables and chairs whenever."

Iris gave Emma a hug. "Good night, and thanks again."

"You're more than welcome." Emma went up to Ben and patted him on the shoulder. "Take your time."

Ben watched Emma leave, then walked over to Iris. "Just the two of us. I was hoping to sneak a moment or two alone with you." Iris smiled, and Ben moved closer to her. "This was a great party. You're really good at this."

"Thanks."

"And you look beautiful tonight." He took her hand in his. Iris looked up and smiled, and Ben bent down and kissed her. They looked at each other for a moment, then Ben said, "Wish I could stay longer, but I'd better go. I'm sure you're tired and I have an early report time in the morning."

"I am a little tired, but it's been a good day. Thanks for your all help." Iris put her arm through Ben's and walked him to the driver's seat. He turned and kissed her once again, then hopped into the truck.

"Goodnight, Iris."

"'Night. Stay safe tomorrow." Ben nodded, and Iris walked back to the sidewalk and watched Ben pull away. As she turned to go back inside, she noticed Frank's lights were still on. She stared at Frank's house for a moment.

Should I? Why not.

She went back to her kitchen, pulled out the leftovers, assembled some on a plate, covered it, then went out her front door and over to Frank's. She stood staring at his door.

What am I doing? Is this a mistake?

Just as she determined it was, Frank opened the door.

"Thought I heard someone out here. It's late. What are you up to?"

"I saw your lights were on. I know you couldn't come to the party tonight, but I at least wanted you to share in some of the spoils," Iris said, nodding toward the plate.

"That wasn't necessary, Iris," Frank said, changing his tone.

"I know, but I wanted to. I couldn't have you miss out on Emma's special potato salad," she said with a smile. "Here you go." She handed him the plate. "Goodnight, Frank."

Frank stood still, held the plate, and looked at Iris. As she walked away, Iris thought she heard Frank say in a voice that was barely perceptible, "Goodnight . . . Iris.

CHAPTER 9

Small Town Living

Emma did call on Iris for some help over the Memorial Day weekend. Iris was more than happy to pitch in since she thought doing so would give her a chance to get to know Emma better, as well as meet new people. So, Saturday morning, Iris assumed breakfast bar duties, while Emma posted herself at the front desk. When breakfast hours were over, Iris came back to the lobby and began to straighten up the area.

Emma entered the last bit of information into her computer for the morning, then she stood and leaned on the counter. "Iris, I was wondering, would you like to go to church with me sometime? Oh, I guess I should have asked if you even go to church first, sorry."

"You don't need to apologize, Emma. I do go to church, and I was thinking about that this past week. You must have been reading my mind. Now that I'm settled in, I thought it time to find a church home."

"Well, I would go tomorrow, but Mary's off for the holiday weekend and with the inn being so full, I need to be here. I'll be going next Sunday though, and if you'd like to join me, we could go out for lunch afterward. That's kind of a thing around here."

"It's kind of a thing around most places I've lived. Something I've found remarkable as I've traveled around the world is it doesn't matter where I'm living, if I can find a good church, I've found a good home. And I can always count on having lunch with someone after Sunday service." Iris laughed.

"Agreed. Would you like to join me next Sunday, then?"

"I'd love to. Thanks."

Is this what it's like to have a genuine friend?

"So, how are things going with Frank?" Emma asked as she straightened out the brochures on the counter.

Iris rolled her eyes, flopped onto the nearby overstuffed chair, and let out a groan. "That's about all I have to say on that subject."

"Oh, I know. He can be intimidating. I'm glad that didn't stop you from moving in, though. It's been fun having you nearby."

Iris sat up. "It's been fun being here and getting to know everyone. But Frank intimidating? Him? No, he doesn't intimidate me."

"Really? Scares the blueberry stuffing out of me at times." Emma shivered. "How do you deal with him?"

"Same way I deal with anybody who wants to bully me or tries to intimidate me." Iris walked over to the front desk and rested her arms on the counter. "I've learned most people, they don't like conflict. And I must admit, I'm not exactly conflict adverse." She gave Emma a sly grin.

"My opinion is—a little trouble now and again is good for the circulation. So, if I come up against someone who thinks they can get the best of me, I stand taller." Iris stood up straight. "I look them in the eye. I do not release my gaze." She peered at Emma. "I speak slowly and firmly with my quietest voice. That draws them in." Emma stared wide-eyed at Iris. "And I state my case plainly, precisely, without reservation, and absolutely no hint of fear." Iris stood back and then said with a shrug of her shoulders, "Most people back down."

"Wow," Emma said, shaking her head. "I can see why. But what about the ones who don't?"

"Well, then it gets interesting." Iris moved her eyebrows up and down. Turning serious and with a most somber look, she deepened her voice and said, "I *will* hold my ground." Iris lowered her chin, and focused on Emma, her almond-shaped eyes darkening from emerald green to smokey midnight. "I *will* go toe-to-toe. I will show no mercy." She paused. "Most often things end with an apology, frequently from me." Then leaning over, she whispered in Emma's ear, "But not always."

"Remind me never to go toe-to-toe with you." Emma shook off another chill.

"Like I said, most people back down." Iris laughed and Emma laughed with her.

"How do you get your eyes to change color like that?"

"I have no idea. They've done that my whole life. My dad said he could always tell my mood based on the color of my eyes."

"Well, I'll be sure to keep an eye out for the midnight green." Emma shuddered again.

As May turned into June, Iris found another flower to add to her favorites collection, the lupine. Lupines bloom for a short period in June, only two to three weeks, and Iris saw them everywhere. While some people considered them to be an invasive nuisance, Iris loved them. Their pointy spikes of pink, purple or white could be found anywhere sandy soil existed—along roadsides, at the edge of cliffs overlooking the sea, and even between sidewalk cracks. To Iris, they were a reminder to "bloom where you are planted".

Iris's favorite's collection included more than flowers. With each passing day, she found another thing to love about Eastport. First, there was the view of the bay, and the picturesque beauty of the surrounding area. Then, the people. With few exceptions, they were as kind and as friendly as she had found anywhere. And now, the festivals.

Iris was determined to take part in as many of the celebrations as possible, hoping to get familiar with local customs and traditions. She and Ben went to the Rhubarb Festival together the second week of June. Emma joined her for the Artwalk at the end of June. Then there were Moonlight Movies and Music on the Rocks scattered in between.

"Iris, I hate to ask, but would you be willing to give me a hand at the inn during Old Home Week?"

"Old Home Week? What's that?"

"It's a celebration of Canada's and the U.S.'s independence days. It starts on Canada Day, July first and continues through the Fourth of July. Eastport hosts the largest Fourth of July celebration in Maine, and people from all over the state and Canada come. It's the highlight of the summer here and there will be thousands of people in Eastport. The inn is fully booked!"

"Well, now, this should be fun. Count me in."

This year, the Old Home Week festivities began with welcoming a naval ship to port, which, considering her ties to the Navy, Iris was thrilled to see. This was followed by a community-wide wild blueberry pancake breakfast and the Sunrise Inn was one of the host sites. Iris helped keep the breakfast bar stocked and Mary manned the front desk, while Emma and her chef flipped what seemed to be hundreds of pancakes. Iris cheered on Emma when she and the chef got into a flipping contest, which Emma won, much to her own surprise and delight.

Working at the inn gave Iris an excellent vantage point for some of the celebration's activities. She had a good laugh when she found out one event was the Annual Codfish Relay Race, where teams competed in a race using a codfish as a baton. She had more of a laugh when the race took place outside of the inn and she could see the various techniques of passing a cod from one person to the next.

Following the race, Iris and Emma took a break from the inn and had lunch together at The Happy Crab, a restaurant near the inn.

"I'm sorry you and Ben haven't had much time to spend together this week," Emma said.

"Yes, I know he's disappointed."

Emma eyed Iris. "What about you? Are you disappointed?"

Iris gave Emma an uncomfortable smile. "Yes. . . and no. I like Ben. He's a good man. It's just this dating stuff. I'm not used to it. I'm feeling a bit like a fish out of water."

"Ben is a wonderful man, Iris. Give him a chance."

"I know he is. I'll keep an open mind. . . at least, I'll try."

Ben was on duty through most of the celebrations, but he managed to take some time to be with Iris throughout the day on the fourth. At sunrise, he joined her for the annual flag raising at breakwater, then later in the day, he stood beside her for a few minutes during the Grand Independence Day Parade that marched its way past the inn.

In the evening, Ben met Iris at her home and the two watched fireworks over the bay from her backyard. As the last blast faded into smoke, Ben kissed her and said, "I guess that's the end."

She looked at him and smiled. "Or maybe, it's the beginning."

"Iris, I have the perfect event for you," Ben said one Sunday afternoon. "Fogfest on Campobello Island."

"Fogfest? Is that a lighthouse tour?"

"Good guess, but no. Fogfest highlights local musical talent, and other local artists. There's a ton of concerts, and things about local history. You know Campobello was the summer home of the Roosevelts. I figured since you love music and you love history, you'd enjoy going to the festival."

"Sounds perfect. Since I can see the island from my backyard, that's been on my list of places to visit, so yes, I'd love to go!"

On the day of the festival, Iris hoped to spend some quality time inside of the Roosevelt estate, but she knew Ben preferred outdoor activities, so she decided she'd pay a lengthy visit to the interior of the estate another time.

They made a day of it at the festival, taking in several musical acts, everything from classical to jazz to rock. Iris enjoyed the jazz portion of the programming, particularly a saxophonist trio, which she thought to be exceptional. Ben's tastes leaned more toward rock music, and Iris noticed a wistful look in his eyes while they relaxed, seated on the lawn during one of the rock concerts.

"What is it, Ben?"

"Nothing. I'm good." He put his arm around her

waist.

"No, tell me. I can see a look in your eyes. What's going on?"

"Eh, it's nothing, really. I was just thinking, remembering the old days. When I was a kid, a teenager. I had a band, then again, didn't everybody in the seventies?" Ben said with a laugh.

"Almost everybody," Iris smiled. "A band, huh? Did you want to pursue music?"

"Yes, but it was just a dream. I love the work I do. I've enjoyed my career. It's just every so often, I think *what if*. So, would you date a long-haired hippie rock-n-roller?"

Iris burst out laughing. "You were a hippie! No way!"

"Well, as much of one as my Pops would allow. I think that phase lasted about as long as it took my hair to grow to my shoulders, then that was the end of that. My old man made me get a haircut, and then he gave me some advice. He didn't tell me outright to pursue another path, but it didn't take me long to figure out that's what he meant. Secretly, I was glad. I knew I didn't have enough talent to make it in the music industry, but I hadn't been ready to give up on the dream and that hair was annoying."

Iris studied Ben. "How did you know?"

"How did I know what?"

"How did you know you weren't talented enough or

you couldn't have made it? I've heard you sing. You have a wonderful voice. Did you try?"

Ben took his arm down from Iris's waist and pulled up a few blades of grass. "I did, but it was all dead-end streets for me. Iris, it was a fool's dream. I didn't have what it took. Look at these performers, what they're doing." Ben pointed to the stage. "It's like the air they breathe for them. They could no more stop playing music than stop their hearts from beating." He tossed the grass to the side. "It wasn't like that for me. I had fun. It was a great way to pick up girls," he said with a wink, "but it was not my life's breath. When I put that badge on for the first time, that was my oxygen."

Iris smiled up at Ben, then leaned into him, and he received her in his arms. "Sad to give up on a dream though, even a fool's dream."

"That's all right, I have others," he pulled Iris close and kissed her tenderly.

CHAPTER 10

Wild Blueberries

Throughout the summer, as Iris continued to explore the ins and outs of Eastport, she also continued to try to forge a neighborly relationship with Frank. She invited him to join her and Ben to do various things—picnics, downtown parades, even the Passamaquoddy Tribal Days, but Frank's answer was always the same, a simple, "No." Then one mid-August day, while Iris was sitting on her back porch with Mo on her lap, Frank called from across the fence.

"Iris."

"Good morning," Iris said sitting up straight.

Uh-oh. What did I do now? Or is it Mo?

"Been awhile since I've seen you, Frank. How are you?"

"Right out straight." Frank opened the gate and walked through.

That's a new one.

Frank stopped and rested one foot on the bottom porch stair. "I know you like festivals. I'm going to the Wild Blueberry Festival in Machias this Friday. It's a pretty big one, and I thought you might like to go."

"Blueberry festival? You like blueberries? I guess that's a silly question to ask someone from Maine."

Guess we're not in any trouble. That's a relief.

"I've got a few entries for the preserve and jelly categories."

"Well, that's exciting." Iris tightened her grip on Mo.

I feel you, cat. Stay put. No pouncing on the enemy.

"It's a good festival, plenty of things to do and see, been taking place for a long time. You've been trying to get to know what it's like to live here, so if you're free and would like to go. . ."

Iris narrowed her eyes. "Frank, are you being nice to me?"

"Listen, if you don't want to go—" Frank took his foot off the stair.

"Sorry, I'd love to go. I'm just teasing you. Besides, someone needs to cheer on the local team. And I am free this Friday, so I'd be honored to be your rooting section."

"It's about an hour from here, so we'll have to leave around 8:30. Wear comfortable clothes and shoes. It'll be a long day."

"Okay, I will. Thanks for the tip and the invite." Iris smiled.

"Ayuh." Frank gave Iris a nod and went back through the gate.

Iris watched him leave, then she picked up Mo, and looked him in the face. "Will wonders never cease, Mo, will wonders never cease." Mo meowed. Iris laughed and put him back on her lap. She continued to rock, pet Mo, and smile.

The day of the Wild Blueberry Festival arrived, and Iris woke early. She had breakfast and took care of a few quick chores.

It's almost time. Get a move on, Iris. Let's not give Frank an excuse to be grumpier than usual.

She grabbed her purse and stopped by the mirror before she walked out the door.

"One last check. Why am I bothering? It's only Frank."

Satisfied that she was presentable, she opened the

front door, and there Frank stood with his hand extended, ready to knock.

"Oh!" she gasped, then gathering herself, she said, "Good morning, Frank. I was just on my way over."

"Mornin'." Frank gave her a nod as he went backward down the steps, allowing Iris to walk out the door. The two walked over to his truck without speaking a word and then they were on their way.

Unlike her car rides with Ben, silence marked Iris's ride to Machias with Frank. Iris gave a sideways glance toward Frank.

Aren't we being Mr. Chatty today? Iris, don't go poking the bear. Leave the man be . . . at least until you figure him out.

As they approached the town, a welcome sign greeted them. "'Machias, Shiretown of Washington County,'" Iris read aloud from the sign. "Reminds me of *Lord of the Rings*."

"Great book," Frank said. "I know everyone thinks Frodo is the hero, but for me, it's Samwise Gamgee."

"Sam, hmm? Why do you think it's Sam?"

Interesting Frank chose to break his silence with this.

"Sam's a man of the earth. He understands hardship and patience. He knows how to make the best from what he's been given. All those times Frodo wanted to give up, it was Sam who convinced him to keep going. The lore of the ring didn't sway him, neither did the likes of Gollum." Frank shook his head. "And when Frodo couldn't take another step, who put him on his back and carried him the rest of the way?"

"Sam," Iris said, nodding.

"And what does Sam want in return for making the journey with Frodo? Nothing. Not a thing. All he wanted was to take care of his friend."

"I think I'd have to agree with you. Never thought of it that way before. Sam certainly was heroic."

Frank nodded.

"So, what can you tell me about Machias? What's the town like?

"It's a unique place. Machias is the Passamaquoddy word for "bad little falls". The town is named for the waterfalls along the Machias River that cuts through the center of town. There used to be a variety of mills that the river once powered, but they've long since disappeared."

"The river runs through the town? Can't wait to see that."

Frank made the turn into downtown and parked his truck in one of the festival parking areas. He opened the door for Iris, then the two walked toward the grounds.

"Wow, there's a lot of people here already. And it's such a beautiful day. This should be fun."

Frank nodded.

"How did this festival start? Has it been going on long?"

"See the white spire over there?"

"Yes. It's gorgeous."

"That's the Centre Street Congregational Church of Christ. They started the festival over four decades ago. Like most things, the festival started out small, but now it brings in thousands of visitors every year. It's a pretty big deal around here."

Iris picked up a brochure at the information table as they entered the church grounds.

"Look at all this, Frank." Iris held out the brochure. "A children's parade, quilts, and artisan crafts, live music, wild blueberry farm tours. Goodness, there's even a blueberry pie-eating contest. Did you enter?" Iris asked with an impish grin. Frank simply gave her a look in return.

Frank dropped his entries off at the competition tent, then he led Iris straight to the church.

Is he intending to join in the worship service? Does he realize it would have started already? Ugh. I hate walking into a place late, especially church. Wait a minute, what's all that?

A large crowd had gathered in front of the church, and they were all looking up. Iris looked up too and tried not to laugh when she saw a giant "blueberry" hanging from atop the steeple. At the appointed time, the colossal cobalt copy dropped to the bottom of the steeple, much like the New Year's Eve ball drops in Times Square. A rousing cheer ensued, and the Wild Blueberry Festival officially opened.

Frank and Iris toured the various booths, admiring the crafts from the many talented artisans and sampling an array of blueberry treats along the way. Every so often, Iris coaxed a smile out of Frank, which pleased her immensely. About mid-afternoon, they took a break from the festival and visited Bad Little Falls Park.

There are several points where you can catch an up close and personal view of the falls that course through the center of town, the park being the most accessible point. Iris and Frank made their way to the viewing platform, and then to a footbridge suspended above the falls, after which they found a shady spot at the foot of the falls, where they could sit and relax.

Storms to the north the day before caused the river to rush into town in a torrent that swirled and foamed at the bottom of the falls. Captivated by the water that danced off the rocks, Iris sat spellbound.

"Frank, thanks for bringing me today. The falls are

beautiful. I'm wondering about something though. Do you know why the water is a reddish-brown color? Is there copper in the soil?"

"It's not that. The river is fed from tributaries that run through peat bogs. Those bogs are filled with cedar trees and decaying vegetation."

"Trees and rotting vegetation? I don't see the connection."

"You like tea, right?"

"Yes," Iris said with a nod.

"Well, the same thing that makes tea brown is what's turning the water this color. It's called *tannin*, and it comes from the cedar mostly."

"Interesting. Tannin. Frank, you're an amazing source of information."

"Not really. I've just lived here a long time."

"So, you were born a Downeaster?"

"Ayuh. Lived in Maine all my life. I was born in Camden. My dad was a lobstah man," Frank said, giving into the accent of his heritage.

Iris smiled a cagey smile as she nodded at Frank.

Frank squinted his eyes at Iris. "What?"

"I believe you are just the man to answer a burning question I've had since the day I arrived here," she said, pointing at him.

"Okay, what's that?"

"Please tell me. Why, oh why are Downeasters called *Downeasters*? It makes no sense."

Frank laughed. "Actually, it does and you're right, I can explain. Would you like the long explanation or the short one?"

An actual laugh out of Frank Happy. Mark this day.

"Oh, the long one, please. I've been waiting for this." Iris sat up and leaned in as if she were getting ready to hear a bedtime story.

"All right. Well, originally, the term 'Down East' referred to a boat."

"A boat? Really? Was that the name of the boat, or was it a type of boat? Was it from this area? Was it built here? Of course, it was built here. This is seafaring territory. If it's the name of a boat, though, it's an odd name."

Frank paused for a moment, eyebrows raised, staring at Iris.

She stopped, looked at him, her cheeks turning a bright pink. "Sorry. I had questions."

"I know. Occupational hazard."

"I'll be quiet now. Please continue," she said, motioning with her hand.

"As I said, 'Down East' refers to a boat—*a type of boat*," Frank said with a tilt of his head. "It was a class of schooner used during the 1800s to haul goods to and from the coast of Maine. On return trips to Maine, the schooner would travel in a northeasterly direction, or *nor'east*, as sailors would call it. Most often, the wind would be at their back, essentially pushing the schooner along." As he spoke, Frank demonstrated the movement of the schooner and the wind with his hands. "This type of sailing, when you're moving in the direction of the prevailing wind, is called 'sailing downwind'."

"Wait, so the sailors are sailing *down*wind, but they're also moving nor'*east*, so they dropped the 'wind' and the 'nor' and it became 'downeast'?"

Frank grinned at his pupil. "Ayuh. They merged the two phrases and used it as an expression of *how* or *where* they were traveling."

"So, if Downeast refers to a location, are Downeasters only the people who live along the coast?"

"Yes and no. The expression used to be a regional term and was used to refer to anyone who lived in New England in general. Over the years, it's become more specific to Maine and you're right, even more specific to people who live along the coast." Frank made the shape of Maine with his hand and pointed to his thumb". "Now it refers to people who live in the most eastern territory of Maine along the coastline. It starts in Ellsworth and stretches east through Washington County and the Maritime provinces. Does that solve the mystery for you?"

"Yes, quite."

An actual laugh, an answer to my question, and now a conversation. This *is* a big day.

"Thank you, Frank."

Frank nodded and gave Iris a small smile.

"Now, back to your father," Iris said with a bounce. "Did you want to follow in his footsteps?"

Frank shook his head. "I was right about you. You are the curious sort."

"Yes, I am. Sorry if I'm being a nuisance. Can't help it. You intrigue me, Frank."

Frank sighed. "No. I didn't want to follow in my father's footsteps. Lobster fishing is a tough life, and my father, he was a tough man. It suited him. That type of life doesn't leave you much time or energy for anything else. I saw what a toll it took on my mother, and I decided I wanted something different. But I loved the land, and I loved the sea, so when it was time, I went to college and got a degree in geoscience."

"Really?" Iris sat back.

"Surprised, are you? Bet you thought I didn't have much of a brain."

"I figured you had something going on upstairs,

Frank, but you hide it well."

Frank grinned.

"So, what did you do after you graduated?"

"We had moved to Eastport by then, so I got the first job I could, working the nightshift at the American Can factory. Wasn't exactly what I went to college for, but it paid the bills. Went on to earn my masters and a couple years later, I landed a job with the state government as a geoscientist. Traveled all over Maine doing various studies. Can't say I enjoyed working for the government, but I loved my job, especially because it allowed me to be outdoors."

"I can see how you'd like that. And did your wife like that lifestyle, too?"

"What do you know about my wife?" Frank scowled.

"Nothing, other than you had one."

"Well, that's all you need to know. We should get back to the festival. They'll be doing the judging soon." Frank stood up, offered Iris a hand, then walked her at a brisk pace back to the grounds.

What did I say? Just when I thought I was making progress. I must have offended him somehow. Either that or he's moodier than Mo. Frank Happy, you are a tough nut to crack. Bet it's going to be a long, quiet ride home.

Frank won two blue ribbons for his blueberry preserves, "Best Preserves" and "Best in Show". He didn't show it, but Iris thought he was pleased with the results. Following the ribbon awards, the two made their way back to Frank's truck, and as predicted, it was a silent trip home.

CHAPTER 11

Lighthouses & Kayaks

The summer months hummed along, as did the many Eastport festivals. Iris loved being a part of it all. With the numerous events held in town, it was necessary for Ben to work longer hours though, not leaving much time for a personal life.

"You know, I didn't use to mind the extra shifts, but you've changed that for me," Ben confessed to Iris one evening over dinner. "I'm sorry we haven't had much time together lately."

"I understand. It's the nature of your business. Don't feel badly about doing it well. And I'm sure the people of Eastport appreciate knowing Sheriff Ben is on duty."

"That may be true, but Sheriff Ben could use a vacation. We're getting close to September, so my workload should lighten up. I thought maybe you and I could make up some lost time."

"I'd like that," Iris said as she stood to clear away the dishes.

Ben got up from the table to assist. "What would you think about joining me for a few day trips? I could introduce you to more of the areas around Eastport, and who knows, maybe you'll like enough of what you see to stick around."

"You're very subtle," Iris said with a smile. "I think that sounds like a great idea. What did you have in mind?"

"I'd like some of it to be a surprise, but our first trip could be to Lubec to see the West Quoddy Lighthouse. I could put in for vacation starting the day after Labor Day and we could begin our adventure then."

"Sounds like a plan. I'm in your hands."

Ben wrapped his arms around Iris. "That's my favorite place for you to be."

Lubec is a little over three miles from Eastport as the cormorant flies, but it's a forty-two-mile drive by car, rambling along the coastline, through rural areas, state forests, and a handful of small towns. While Eastport may be the easternmost city in the United States, Lubec lays claim to being the easternmost municipality. Like most of the towns in Maine, it is small, with a population just over one thousand souls, but it's home to one of the most iconic lighthouses in the nation, West Quoddy Head Lighthouse.

On Labor Day, Ben called Iris and said, "I know it will be early, but if you only do it once in your life, you need to see sunrise from West Quoddy. You know, it's on the easternmost point of the continental United States, so that's where the first rays of sunlight hit the country."

"This 'easternmost whatever' is a real thing up here, isn't it?" Iris laughed.

"Yes, I guess it is. What can I say? It's a source of pride for us Downeasters. And it's true, so why not brag about it?"

Iris agreed to experience dawn over the U.S., so their first day was planned and they were at Quoddy Head State Park by four forty-five on Tuesday morning. Iris brought along a picnic breakfast, and the two shared a meal and coffee as the sun inched its way over the ocean.

It began as a pinpoint of light on the horizon, then grew to a glow. The glow increased to a brilliant ball that perched itself above the sea. Iris was afraid to blink for fear she would miss something as she watched the sun's rays shoot across the waves, turning the black water into a glimmering mirror.

As if nature's alarm clock had sounded, the fish and fowl awoke to begin their day. The silence that surrounded them in the darkness was now replaced by the laughter of herring gulls soaring overhead and the peeps of arctic terns. Iris watched the cormorants, their iridescent black feathers slick against their bodies as they dove underwater, then emerged several feet away with a fish wriggling in their hooked beak.

"You were right, Ben, this is well worth the early rise," Iris said as she marveled at the heavens transitioning from deep purple to pink to blue.

Once the morning sun filled the sky, the couple went on a leisurely hike along the coastal trail. From their vantage point, they could see seals sunning themselves on the rocks below, some peeking their heads out of the sea as if they were playing a game of Marco Polo. A cormorant perched on the tip of a pointed rock, its wings splayed out in the wind to dry, fascinated Iris. Her attention shifted to the sky as a raft of eiders flew by.

Ben found a bench carved out of a boulder on the side of the trail. The two took time to sit and watch the waves buffet the craggy shore as rhythmically as a heartbeat. The sweet aroma of wild sea roses mixed with the salty scent of the ocean perfumed the air. Ben put his arm around Iris, and she felt as if she could cry from sensory overload. He pulled her close and pressed his lips into hers. Iris nestled herself under Ben's arm and they rested for a while, then Ben took her hand, and they rejoined the trail.

When they reached the trail's end, they visited the West Quoddy Head Lighthouse, which is the only lighthouse in the United States with a candy-striped tower. And as Iris had guessed, it is also the easternmost lighthouse in the United States.

A park ranger stationed himself outside of the museum that day, and once Iris spotted him, her journalist's mind kicked into gear.

"Good morning, sir," Iris said.

"Morning. Thanks for visiting the lighthouse today," the ranger said.

"Tell me, is it still operational?"

"Yes, it is."

"So, there's a lightkeeper here?"

"No, not anymore. The lighthouse is automated now, so a lightkeeper is no longer necessary."

"I guess that's a good thing. Shame that it sits empty though."

"Oh, it's not empty. There's a museum on the first floor and my family lives in the apartment on the second floor."

"You don't say! Well, that's fascinating." That prompted a peppering of questions from Iris. After a few minutes, Ben interrupted.

"Iris, did you know you can spot seals off the coast here? Let's go see if we can find one." Ben led Iris away from the ranger.

"Nicely done," Iris said with a smile.

"What's that?"

"I can get carried away with questions. I appreciate your polite intervention."

"Sorry if I offended you."

"No offense taken. I know how I can be, and I know you mean well."

"Good. The last thing I'd want to do is offend you."

He is a good man. Keep the door open, Iris.

After lunch, they decided to take one more hike, the trail to Bog Brook Cove Preserve. The hike went through a quiet part of the woods, so quiet at one point, Iris stopped, and closed her eyes.

"Keep your eyes closed and take a deep breath," Ben said softly. "Listen."

Iris obliged and breathed in the scent of the white pines surrounding her and listened to the gentle breeze sifting through their needles.

"Places like this," Ben whispered. "They remind me

of that old hymn. You know the one, 'When through the woods, and forest glades I wander . . . then sings my soul, my Savior God to Thee, how great Thou art.'" Iris nodded. Ben took her hands as they stood in silence, each taking a moment to thank their Creator for the peace and beauty that surrounded them.

After such a full day, Iris was happy to get home and spend a little time with Mo before heading to bed. "What a great day, Mo. The sunrise, the ocean, the hikes. Beautiful. Day one of exploration, a success. And Ben, he's a good man. There are times when we're together that I couldn't be happier, but there are other times . . . Oh, I don't know. I'm tired. Let's go to bed, there's another big day coming tomorrow."

The next morning was another early rise for Iris and Ben as they traveled inland to Moosehead Lake. Forty miles long, Moosehead is the largest lake in Maine, covering nearly seventy-five thousand acres. Over the years, Ben spent a great deal of time at Moosehead camping, kayaking, and hiking.

"When we get to the lake, would you like to go on a cruise on the steamship Katahdin? It's a historic vessel and you get a great view of the lake and surrounding shore areas."

"I'd love a cruise! Especially on a historic ship.

Sounds like fun."

They arrived at Moosehead in time to take a brief stroll around the town before boarding the ship. Once onboard, Iris stood by the rail. A soft breeze caressed her face as the ship set out. Ben joined her, and they stood side-by-side, arms around each other. Ben pointed out Mount Kineo, which rises from the eastern shore of the lake and in the far-off distance, Mount Katahdin, two places he spent many hours hiking. Iris watched Ben as he spoke of these places, as if they were old friends.

Ben stopped and looked at Iris for a moment. "What is it? What are you thinking in that red head of yours?"

Iris smiled and looked at Mount Kineo. "I was thinking, it must be nice to have spent so long in one place. To have that kind of foundation, that sense of belonging."

Ben nodded. "I never really thought about it, but yes, it is nice. It's nice to belong." He pulled Iris close, and she settled into the comfort of his body.

The next evening over dinner, Ben told Iris about the surprise he planned for her.

"The Bay of Fundy? You're taking me to the Bay of Fundy?"

"I thought it was high time you see it. Let's get that crossed off your bucket list."

Could he be any nicer to me?

"Now, the thing is this trip will require more hours than we can fit in one day," Ben said. "We'll have to stay there, but don't worry. I've booked two rooms at a bed-and-breakfast, and I promise, I'll be a gentleman."

"When are you not?" Iris said, kissing Ben on the cheek. "The Bay of Fundy. What an amazing surprise. Thank you. I can't wait!"

Ben planned out a full day for the two of them. They would begin at the Fundy Tidal Interpretive Center early in the morning for an introduction to the Bay and a brief look at high tide. He picked up Iris and the couple chatted about their adventures earlier in the week and they wondered what this day would hold. Once they arrived, Iris felt like her insides were a bottle of soda someone had shaken up.

"I'm so excited I could burst. Thank you for this, Ben." She gave Ben a hug then took his arm as they made their way into the Interpretive Center.

Once inside, Iris read every word from every display, or at least she wanted to. Though he followed behind her without complaint as she went from display to display, Iris could tell Ben would prefer to be outside exploring.

He's bored. He's been very patient with me though.

"Come with me." Iris took Ben's hand.

"Where to? You're not done here yet."

"I'm done for now. Let's go outside."

Ben smiled and squeezed Iris's hand. Together they went to the observation deck, a former trestle bridge that had been transformed into a platform. The deck provided a spectacular view of the Shubenacadie River and its red clay slopes.

While viewing the river, Ben caught sight of a Great Blue Heron soaring over the landscape and pointed it out to Iris. She watched the elegant bird as he glided over the river. He landed, stood on the shore for a few moments, scooped up a fish, then took flight. Iris shook her head in wonder as a thousand questions about herons, the river, and the bay formed in her head.

While Iris was happiest taking in new information from whatever source was available, she knew Ben would be happiest when they were on the river kayaking. Ben was an experienced kayaker, but given the tidal changes and the precarious conditions that can result he suggested they take a guided kayaking tour.

"I'm so glad you booked us a guided tour and a two-person kayak. I've only been kayaking a few times, and it's a relief knowing I won't be left to my own devices. I'd much prefer to share a kayak with you."

"Well, I'm usually a loner, but I think I can make an exception for you . . . this one time," Ben said with a wink. "You don't have to worry. I'll take care of you, Iris."

They began their tour at Hopewell Rocks Park with their tour guide, Jack Jackson. An experienced guide, Jack told story after story about the Bay of Fundy, its history, and its value to the local communities as they paddled along in the Bay. He sprinkled those stories with anecdotes of some of the ludicrous things tourists have done over the past years.

Pay attention, Iris, you will not become another entry in Jack's diary, *Stupid Things Tourists Do.*

Following Jack's lead, they paddled near the sea stacks called "The Flowerpot Rocks". The stacks, standing like amoebic pillars ascending from the sea floor to the sky, have been carved out of the Bay of Fundy's sandstone cliffs by the rising and falling tides. These pillars were given the nickname "flowerpot" because the trees on top of the brown stacks resemble plants growing in clay pots.

Not limiting itself to pillar shapes, the tides also carved out arches, one of which was on their tour. The color and shape of the rocks fascinated Iris and she marveled at the stacks and archway as Ben steered the kayak in, out, around, and through them.

Toward the end of the tour, Jack shared the

Mi'kmaq legend of the Bay and the tides. "The Mi'kmaq are the indigenous people of the area and were among the original inhabitants of the Atlantic provinces of Canada. The legend says in ancient times, Mi'kmaq people were slaves of angry whales who resided in the bay. One day, some slaves tried to escape but only made it as far as the beach before being turned into stone by their whale captors. It's said those slaves remain encased in the rock formations still today."

As they paddled by, Iris let her imagination roam through the rock formations, looking for any evidence of Mi'kmaq slaves . . . and angry whales.

Following the tour, Ben and Iris stopped for a cup of coffee by a seaside cafe, waiting for the tide to go out before heading back to the bed-and-breakfast.

"Are you enjoying yourself?" Ben asked as he pulled a chair out for Iris.

"Absolutely, this place is fascinating. Can't wait to see what low tide is like. I've lived in a lot of different places in my life, but I can't think of anywhere as unusual as this."

"Have you ever totaled up how many places you've lived?" Ben asked as he sat down.

"No, and honestly, I don't think I could remember them all, if I tried."

"I understand why you moved so much when you

were a kid, and when you were married, but why keep moving after your husband was gone?"

"I don't know." Iris looked out at the bay. "I knew I wanted to move after Danny died because I wanted to remove myself from all that happened, and I wanted to be near family. I moved closer to my sister at first, which was helpful since my son had just turned two. She was so good with him and with me. We'd been there a couple of years when I got an offer for a fantastic writing job, but it required a move. I thought it would be worth the upheaval, so I accepted, and off we went. After that, it was either my work or me getting restless that made us pick up and move again. When my son got into high school, I promised him we would stay put until after he graduated. Other than when I was in college, that was the longest I've ever lived in one place."

"Was it hard on him? Moving around so much?"

"Maybe. Probably. I guess so." Iris blew on her coffee, as if blowing away a distant memory. "I didn't think too much about it at the time. It's how I grew up, it's what I knew. And while it is difficult at times, there are a lot of pluses. You get to see a lot of places, meet a lot of different people, experience different cultures. You learn how to be independent. My son knows how to meet people. He knows how to connect, where to spend his time wisely. He's a lot better at it than I am," Iris said with a smile. "After he enlisted in the Navy, I thought it was time to move again, and I've been moving ever since."

Ben took Iris's hand. "Don't you get tired of it?"

"Sometimes. The last few moves have been hard, physically. I don't like to admit it, but I need to slow down and find that one place to stay. The thought frightens me, though."

"Why? I'm surprised anything frightens you."

"Ah, it's an act." Iris waved her hand at herself. "I know how to seem fearless, but I don't know how to set my roots in one place." Iris paused and looked out at the bay again. "I don't know how real friendships work. What if I can't do it?"

Even though she could feel tears welling up, she continued, almost in a whisper. "What if . . . what if the reason I keep moving is I'm not meant to have friends or build relationships?"

Ben put his other hand on top of Iris's. "I don't think you need to worry about that. I've only known you a few months, but I could tell in the first week you knew how to read people, how to find out what they needed, and then how to meet that need. You know how to build relationships. You've been doing it all your life. You just didn't realize it."

Iris smiled and nodded. "Well, we'd better be going if we don't want to miss low tide."

CHAPTER 12

The Earring

I am so stiff today! Ibuprofen, you are my new best friend. I'm sorry Ben had an emergency, but my body is grateful for the reprieve," Iris said as she put on a sweater.

The Bay of Fundy was the last day trip Ben and Iris shared. Ben planned one more excursion inland for them, but there was an emergency in town, so he had to call it off.

Iris gave Mo a pet, then made herself a cup of tea. She grabbed a book, and her tea, and headed for the back porch with Mo.

"A little sunshine, a good book, and a friend." She petted Mo. "All is right with the world. Or at least it will be as soon as the ibuprofen kicks in."

After a weekend of rest, Iris felt like herself again

and decided it was time to address one area in her home she'd been ignoring.

"Well, Mo, I think it's time to get that storage area straightened up. Haven't been up there since we moved in, and I want to take care of it before cold weather arrives. The leaves are already falling, so let's get it organized." Iris put away her breakfast dishes, then climbed the stairs to the second-floor storage room with Mo following at her heels.

"My mom used to say, 'The best way to get something done is to begin.' So, let's begin." Iris put her head down and went to work. From her many moves, she learned the value of having few possessions, so there wouldn't be much to organize. She thought she would just need a few hours to set things in order. Well on her way to completing her task, she noticed Mo pawing at something in the corner.

"That better not be a mouse. And if it is, don't even think about bringing it to me as a present." Iris walked over to investigate, and on her way, she picked up a tennis racket, should a weapon be required. Mo sat up straight, his tail flicking like a flagman, warning something was amiss. Iris approached with caution.

She looked in the corner and didn't see anything moving, so she put the tennis racket down, took out her phone, and turned on the flashlight. As she shone the light in the corner, she noticed a sparkle on the floor. She bent down and found a beautiful teardrop diamond earring. She scanned the area with the flashlight to be sure there wasn't another, then sat on the floor, staring at the earring. Mo rubbed up against her side, then curled up on her lap.

"Well, what do you think of this, Mo?" Iris held the earring up to the light from the window. "It's beautiful. How'd it get up here? I bet a previous renter lost it. Wait." Iris pulled herself up, sending Mo scurrying. She went to the window, looked out and saw Frank in his backyard raking leaves. She tucked her phone in her back pocket, secured the earring in her hand, and hurried out of the storage room. She left the house and went straight to Frank's backyard. As she came through the garden gate, he looked up and stopped his raking.

"Hi, Frank. I found something, and I think it may belong to you, or at least with you," Iris said, with a wide grin. She held out her hand to show Frank the earring.

Frank's face grew white, then red. He snatched the earring out of Iris's hand. "Where did you find this?"

Frank's gesture startled her. "In the storage room upstairs."

"How long have you had it?" Frank's tone was as sharp as the look he gave Iris.

"I just found it, just now. I went up to do some

organizing. Mo came with me, and he was pawing at something in the corner. I thought it might be a mouse."

"Of course, *Mo*," Frank sneered.

Careful, Frank. That's *my* cat you're talking about. I'm the only one who gets to dislike him.

She glared at Frank. "I went over and saw something shiny. This was it. I picked it up, realized it probably belonged with you, and I brought it to you. End of story."

I'm beginning to think I shouldn't have bothered showing it to you.

Frank jutted his chin out. "What do you know about where it belongs?"

"Frank, I didn't mean anything by that. It's an earring. It was in your house. I thought it could have belonged to your wife."

Frank stared at the earring in his hand, then curled his fingers around it. Iris caught his motion.

It was, wasn't it.

She gave him a moment, then asked, "Was it hers?"

"What business is it of yours?" The venom with which he spit out these words caused Iris to shudder.

"None. I just thought considering your loss—"

"What do you know about my loss? About *any* loss? You and that cat of yours. You know nothing. Mind your own business, Iris."

144

Iris inhaled at the shock of Frank's tone and took a step backward. "I'm sorry, Frank. I didn't mean to upset you." She looked at Frank's hand and nodded. "You have the earring. I'll leave you be." She turned and hurried back to her house.

Once inside, she closed the door and leaned on it for a moment, then paced back and forth in the living room, hot tears stinging her eyes.

Of all the selfish, hard-nosed, bad-tempered men. What nerve. Why did you let him talk to you like that? What is wrong with you? What's wrong with *him*?

A few minutes later, there was a knock on the back door. Iris wiped her eyes. She went to the door and opened it to find Frank standing on the porch. She stared at him, lowered her chin, and pressed her lips together. Her eyes turned from emerald to midnight green. She waited.

"Iris, I'm sorry but—,"

Iris lifted her chin and interrupted. "My mother always told me to never allow the word 'but' to follow the words 'I'm sorry'. If you do, you're not apologizing. You're making an excuse." Frank looked down.

"I'm not sure what I've done to you, Frank. I've tried to be friendly since the first day we met, but you don't make it easy. I can barely get a civil word out of you most days. I've met some hard sorts in my time, but you take the cake.

"You have no right to speak to me as you did. No right. You don't think I know anything about loss? You don't know me. You have no idea what I've been through, what I've experienced. You know nothing about me and yet you choose to be my judge? How dare you.

"You stay in your backyard, leaning on your hoe as if it's a great scepter and you, the amazing vizier casting aspersions on anyone who dares look at you, much less speak to you, or God forbid, attempt to be kind to you." She stopped. Her body shook, and she began to clench and unclench her hands.

Frank looked up at her, his brow furrowed. Iris met his gaze with a frown. "Well, if I've done something to offend *you*, I apologize, sincerely. I'll do my best to leave you alone in the future." Iris stepped back and closed the door.

Iris paced around her living room. "Maybe it's time to go, Mo. Maybe we should leave." She continued to pace while clenching and unclenching her hands. Mo jumped on her rocker and stared.

Iris stopped and looked at him. "You're right. It's never a good idea to make a decision out of anger. Better to calm down and think about it."

She built a fire, grabbed her favorite book, and settled down with Mo on her lap. For the next few hours, she alternated between staring at the fire and staring at her book.

Another knock came on the door, this time the front door. Mo jumped from Iris's lap and arched his back.

"What now? I am not in a people mood."

Iris put the book down, took her time standing up, then went to the door. She opened it halfway. Frank stood on the bottom step, holding a potted orchid in his hands. He held it out for her.

"What's this?" She stared at Frank as she cradled the door in her elbow.

"A peace offering," Frank said, holding the orchid out for Iris. "May I come in? Please?"

Iris looked at him and hesitated.

This is against my better judgment.

She opened the door wide and motioned for Frank to enter. She accepted the orchid from him. "Would you like some coffee or tea?"

"Will you allow me to stay that long?"

"It depends. Are you gonna behave?"

I doubt that's possible.

He nodded a slow 'yes'. "Tea would be nice. Thank you."

Iris went to the kitchen, set the orchid on the breakfast bar, and put a kettle on. Frank watched her, Mo watched him, and no one spoke a word. When the water was ready, Iris made two cups of tea and brought them to the living room. Frank followed.

Iris sat upright on the sofa, her body tense and straight.

You know the drill, Iris. Stay armed and ready just in case there's a round two. If he's here for a fight, he'll get one.

Mo sat close beside her, his body just as rigid. Frank took a seat in the chair nearby.

The two sipped their tea in silence while Mo shifted his eyes between them. Frank put his tea down and turned toward Iris. "Iris, I'm very sorry. I was out of line earlier. I was rash and I spoke harshly. You were right, you didn't deserve that. You have my sincerest apologies."

A genuine apology, that's a surprise.

Iris took a deep breath. "Thank you. Apology accepted." The two sat in awkward silence while Frank stared at the floor. Iris tried to relax her face but failed in the attempt.

"Would you like me to stoke the fire?" Frank asked, gesturing toward the fireplace.

"Yes, thank you," Iris replied with a small smile. Mo nuzzled Iris's hand and pawed at her to be petted. Iris obliged while Frank went to work. He put a few more logs on the fire, and in moments, the room was filled with a warm glow.

Frank sat back down in the chair, looked at the floor, then folded his hands together. "The earring was my wife's. I haven't seen it for well over a decade now." Frank unclasped his hands and placed them on his knees. "She lost it one day, and we turned the house upside down looking for it. Broke her heart it was gone. She didn't care much for jewelry, but she loved those earrings. I'd given them to her on our twenty-fifth wedding anniversary. She thought they were too fancy, but she wore them almost every day." He smiled. "Must have had them on when we were cleaning out the storage room for the next renters. Never thought to look there."

Iris nodded. "I'm sure she was upset over losing something so special. I know I would be."

"She was. Bothered her for the longest time. I wanted to replace it, but she said no. She said she'd rather hold on to the memory. My wife was pretty sentimental. I didn't think I'd ever see it again. I wish she knew . . ."

No wonder he got angry. It *was* his wife's. His dead wife's. Oh, Iris, what were you thinking? You should have been more careful. You know what that's like.

She sighed. "Frank, I'm sorry too. I shouldn't have spoken to you the way I did when you came over to apologize the first time. When I found the earring, I just thought, well, I guess I didn't think. I surprised you with it, and I understand now why you reacted the way you did. I wish I'd handled the situation better."

"You handled it just fine. I have a bit of a temper, in case you haven't noticed."

Iris smiled, relaxed at last, and sipped her tea.

I wish I knew more about her. Should I ask or leave things be? Ah, let's test the waters.

"Would you mind telling me about your wife? I understand if you'd rather not."

Frank leaned back in the chair, then said, "Her name was Claire." Iris could see a glisten in Frank's eyes. "She was the kindest person I've ever known."

"How did you two meet?"

"I ran into her. Literally. Eastport was an even smaller town back then, and the big excitement was a new stop sign being installed. Can you imagine getting excited over a stop sign?"

Iris laughed, "No, I think not."

"Well, I had just finished the night shift at the factory, and Claire was on her way to work. She was sitting in her car, stopped at the brand-new sign. I wasn't paying attention. I was on autopilot, and I didn't notice. Plowed right into her. Thankfully, I wasn't going very fast, and I only did some damage to her fender. She got out of the car, and you know what she said?”

Iris shook her head no.

“She asked, ‘Are you all right?’ She wasn’t upset about the car. She wanted to know if I was all right, if I was hurt in any way. That’s the type of person she was. Things didn’t matter to her. She was all about people. I told her I was fine, but her car wasn’t. She was concerned about being late for work, so I offered to drive her there. I was driving a truck, and it was okay, no real damage. I told her I’d take care of her car, get it all fixed, and have it back to her by the end of the day. It took a little persuasion, but she accepted, so I took her to work. She was a nurse. Makes sense, right?”

“Yes, it does. And were you able to fix her car?”

Frank gave Iris a wily grin and said, “Well, yes and no. I could fix it all right, but I wanted to see her again, so I told her it would take a few days, but I’d be happy to give her a ride to and from work in the meantime. I have a feeling she knew what was up, but she went along with it.”

“Oh, she knew, Frank. We always know.” Iris smiled as she leaned back on the sofa and continued to pet Mo.

“After the first week, I knew there wasn’t anything I wanted more in this world than to be with Claire. Over the next year, I worked like a dog, paying off debt, getting a better job. That’s when I went to work for the state. When

I had myself together, I asked her to marry me. She asked me what took so long. God, I loved that woman."

Iris smiled and nodded. She took another sip of her tea and placed her cup down. "How long were you married?"

"Twenty-nine years. I was twenty-six when we pulled the trigger. She was twenty-three. Best years of my life."

"Did you have any kids?"

"One, a son," Frank replied. "Claire wanted to name him after me, but I didn't think the world needed another Franklin B. Happy, so we named him after her dad instead, David."

"Nice name. I don't remember ever seeing him here. Does he live far?"

"No, he's over in Perry. We had a falling out a couple of years ago. We haven't spoken since." Frank looked down at the floor, and even so, Iris could see the regret in his eyes.

"I see," Iris nodded.

What a shame for a father and son to be estranged. Life's too short for that. I wonder what happened between—. No, don't push it. Ask more about Claire instead.

"Frank, if you don't mind me asking, what happened to Claire?"

Frank took a long breath, set his teacup down, then looked at Iris in a way that brought tears to her eyes before he spoke a word. She took a quick sip of her tea.

"Cancer. She had cancer." Frank knitted his eyebrows and swallowed hard. "She woke up one day like normal, but by the end of breakfast, she was exhausted. It was unusual for her. She always had a lot of energy. She thought she may be coming down with something. I wanted her to take the day off and stay home, but not Claire. She wouldn't do that to her patients so, she went to work."

"She was just a few hours into her shift and she complained about having a headache, then she passed out. The other nurses insisted she let a doctor check her out, and when he did, he admitted her to the hospital right away. They found a mass in her brain, a tumor the size of a grapefruit." Frank's chin quivered. "It was inoperable. Too large, too complicated. There were some treatments available that would have extended her life, but the thing about being a nurse, you know what's coming. She didn't want any part of it. She knew it would be hard on me, and on her, and in the end, it wouldn't change a thing. So, she insisted on leaving this world on her terms, and she did. Four months later, she was gone."

Iris pulled Mo closer. "October twenty-sixth," she whispered, nodding her head. Frank looked up at her.

"October twenty-sixth. That's the day she died?"

"Yes, how did you know?"

"My rent. I've always thought $1026 was a curiously specific amount, and a little less than what this house is worth."

"Well, $2008 seemed overpriced."

Iris smiled. "And it was a Sunday?"

Frank nodded. "One more way of remembering her." Frank stared at the fire. "Claire would have liked you. That's why I came over. She would have been angry with me for how I treated you, so I had to make it right."

Iris smiled and took a breath, fighting back her tears. "I'm sure I would have liked her. Thank you for sharing all that with me." Iris sat up and composed herself, "And thank you for the orchid. It was my favorite one from your greenhouse."

"I could tell. That's why I'm giving it to you." He smiled. "I saw how much you liked it."

Look how his face softens when he smiles. There's something else behind this gift though.

"Frank, what aren't you telling me?" Iris searched his eyes for any clues about what he may be thinking.

"Ah, it's nothing. It's just that orchid, it's called a dendrobium. Its name comes from the ancient Greek. *Dendro* means tree and *bium* refers to life. This orchid draws its life from the tree it inhabits."

"Oh my." Iris shook her head at the connection.

"Yeah. It's always been one of my favorites too. Kinda reminds me of a sunrise and a sunset all in one flower. Happy to share it with you, Iris," Frank paused. "I am sorry. I'd like to say I won't lose my temper again, but I'm an idiot, so I probably will."

Iris shook her head and laughed. "Frank, you are different. I'll give you that, but let's not make this a habit. Although I should warn you, I'm usually up for a good fight."

"I can tell. I'm still stinging from the verbal upper cut you gave me earlier on the back porch." Frank rubbed his jaw.

"I guess we both have a little temper. This red hair of mine is no lie." Iris stood. "More tea?"

"Sure, thanks."

Mo flicked his tail, moseyed over to Frank, then jumped up on his lap. Frank unconsciously began to pet him. Iris watched the scene unfold.

Interesting.

CHAPTER 13

The Harvest Fair

Flannel shirts, swirling leaves, pumpkin spice, . . . I love this time of year," Iris said as she gathered Mo up in her arms.

"Me, too," Ben said. "Although, I know all those swirling leaves means swirling winds and snow are in the not too distant future. But October does bring something very special to my family–the Perry Harvest Fair."

"Ooooo, another festival? What's this one all about? Let me guess. It's the easternmost harvest fair in the United States."

Ben laughed. "Good guess, but no. Perry's not the easternmost anything, but it does have its own claim to fame. It sits on the 45th parallel, halfway between the Equator and the North Pole."

"Well, now, that's something."

"Yes, and the Harvest Fair is the last festival of the season and Perry does a great job. While it may be small, what Perry lacks in numbers, it makes up for in community spirit."

"That does not surprise me. You Downeasters are a spirited bunch."

"That we are." Ben put his arm around Iris and escorted her back inside her home. He built a fire while Iris heated up some cider for them to share.

"Ben, you said the Perry Harvest Fair was special to your family. Why is that?" Iris brought in the cider.

"You know I come from a big family."

"Yes, still can't believe there are five of you Hudsons. And you grew up in Boston, a proud Scottish family," Iris said with a tilt of her head.

"Aye, we are." Ben grinned. "Now that we're all adults, we're spread out from Boston to Eastport. You remember Jennifer, my youngest sister?"

"Yes, she's in Perry and your parents live with her and Bill, right?"

"Right. Well, we learned years ago that it's next to impossible to get six family schedules coordinated for the holidays, so the Perry Harvest Fair became our Thanksgiving, Christmas, and New Year's celebrations wrapped into one. The fair also coincides with my parents' birthdays, so after spending the day at the fairgrounds, we all head back to Jennifer's to celebrate my parents. Now that they're older, this time has become very special to us. Everyone makes it a priority, and we share it together." Ben took a sip of his cider. "This year, I'd like to share it with you. Would you come?"

Iris felt a catch in her breath.

Oh dear, meeting the family.

"Thank you, Ben. That would be very nice."

I hope.

Iris went for a stroll the next morning, and after a thoughtful turn along the water walk, she made her way to the inn. She sat down with Emma in the west wing, Emma's private quarters, for a cup of tea.

"So, what's bothering you, Iris?"

"Who said something was bothering me?"

Emma tilted her head.

"You know me pretty well."

"I'm getting there." Emma smiled. "What's on your mind? What's the trouble?"

"It's Ben." Iris sighed.

"Ben? Is there a problem?"

"Not exactly. Things are good. He's a nice man."

"That he is, the finest kind. And he's smitten with you."

Iris rolled her eyes.

"Well, he is. It's obvious."

"Ben's a good man. He's easygoing, thoughtful. I've enjoyed getting to know him, spending time with him. He's the closest thing I've had to a relationship in decades, so I guess I'm making progress."

"Progress is a good thing."

"I am a little worried though."

"About what? Can I help?"

"I don't know. It's just. . . Ben wants to introduce me to his family."

"Is that all? I thought there was something serious."

"You don't think this is serious? Emma, he wants to introduce me to his *family*. All of them. And I think there's a million Hudsons."

Emma laughed, "Not quite a million, but there are a lot of them. Listen, the Hudsons are a great bunch. You'll love them. And it's natural that Ben would want you to meet them. You two have been dating for a few months now."

"I guess so. I like Ben, I do. But I'm still not used to this. It's making me nervous."

"Well, my suggestion would be to relax. The

Hudsons are a wonderful family, and Ben is a wonderful man. Enjoy this time. Get to know him better, get to know them. It'll all sort itself out. You'll see."

"I hope you're right."

Iris picked up Mo and set him on her bed. "Okay, Mo. Let's talk about this. Ben will be here in a couple of hours. There's nothing to be nervous about. Emma's right. Ben is a wonderful man, I'm sure he comes from good stock and his family will be just as wonderful. Our job is to relax, be ourselves, and have a good time today. Right?"

Mo nuzzled into Iris.

"Right. Thank you. Good talk. I feel better."

Ben arrived on time, and after greeting him with a kiss, Iris noticed the tension in his eyes.

"Ben, are you all right? You seem a little anxious."

"Anxious? I'm not anxious. How 'bout you? You anxious?"

"I was a little nervous, but I'm okay now. Should I be nervous?" Ben held her jacket for her while she put it on.

"No, not nervous." He paced in a circle. "It's just I know my family can be a little overwhelming at times. Mostly because there's so many of them. Just be prepared for a lot of—loudness."

Iris wrapped her arm around Ben's waist and stopped his pacing. "I'm sure it'll be fine."

"Hope you'll still feel that way by the end of the day," Ben gave her a crooked smile.

On the trip to Perry, Iris had Ben quiz her. "Okay, I want to be sure I have this straight. Fire away."

"Janice," Ben said.

"Janice. The eldest. Recently retired from the Boston police force. A mentor of yours when you joined the force yourself."

"Very good. Jacob."

"Jacob. Next in line. Used to be on the Boston force too, but left to become the head of security for a local university."

"Right. Jennifer."

"Hah! You're trying to trip me up. Jennifer is not the next line. She's your youngest sister and is an elementary school teacher in Perry. And she's awesome. We love the same books, and she doesn't let you get away with anything. My kind of girl."

"You are so right about that! She's small, but mighty as they say. You're doing very well. Okay, Oliver."

"Oliver looks just like you, at least from the pictures you've shown me. Only a year younger, he's the brother you're closest to. Lives in Bangor and is a public defender."

"Okay, last one. Ben."

Iris smiled. "Benjamin Philip Hudson. Named for his grandfather and his father. Middle child and it shows. Always taking care of everyone. One of the kindest people I know."

Ben smiled. "Well, I guess I have to pass you with flying colors for that answer. Looks like you're ready, Ms. Hornbeam."

The trip to Perry was a quick one, and they found the family at the fair right away.

Wow, there are a lot of Hudsons. Ben wasn't kidding!

Between the siblings, their spouses, and the children, there were over thirty of Ben's relatives. Iris had a hard time keeping up with who belonged to whom, since people were coming and going so quickly. She felt a little like Dorothy when she first landed in Oz.

Iris held her own throughout the day as she interacted with Ben's nieces and nephews, as well as his siblings. She even joined in the pumpkin carving contest, something the siblings made into a competition among themselves. As the day progressed, Iris noticed just about everything became a competition among the siblings, especially the siblings of the male variety.

"Jennifer, may I ask you something?" Iris said to Ben's sister.

"Sure. How can I help?"

"Are they always like this? The guys I mean. It seems like they make the simplest things into a competition."

"Oh, yes, that's the Hudson genes kicking in. They've been like this since they were boys . . . well, they're still boys in my mind. Don't think they'll ever grow up." Jennifer laughed. "It's best to go along with it, Iris. They'll tire themselves out by the end of the day. Then they'll compete to see who can fall asleep the fastest."

When the fair ended, everyone made their way back to Jennifer's home. Jennifer had a picturesque home on Boyden Lake, and it was the perfect setting to conclude the day. The brothers built a bonfire in the backyard while the sisters prepared hot chocolate for the kids and mulled cider for the adults. Everyone gathered round the fire, and as the sun went down, it became apparent to Iris where Ben's musical talent originated. Ben and his brother Oliver brought out their guitars, Jacob retrieved his concertina, and the rest of the clan formed a family choir. Ben's father, Phil, had a rich baritone voice and his mother, Elsie, added her silky alto tones to the ensemble. Even in their late eighties, their voices were strong.

Oliver started the singing with a song for the kids,

from there they moved to a rousing rendition of "Sweet Caroline", which included some very enthusiastic "whoa-oh-ohs". After several other selections, the songs became more reflective and meaningful. The evening music session ended with an acappella version of "Amazing Grace" with harmonies so beautiful they brought tears to Iris's eyes.

When the song was over, everyone sat still for a few moments, then Ben's father stood. "Let's pray." He bowed his head. "We thank you, God, for one more year. We thank you for your provision and for your care. And Lord, I am grateful for those gathered around this fire tonight and pray an earnest blessing on them all. Thank you for this wonderful family you have created and may we gather once again next year. In Jesus's name." And everyone joined in with, "Amen."

Ben looked at Iris and seeing her tears, he whispered, "You okay? I know this was a lot today."

"It was beautiful, Ben. Thank you for sharing this with me. It's been a wonderful day." Ben put his arm around her, and she settled into his embrace. There they remained, staring into the fire, enjoying the night air, each other, and the closeness of family.

The day following the Harvest Fair, Ben and Iris went to church together, then went to her home for lunch. They shared sandwiches on her porch, then walked to the back of her property. They made themselves comfy on the bench, keeping close to stay warm.

Ben's phone buzzed. He pulled it out, read a text and smiled.

"What is it?" Iris asked.

"My family. They've been texting me all morning. My nieces especially want to know when they'll see you again," Ben said with a grin.

"Aw, that's nice. They're sweet girls. You are a blessed man, Ben Hudson. You have a wonderful family."

"Yeah, they're pretty great and I'm glad you think so." Ben paused, then took Iris's hand. "Iris, meeting you has been, I don't even think I can come up with a word for it. Life changing? You're an amazing woman."

"That's kind." She blushed.

Ben turned toward her and held her cheek in his hand. He lowered his head toward hers, kissing her forehead, then her cheek, then pressing his lips against hers in a lingering kiss. They separated, and Ben cupped her face in his hands. "Iris, I love you."

Iris took a breath, then looked down. She shifted on the bench. Ben let go of her. "Have I spoken too soon?"

166

Iris took Ben's hand. "Ben, I've enjoyed spending time with you, getting to know you. You are a wonderful man."

"But you don't love me."

Iris stared at him for a moment, then shook her head slightly and whispered, "No."

Ben looked down and released Iris's hand.

She took it again and said, "Ben, I do care for you. More than I've cared for anyone in a very long time."

Ben nodded. "I see."

"Do you? I'm not sure you do." Ben looked up at her. "When my husband died, I had no interest in ever having another romance, none. And I didn't for a very long time. He was gone a good ten years before I even considered going on a date with anyone. Since then, I've dated a few men and even then, I would only go on a date with them once or twice. No one ever made it to date number three. The past few years, no one made it to date number one."

"Why? What was wrong with these men?"

"Oh, they were very nice men. They weren't the problem. It was me. I've moved so much in my life, it became very difficult for me to make any meaningful connections with people. I just couldn't do it. I knew as soon as I arrived in a place, I'd be gone in a few short years. It became too painful to keep saying goodbye, so I'd hardly say hello.

"When I arrived here in Eastport . . . this place, there's something special about it. It's the first time I ever felt like I belonged, like I was home. I'm fifty-nine years old and this is the first time I've ever felt that, Ben," Iris's eyes glistened.

"You were a surprise. A nice surprise." She squeezed his hand. "I've enjoyed spending time with you, right from the start. And I thought this time, I'm going to give it a chance. I won't close a door that's been opened. At least, I won't close it right away." She rolled her eyes, acknowledging her tendencies. Ben smiled.

"Do you remember when we went to the Bay of Fundy and had lunch at that harbor restaurant?" Ben nodded. "You told me you were surprised anything scares me. Well, this, you and me, this terrifies me."

"You're scared of me? I'm sorry. I don't mean to scare you." He took both of her hands in his. "I want to protect you, love you."

"I know. It's not *you*, exactly. It's the idea of being in a serious relationship with someone, anyone. Emma and I have become close friends, best friends. Before her, I never had a real friend like that. Never. I was never around long enough to make one. And I'm just learning now how friendships work.

"My husband was the second guy I dated—ever. The first one lasted for a single date, and that was back in high school. If Danny hadn't pursued me as he did, I'm not sure we would have gotten married. And now, so much time has passed, I'm not sure how this kind of relationship should work either."

Ben held Iris's face in his hand. "We'll figure this out together, if you're willing to give us a chance."

Iris nodded and smiled with tears in her eyes. "Yes, I'd like that." Ben pulled Iris in and held her. After a few moments, she pulled herself up and looked in Ben's eyes. "I'm sorry I can't say those words to you. When I say them, I want to mean them completely."

Ben nodded, "It's okay. I'm glad to know where I stand, and you'll give us a chance. I have to admit, it's been a while for me too, so it's good for us to take our time." Ben held out his arm. Iris smiled, leaned into him, and rested her head on his shoulder as they watched the afternoon sun fade into evening.

CHAPTER 14

A Vagabond Thanksgiving

For more years than she could remember, Iris hosted what she called a "Vagabond Thanksgiving". Holidays used to be a lonely time for her. She often found herself in a new town, not knowing anyone or very few people, and as a result, she would spend the holidays alone. One year, she realized there were several others she met who were also going to be alone, so she invited them to Thanksgiving dinner. The dinner was the best she'd had in a very long time and from that point on, she was determined no person in her circle of friends, family, or acquaintances would spend Thanksgiving by themselves.

"Okay, Mo. Time to bring Eastport into the Vagabond Thanksgiving tradition! Now, who should we invite?" Mo hopped up on the sofa and curled into a ball.

"Well, you're no help. We'll have to invite Ben, of course, and Emma. She's going to see her kids after the holiday, so she'll be around. I'd like to invite the Westheimers and the McNamara's, oh, and Eddie and his parents. It would be nice to get to know them better. Am I forgetting anyone?"

Mo picked his head up and stared at Iris.

"You're right, Frank. Ugh, that will be a tough sell. Good thing I'm tough."

Iris decided to take the direct approach with Frank. On the first day of November, she walked over to his house and rapped on the front door. When Frank answered, she looked him straight in the eye and said, "Frank, I want you to come to my place for Thanksgiving."

"No," Frank responded, returning Iris's look. "Thank you."

"Let me rephrase. Frank, you're coming to my house for Thanksgiving," Iris remained in solid eye contact.

"I don't think so, Iris," Frank said, still meeting her gaze.

Iris squinted to intensify her stare. She lowered her chin and her tone. "Yes, you're coming. I'll explain. If you say no, between now and Thanksgiving, I'm going to continue to ask you. Every. Single. Day. Probably several times a day. I'm going to bother you about this every time I see you. *Every time.* My voice will be the last thing you hear in your head before you lay down on your pillow each night. I will visit you in your dreams and haunt you in your nightmares. When you wake up in the morning, your tea kettle will whistle my name. Your microwave? It'll beep the date and time. I will not leave you alone, Frank. That's a guarantee." Iris stopped. Frank stared. She continued, "So, why don't we just skip all that and go right to the part where you say, 'Thank you, Iris. I'd love to come.'"

Frank sighed.

"Dinner's at four. Don't be late." Iris smiled, turned and went back home, swinging her arms and whistling a merry tune.

The rest of the invitations went without incident. Ben was delighted to come, as were Emma, and Eddie and his parents. The Westheimers planned to take a trip to visit family in Florida, so they declined, and the McNamara's already had a houseful coming to their home. There was no official word from Frank, but Iris was certain he would come. Mostly certain he would come. Actually, she had her doubts.

Thanksgiving Day arrived, and Iris couldn't wait to

gather with her new friends. She'd been chopping and peeling, and braising and roasting all week, and she was ready for the final push. Ben came early to lend a hand, as did Emma. Eddie and his parents, Kevin and Charlotte, arrived around three-thirty and brought along blueberry pie for dessert. Iris couldn't help but look at the clock several times and wonder if Frank would show.

At two minutes to four, there was a knock on the front door. Iris opened it and smiled when she saw Frank holding a basket filled with preserves, jams, and jellies.

"Welcome, Frank. I'm so glad you could come. What's all this?"

"Just a few things I put together from over the summer." He handed Iris the basket.

"How nice, thank you. Please, come in." Iris welcomed him in and made introductions, forgetting in Eastport, everyone knows everyone. After introductions were made Iris's guests scattered to different parts of the room. She slipped beside Frank and whispered, "I wasn't sure you'd come."

"How could I not? You've been hounding me in my sleep for the past three weeks. I needed to get some shuteye," Frank whispered back, trying to sound irritated, but Iris could see the smile in his eyes. She tried not to look too triumphant.

Iris went back to the kitchen to check on dinner and Ben joined her. He nodded toward Frank. "What was that all about?"

"Oh, nothing. Just me winning an argument with Frank," she said with a satisfied grin.

Ben nodded, then looked away from Iris and stared at Frank as he sat down and began a conversation with Charlotte and Kevin.

When it was time for dinner, Ben brought out the turkey and sliced it up as plates were passed to him. Iris set the side dishes on the breakfast bar, and there was much chatter and *oohs* and *ahs* as everyone admired the spread. As was her tradition, Iris had made dishes from various parts of the country and the world where she had lived, everywhere from California to Italy. Eastport became the newest addition to Iris's geographic feast as she added oyster stuffing and lobster risotto to the menu.

Once everyone had their plates full and returned to their seats, Kevin offered to say the blessing. Hands were clasped around the table. The blessing was given, and the conversations began.

During dinner, Iris found out more about Kevin and Charlotte. They met at work, fell in love and a year later, they were married. Eddie came along a little over a year after that.

"Iris, did you know Ben is Eddie's godfather?" Charlotte asked.

"No, I didn't. That's nice." She smiled at Ben.

"Guess he didn't tell you the story then," Kevin said.

"No, he didn't." Iris glanced at Ben and tilted her head. He shrugged. Then, turning to Charlotte, she said, "I love stories, so do tell."

Charlotte smiled. "I wanted to work as long as I could before Eddie was born. I still had a few weeks to go, so I went to school, as usual, but right around lunchtime, I felt some pangs, so to be cautious, I took myself to the nurse's office, and she immediately called 911."

Kevin continued the story. "I was working at a remote location in the county when this happened, so I had no idea Charlotte was about to give birth. And you know what cell service can be like around here, well, where I was, it was practically non-existent."

Charlotte took Kevin's hand. "I was so nervous. I thought for sure he'd miss everything. Ben was on duty that day, and when he heard the address over his police radio, he made a beeline to the school and found me in the nurse's office. This man," Charlotte said, pointing to Ben. "he stayed by my side until the ambulance arrived. He kept me calm, even did breathing exercises with me. Once the EMTs got me packed away and headed to the hospital, Ben turned his sirens on and sped off to retrieve Kevin."

"I couldn't imagine what I'd done when I saw the police car pull up. Next thing I know, Ben's jumping out of the cruiser saying, 'Time to go, Kev. You're gonna be a dad!' I jumped in my car and followed him to the hospital. I don't know what scared me more—driving ninety miles an hour or becoming a father. I think it was a tie. We arrived at the hospital just before Charlotte delivered." Kevin squeezed Charlotte's hand.

Charlotte wiped a tear from her eye and Iris smiled at Ben. "It was an amazing day, and it would have turned out much differently, if it hadn't been for Ben."

"That is a wonderful story. Thanks for sharing," Iris said as she got up to refill the water pitcher. She patted Charlotte on the shoulder on her way.

Charlotte turned to Frank and asked, "Frank, all those jams and preserves, is that something you do every year?"

"Yes, it's a little thing I enjoy."

"He's being modest, Charlotte." Iris said from the kitchen. "Frank won two blue ribbons for his preserves at the Machias Blueberry Festival this year."

"You don't say. Congratulations. Well, I can understand why. They're delicious, and they're a little different from what I'm used to. Can't quite put my finger on what it is." Charlotte leaned in Frank's direction. "Not as sweet, maybe? How'd you learn to make them like that?"

"I was taught at the feet of the master, my mother. They're her recipes. Every summer she'd have my brother, Will, and I out gathering berries of one kind or another, then we'd help her make her specialties. When we'd complain about berry picking, or helping with the canning, she'd tell us the story of the little red hen. You know the one."

"Oh yes, I read it to my students every year, 'Who will help me plant the wheat?', 'Not I,' said the dog. 'Not I,' said the pig. 'Not I,' said the cow. 'Then I'll plant it myself.'" Charlotte recited with a laugh, "Great story, great lesson."

"Right. Well, my brother and I got the message, no work, no reward, so we picked, and we canned."

"You know," Charlotte said, finishing a bite of roll with jam. "This reminds me of my childhood. There used to be a little tea shop in Eastport and my mother would take me there on Saturdays after we'd do the grocery shopping. We'd have these wonderful little scones with jam and hot tea. It always made me feel so grown up."

Frank smiled, "A Happy Place?"

"Yes! That's the one. The woman who owned it was so kind, and I thought it was the perfect name. I always felt happy there."

178

"That was my mother's tearoom."

"No, really? Oh, the *Happy* place. How about that. Well, she was wonderful. I have a lot of fond memories of the place and of your mother. You learned well from her. She must be very proud."

"A Happy Place? I don't remember that, Frank," Emma said. "Was it in town?"

"I'm sure it was gone before you took over the inn, Emma. We converted a small house on Water Street, just past Sullivan. She opened it in 1970." Frank paused. "There was a fire in '77..."

"Ohhh, I remember now. Tragic," Charlotte said, furrowing her brow. "Terrible thing that happened. I'm so sorry, Frank. I wouldn't have brought it up. I'm very sorry if I upset you."

Frank shook his head. "No, it's nice to hear you enjoyed her place. She would have loved that. And you were right, Charlotte. She was wonderful. I still miss her." Frank took a sip of water.

Iris came by and filled his water glass.

More tragedy? I wonder what happened. Never mind. Now's not the time to find out. Let's get him thinking about something else.

"Frank, I've been wondering about something since the festival." She put the pitcher down and took a seat. "The blueberries here are so different from what I've had in other parts of the country. Why is that?"

"Isn't it obvious? It's because Maine blueberries are the best." Frank stated, raising his chin.

Emma, Kevin, and Charlotte applauded. "Here, here, that's right, Frank." Iris laughed at the group of blueberry aficionados.

"They're different for several reasons, Iris." Frank said with a grin. "First, they're wild. While there are many commercial farms in Maine, the blueberries they farm aren't planted as much as they are allowed to grow."

"What do you mean?" Iris asked.

"Not to get too technical, but wild blueberries grow on a low bush that's spread by rhizomes. Think of rhizomes like fingers." Frank held up his hand to demonstrate. "These fingers spread, and as they do, they produce new roots, and eventually, new bushes with new berry clusters. Instead of planting more bushes, farmers clear new patches of land which allows the bushes to spread."

"I see, so, does their being wild account for their size? Maine blueberries are so much smaller than what I've seen in grocery stores in the past. Or is it the climate? Not enough growing time?"

"The size difference is due more to genetic modification than anything else. Most blueberries you find outside of Maine and parts of Canada have been genetically modified to grow larger."

"The bigger, the better?"

"You'd think so, but in this case, it's not true. Those blueberries may be bigger in size, but they are not bigger in taste or in nutrition. I'm sure you've noticed Maine blueberries are sweeter and firmer."

"Yes, I have, now that you mention it."

"Wild blueberries also have double the number of antioxidants and fiber than their modified counterfeits. I mean, counterparts." Frank smiled.

"Wow, you're an encyclopedia of blueberry knowledge there, Frank," Ben said.

"Just answering the question, Ben," Frank said with an icy glare Ben's way. Then, changing his tone and his expression, he said to the group, "Sorry everyone, just reverting back to my geoscientist days."

"No need to apologize, Frank," Iris said quietly, with a quick glance to Ben.

Charlotte looked at Frank, then at Ben and Iris, and changed the subject. "So, Iris, Eddie tells me you're almost retired. What kind of work do you do?"

"I'm a technical writer. Mostly, I write manuals, handbooks, and the occasional research summary. Can't believe I've been doing this for almost thirty years."

"Wow, that's amazing," Charlotte replied. "Do you have a date when you'll be officially retired?"

"Not yet, but I submitted my final manual for review this week. Once that's finished, that's the end."

"Iris Hornbeam..." Frank said, staring at Iris.

"Yes, Frank?"

We're using full names now?

"Iris Hornbeam, the writer." Frank said, bobbing his head up and down.

"Yes, that's me."

Has he been sampling too much spiced wine? Maybe it's the eggnog.

He leaned in with his arms on the table. "Are you the same Iris Hornbeam who wrote *Summary Effects of Precipitation, Erosion, and Deposition on Landforms*?"

"You're playing with me, right Frank?" Iris narrowed her eyes at him.

"No, of course not. I used that research summary all the time in my work for the state. Well written, clear, had all the pertinent information. Kept a copy on my desk. I referenced it often. Well done, Iris."

Iris sat in stunned silence, mouth agape, blinking.

Emma looked at Iris. "I think you've done it Frank. She's speechless." Everyone laughed, and Frank looked down at the floor, then glanced at Iris with a smile.

"Here, Iris, have a drink of water. It'll be okay, you'll recover soon," Emma said, filling Iris's water glass and giggling.

Ben stared at Frank then changed the subject. "Eddie, what's this I hear about you getting your license?"

"Yes, sir! I turned sixteen on November thirteenth, and Dad took me to the DMV that day. Passed on my first try."

"Good man," Ben said, lifting his glass in a toast. "To Eddie!"

"To Eddie!" everyone replied, raising their glasses.

"Yes, that's excellent news, Eddie. Good for you," Iris said, still recovering from Frank's compliment.

"Thanks! Now that I've got my license, I have to work on getting my own truck. Already started saving a couple of years ago by doing odd jobs for people."

"Like helping them move?" Iris said, patting Eddie's arm, remembering how hard he'd worked the day she moved in.

"Yes, and mowing lawns, and cleaning out garages, whatever people need."

Charlotte chimed in, "Eddie is a good worker. We're very proud of how industrious he is."

Eddie bounced forward in his seat. "I had this idea. I'd like to start my own business, so Dad and I have worked out an arrangement. He's going to lend me his truck so I can get around and shovel driveways this winter and do other jobs for people. When I get enough money, I'll buy my own truck and my own equipment. I figure if I work hard, I'll have enough for a used truck by the time I'm eighteen."

"That's a pretty ambitious goal, Eddie," Ben said.

"Nothing wrong with a little ambition," Frank countered.

Iris gave them both a look, then looked at Emma, who shook her head at the two.

"Miss Iris, I was thinking. I'd like you to be one of my first customers. Could I shovel your walkway and plow your drive this winter? I'll give you the family discount."

A rush of tears filled Iris's eyes. She took a quick sip of water. "I'd love that, Eddie. Thank you. That's very thoughtful." She stood up and started toward the kitchen. "Coffee anyone?"

"We'll start clearing, Iris," Charlotte said, getting up and gathering plates.

Emma picked up a few dishes and followed Iris into the kitchen. Iris filled the coffepot with water and Emma came up beside her. "You okay?"

Iris smiled and nodded, trying to hold back her tears. "Yes, thanks."

Emma patted her on the hand. "We'll talk later."

Iris nodded again and made herself busy with the coffee.

Emma helped organize the clearing of the table and the putting away of the leftovers while Iris concentrated on the coffee and the dessert spread. Everyone else adjourned to the living room.

"Would you like me to make a fire, Iris?" Frank asked.

"I'll take care of it," Ben said, going to the fireplace. Frank stepped aside and took a seat in the corner of the room. In no time, Ben built a roaring fire.

Kevin leaned back in his chair. "This reminds me of our time around the campfire this summer. We love to camp. How 'bout you, Ben? Did you get out much?"

"Haven't camped as much this year, had a few other things occupying my time," he said with a glance and a smile toward Iris as she walked into the room with Mo trailing behind her. Iris smiled, then looked toward the floor, her cheeks blushing.

"Do you like to camp, Iris?" Frank asked.

Iris looked up, then took a seat near Emma, and Mo jumped on her lap. "When I was a child, my family loved to go camping. It was my dad, really. I think he was a frustrated mountain man. One time, it was just him and me on a daddy/daughter weekend and we went to an area I'd never been to before.

"On one of the days, we went on a late afternoon hike, and on our way back to camp, a storm was brewing. We could see the front coming and in just a few moments, everything got dark, like can't see your hand in front of your face kind of dark. My father pulled out his flashlight, which I swear was as old as Methuselah. It had a very narrow beam, and it wasn't very bright, so you could only see about a step in front of you. I walked as close as I could to him because of it.

"We picked up the pace, but the storm was catching up and I was frightened. I had no idea where we were. I looked up at my father and said, 'Daddy, I'm scared. I can't see where we're going. I think we're lost.' He smiled and wrapped his big paw of a hand around mine and said, 'It's okay, baby, Dad's here. You don't have to worry, I know the way. You just hold my hand and take the next step into the light. Trust me, and you'll be fine.' And I did. . . And I was." Iris paused, her mind lost in the memories, then she looked toward Frank. "Yes, I like to camp." She wiped a tear away, took a deep breath, then noticed the room was quiet. "Sorry, just remembering."

"That was a good memory," Emma said with a smile, wiping her own tear and patting Iris's hand.

186

"Pie anyone?" Iris stood.

"I'll give you a hand." Emma joined her.

The rest of the night was filled with laughter and stories and even a little music when Ben brought out his guitar. Frank excused himself at that point, thanking Iris for dinner, congratulating Eddie, and asking if he'd plow and shovel his place too, and assuring Charlotte he'd send over a round of preserves for her. He even hugged Emma and gave a nod toward Ben, who was strumming away. Iris walked Frank to the door. "Frank, thank you so much for coming."

Frank nodded and said, "Ayuh." Then he turned, took a few steps, stopped, and turned back. "Thank *you*, Iris."

She gave him a nod, then Frank turned again and Iris watched him walk back home.

The next day, Emma called Iris and asked if she could come to the inn and lend a hand. Iris was more than happy to help, so she got herself together and went right over. The inn was full to the brim with holiday guests, and Emma was having trouble keeping up with the breakfast rush, and the requests for information about what to see and do. Iris took over the breakfast supervision, which allowed Emma to do what she did best, handle people. By ten o'clock, things settled down and the two women enjoyed a cup of tea in Emma's office.

"Yesterday was a wonderful dinner, Iris. You did an amazing job pulling it all together. You're a fabulous cook!" Emma handed Iris a cup of tea.

"Well, thank you," Iris said with a bow of her head. "I'm glad you had a good time. I enjoyed myself too. It was nice having everyone together."

"So, what happened? Why did you get up from the table so quickly after Eddie asked if you'd be his first customer? You don't like his work?" Emma took a seat.

"Oh no, that's not it. Eddie is an amazing worker. He's very diligent for someone his age. You may want to ask him to do some things around here. He's pretty handy."

"Good idea. I'll do that. So, what was it then?"

"It was when Eddie offered me the family discount." Iris took a sip of tea. "I don't have much family left. My parents passed away when I was in my forties. They were older when I was born. I was a surprise, if you know what I mean. I have two older siblings, a brother, and a sister. My brother's ten years older than me and my sister is twelve years older. When I came along, well, there's not much a twelve-year-old and an infant have in common. By the time

I could interact with either of them in any meaningful way, they were well on their way to adulthood. I was essentially an only child. My sister and I got closer as I got older, but she passed away three years ago this coming April fifth. My brother's still around, but he lives in Arizona. We speak on the phone, but that's about it. I guess I was just touched Eddie thinks of me that way."

"I understand." Emma gave Iris a sympathetic smile.

"You know, Emma, my dad was a Marine, and when you're in a military family, you live a different kind of life. I got used to being a nomad, moving every two or three years. I learned as a child how to meet people, how to make acquaintances, and I also learned it wasn't a good idea to make friends because I knew before too long, I'd be moving again and have to say goodbye. Enough goodbyes and well, let's just say it's tough on the heart. So, I'd move to a new location, get to know a few folks, then prepare myself to move on. I never allowed myself to get too attached to people or places. Right after I graduated college, I married my Navy guy and kept right on moving. After he was gone, I kept the pattern up."

"And now you're looking to settle down. Are you sure you're ready for that? Sounds like it'd be a big change for you."

"I wasn't sure. I was hoping something would speak to me, that God would give me a sign or a billboard or something when I was in the right place."

"And did He?" Emma looked over her teacup.

"I think He did." Iris nodded.

"Really? Explain please."

"Remember the day you told me about the cottage?"

"Yes, I remember. I remember telling you about Frank, too."

"Yes, and you were right. Frank Happy, he was not. He mostly grunted at me when I asked him about renting. Eventually, he walked me over to the cottage and opened the door. I took a few steps inside, then I had to take a step backward. At first, I thought I was overwhelmed by how beautiful the space was, but that wasn't it. I was overwhelmed by the sense that this was home. I can't explain it, Emma, but the feeling was palpable. *I was home.* I've never felt that in my entire life."

"And now you're making friends, not acquaintances." Emma patted Iris on the knee.

"Yes, very good friends." Iris lifted her teacup in a toast to Emma.

"I'm glad. It's time, Iris. You can have a good life here. Eastport, it's a great place. You're finding that out for yourself. There can be a lot for you." Emma gave Iris a sly smile.

"I see that look." Iris narrowed her eyes at Emma. "You mean Ben."

"And?" Emma grinned.

"Oh, I don't know, Emma. It's going well with him, I guess. He told me he loves me."

"What? When?"

"After the Harvest Fair, the next day."

"And you didn't tell me?"

"No. I'm sorry. I'm still working on this friendship thing. And this dating thing." She clenched her hands. "And this being human thing. It's a little overwhelming." A tear perched in Iris's eye.

Emma took her hand. "It's a lot, I'm sure."

"After the fair, the next day, we were sitting out back at my place. That's when he told me he loved me. But I couldn't say those words to him. I feel badly about it, but I'm not there yet."

"I see. You need time. You don't want to say those words unless you mean them."

"Right. Ben's a good man. He's kind, funny. He's a strong man of faith. I like him. But where this will all go? I have no idea. I'm willing to find out though."

"So, you're still giving him a chance then."

"Yes, I am. He understood and we're working on this

together."

"And what about Frank?"

"What about Frank?" Iris grimaced. She changed her tone. "Frank is a pain in the neck. He can be so infuriating. The first six months, all he did was grumble at me. And then last month," Iris paused, and shook her head, remembering that difficult day.

"What happened last month?"

"Oh, we had a big blowup. I was in the storage room, getting it organized. Mo was with me, and he found something in the corner. I thought it was a mouse, turned out it was a diamond earring. Beautiful, little teardrop shape."

"At first, I thought it could be the previous renter's, but then I heard Frank in the backyard raking, and I remembered what you said about him having a wife. I thought it must have been hers, so I went over to return it to him. I thought he'd be thankful, but noooo." Iris shook her head. "When I showed it to him, he got very upset with me, angry really. He snatched that earring out of my hand so fast, and then he lit into me. And I took it. I stood there, letting him yell at me."

"Frank yelled at you?" Emma put her teacup down.

"Well, he didn't yell as much as growl at me." Iris took a deep breath, then looked back at Emma. "Emma, I never let anyone speak to me the way Frank did. *Never*. But I did that day. I think I was so shocked by his reaction that it mummified me. Once he was done, all I could say was, 'You have the earring. I'll leave you be.' And I left, went in my house, and cried. I was so angry with him and so angry with myself for letting him get away with that." Iris took a sip of tea, trying to calm herself from the memory.

"And still you invited him for Thanksgiving dinner?"

"Well, about five minutes later, there was a knock on my back door. I answered it, and there was Frank. He'd come to apologize, sort of. He started with 'I'm sorry, *but*' and for me, that is no apology, so I let him have it. Everything I'd been wanting to say for the past six months, I said. I was not kind. Even while the words were coming out of my mouth, I knew, I was thinking 'Iris, there's more going on here than you realize, shut-up', but no, I kept going. And when I was done, I shut the door in his face."

"You didn't."

"Oh, I did. And then I felt sick to my stomach over it. I knew it was going to be my turn to apologize, but I was still so angry, I couldn't do it. A few hours later, there was another knock on my door, this time the front door. When I opened it, there Frank stood holding the most beautiful orchid. He said it was a peace offering. He asked to come in, and I reluctantly allowed it."

"We sat and had an honest conversation, heartfelt. He apologized, for real this time. The earring was Claire's, it was a special gift from him. He told me about her, how they met, what their life was like, how she died. I could tell he loved her very much." Iris paused and took a sip of tea, then setting her cup down again, she continued.

"I was so embarrassed. I had pushed Frank's buttons with the earring. He wasn't expecting to see it, to see something he'd given his wife, something so precious to her and to have someone handing it to him like, like it was a newspaper delivered to the wrong address. No wonder he behaved as he did. If anyone should have understood, it was me." Iris's eyes filled with tears.

"Iris, you didn't know. Don't be so hard on yourself."

"But I kinda did, Emma. Maybe not everything, but I knew enough that I should have been more careful. I was insensitive and that caused Frank to react the way he did. He was hurt and I did it." Iris wiped away a tear.

"It seems you've patched things up?"

"I think so. We both apologized and we've had a fragile truce since then. It was a big deal that he came to Thanksgiving dinner. I was afraid he wouldn't, but I was glad he did." Iris wiped away one last tear.

Emma sat for a moment, watching Iris. "Iris, forgive me for what I'm about to say, but since we're friends now,

194

I believe I should say it."

"Okay. . ."

Emma looked Iris in the eye. "You may want to rethink your relationship with Ben."

Iris sat back. "Why would I want to do that?"

"Because you're crying over Frank."

CHAPTER 15

Winterizing

J ack Frost painted a mosaic of feathered shapes on the windows of Iris's home one brisk November day. She lifted Mo up on her lap after her morning cup of coffee. "Mo, looks like winter's well on its way and I haven't done a thing to prepare for it. We need to get started. Problem is, I'm not sure what to do." She put Mo down. "Might as well consult the expert."

Iris got her coat on and went next door to Frank. She found him in his backyard, stacking wood.

"Morning, Frank."

"Morning." Frank continued stacking as Iris watched. Minutes passed and as he picked up another log to stack, he said, "You're staring."

"That's a lot of wood."

"It'll be a long winter." Frank stopped and brushed

his hands. "Is there something you need, Iris?"

"Sorry to interrupt. I hate to admit this, but I know winter's on its way and I said I would to be prepared, but honestly, I have no idea what to do to get the house ready. Can you give me a clue?"

"You don't have to worry about the house. I'll take care of all that. What you need to do is make sure *you're* prepared."

"Me? I've got a coat, boots, gloves. I'm set." Frank gave her a dubious look. "I'm guessing by your expression that's not enough."

"Not hardly."

"Care to enlighten me? Please?"

"Well, at least you have the right type of vehicle for this area. Do you know how to get your SUV into 4-wheel drive?"

Iris wrinkled her nose.

"Yeah, get on that. If you need help, I can show you. How are your tires?"

"Round?" Iris squinted her eyes.

Frank shook his head. "I mean the tread. I'll help you check that too. You might want to think about snow chains. Be sure to keep a snow shovel and a blanket or two in your trunk, along with a long-handled brush and some sand or kitty litter. I'm sure you have some of that."

Iris nodded.

"Keep your gas tank full. You have jumper cables and a spare tire, right?"

"I think so. I don't pay much attention to those kinds of things. I wouldn't know how to change a tire or jump my car anyway. I'd just call roadside assistance."

"Roadside assistance around here usually involves Chip from north of Perry, and when the weather's bad, it's anybody's guess when he could get to you." Frank paused a moment, then said, "One other thing, when you go out, carry along some protein bars or other food and a water bottle. Don't leave them in the car, they'll freeze."

"Do I really need all that in my car? And I need to pack snacks?" Iris gave Frank a skeptical look.

"Yes, to both. Storms come up fast around here. You don't want to be stranded on the side of the road without some extra warmth and food or a way to dig out. I was stranded once for a day and a half. That was not a lot of fun."

"I imagine not." Iris shuddered.

"Pay attention to the weather forecasts. Don't roam far if there's a storm coming. The intensity can change on a dime. Us being so close to the shore, we don't always get the snow, but we sure get the ice and wind. You ever experience gale force winds?"

"Only once. We were stationed in the Philippines. That was scary."

"Good. Then you know not to take them lightly. They blow through here often during winter and will pile up any snow they bring with them. And don't think things are fine if you look out the window and see there's just a dusting here. You can drive fifteen minutes to Perry and be in a foot of it."

"Good to know."

"We've had our share of snow, too. Last year, we got seventy-six inches in ten days." Frank started walking to his shed, and Iris followed.

"Seventy-six inches? That's over six feet!" Iris stood wide-eyed. "What did you do?"

"Not much." Frank shrugged his shoulders.

Iris laughed. "I should have figured."

"For home, be sure to keep a push broom and a snow shovel inside the house where it's handy." Frank opened the shed and pulled out one of each. "Here, keep these in your utility room. I have a generator I'll be hooking up in case we lose power. Be sure to keep your pantry stocked with non-perishables. You'll always have some power with the generator, but that doesn't mean you'll be able to get to the grocery store.

"I've asked Eddie to take care of the shoveling and

plowing, but I'll take care of it when he can't, and I'll treat the walkways and driveway. You should have some snowmelt on hand yourself in case you need to get out before I get there. I can give you some."

Should I be taking notes?

Frank picked up steam. "Make sure you keep your phone charged. Do you have a sturdy pair of muck boots and a parka?"

"Muck boots?"

Frank shook his head. "You can get a pair at Moose Island Marine in town. I'll take you. You should have a couple pairs of gloves, too. Not fashion gloves, real ones, lined and waterproofed. Don't forget a hat, and you could use a scarf too. For me, Long Johns are a must."

"Got it." Iris tucked the broom and shovel into the crook of her elbow and counted off the list on her fingers. "Broom, shovel, snowmelt, boots, coat, gloves, snacks, a hanky to wipe my nose and clean underwear." Iris gave Frank a side-eyed glance. "Frank, you're starting to sound like my mother."

"Go ahead, make fun. We'll see who's laughing come the first snowstorm," Frank said, pointing at Iris. He softened his tone and smiled. "I've got some time tomorrow. Can I come over then to work on things in the house?"

"Tomorrow's fine. Thanks." Iris returned his smile.

The next day, Frank showed up at Iris's mid-morning. He told her he wanted to clear the gutters first and do some outside chores, then he'd come inside to seal the windows and shut off the water to the outside hoses. It was a brisk day, but Iris was determined to help Frank, whether or not he wanted it. When they were through with the outdoors, they came inside and took a break for lunch and to get warm before tackling the rest.

Over a lunch of grilled cheese and tomato soup, they had a conversation about the proper way to winterize a garden, and somehow, that led into a conversation about the history of Eastport, then they moved on to a discussion of jazz music and who was the better saxophonist, Stan Getz, or Charlie Parker. Eventually, their talk turned to family.

"So, tell me about your husband. What was his name?"

"Danny, Danny Hornbeam—like the tree," Iris said with a smile.

Frank met her smile. "How'd you meet him?"

"We were in the same grade in high school. We were

assigned to be lab partners in chemistry class our junior year. Of course, that became a big joke once we started dating. I was the bookish type, and Danny, he was more into sports. He was an excellent athlete. He played just about every sport there was, but his favorite was track. He wasn't the fastest person on the team, but he loved the feeling he got while running. He preferred long-distance, speed wasn't as necessary as endurance, and he had plenty of that. He needed it when it came to me. He wanted to date me, and he asked me out for weeks. I kept saying no because I didn't think we had anything in common. I can be a little stubborn."

"I hadn't noticed that about you." Frank took a bite of his sandwich, hiding his grin.

"Ha, ha." Iris took a sip of tea. "Danny kept asking though, and I finally agreed, just to get him to leave me alone about it. I told him I'd go out with him once, then he'd see that we weren't right for each other and that would be the end of it. Boy, was I wrong."

"What happened?"

"On the night of our first date, Danny picked me up in his dad's Oldsmobile Cutlass—freshly washed, and he took me to a little Italian restaurant. It was my favorite place to eat. It wasn't fancy or expensive, just good food. My parents and I had been going there since we moved into town, and we'd gotten to know the owners well. It was family run business and the dad was a former Marine.

"Anyway, we got to the restaurant, and even though they didn't take reservations, there was a table waiting for us in the back with a lovely red and white checked tablecloth on it—the only table that had one. We walked over to it. Danny pulled out my chair, and when I sat down, I couldn't believe what I saw. There on the table was a copy of my favorite book, a mix tape of my favorite songs and a bouquet of my favorite flowers—"

"Irises?"

"No, Lily of the Valley." Iris remembered the little white bouquet with a smile.

"And a mix tape, the man went all out," Frank said with a nod.

"Yes, he did. I was stunned. I couldn't say a word. We didn't speak for a while. All I could do was shake my head at what he had done, and all he could do was smile. I think he was very proud of himself. We'd been there about ten minutes when our dinner came without us ordering, and of course, it was my favorite meal, *osso buco*. I was in awe. If we were old enough, I'm sure Danny would have picked out the perfect wine as well. Instead, we stuck with water and good conversation. Turns out we had a lot more in common than I realized. From that point on, we were inseparable."

"Ah, puppy love."

"You'd think so. We were sixteen at the time. Everyone wondered if we'd stay together after high school. Everyone but us, that is. We knew we were lifers."

"So, did you get married right after high school?"

"No. I went on to college at the University of Maryland to study journalism and Danny was accepted into the Naval Academy. He was so excited. The seventies were an odd time to think about enlisting. It was just a few years earlier when the U.S. withdrew from Vietnam and veterans, well, you remember, they weren't treated respectfully when they returned home. Still, Danny believed in what the Navy stood for, and his dad had served in WWII, and his granddad in WWI, so he was more than willing to do his duty and keep up the family tradition. He did well at the Academy, he graduated as a Second Lieutenant. Shortly after I graduated, we married."

"Sounds like he was a real go-getter. Did you like being a military wife? I would imagine that could be difficult."

"I liked most of it. We moved around with the Navy every three or four years, but that's how I grew up, so I was used to it. That kind of life does have its up sides. We were able to experience many different parts of the world, so many different cultures, and we went on a ton of adventures. The difficult times were the ones we spent apart while Danny was shipped out. Those months were hard on us both."

"Did you have any kids?"

"Yes, one, like you, a son. His name is Birch." Iris stood and picked up a framed picture from a shelf and handed it to Frank.

"Birch, like the tree." Frank nodded. "He's a handsome guy. He's got your smile."

Iris nodded at the photo. "His name, that was Danny's idea. I couldn't talk him out of it. He thought it would be cool to have a son named after two trees." Iris shook her head. "I had a hard time telling Danny no about anything, and it was even harder to tell him no about naming his first son. Little did we know, Birch would be his only son."

"So, what happened, how did you lose him, if you don't mind me asking?"

"You're right about Danny being a go-getter. He was always striving to be better, and he wanted to be a Navy SEAL in the worst way. He trained and studied and eventually, he was accepted into the program, and he reached his goal—he became a SEAL. He loved it, and I was very proud of him.

"A few years later, we were stationed in Virginia and Danny had shipped out and was going to be gone for several months. He was on a mission, which meant I wouldn't hear from him until he got back. Three weeks after he pulled out, there was a knock on my door. When I opened it, there were two servicemen there, an officer, and a chaplain. They didn't have to say a word. I knew why they were there." Iris took a moment and looked out the window.

"They came in and told me Danny had been killed. They couldn't tell me why or where or what happened, not even when, but they did tell me he died a hero, saving others. The two of them stayed with me, helped me call Danny's parents and my parents. They encouraged me to contact some friends on the base and have them come stay with me until our parents arrived."

"How old were you?

"Thirty-one. We'd been married ten years, that's all. We'd been together for fifteen, though. Best years of *my* life. I have no regrets."

"How did you deal with it all? I thought it was a lot in my fifties, but how'd you deal with it when you were just thirty-one and you had a small child?"

"I had an older cousin, Kate. She was an amazing woman. Cheeky sense of humor, a little mischievous, played a mean game of air hockey, and she was wise. When

Danny died, she came for a visit, about six months after the funeral. I was struggling.

"Kate, she knew about loss firsthand. She sat me down one day and said, 'Iris, there's no getting around it. This is the hard part of life. None of us gets through this world unscathed. What you've been through, what you're going to go through, it's more weight than your shoulders should have to carry. You can choose to try and carry it alone or you can choose to get help by calling on your Father in heaven. He's more than willing to bear this with you and give you the strength you need. Let Him. What you choose to do next, that's what's going to determine the next five or six decades of your life. Choose wisely, my girl.'"

"What did you do?" Frank leaned toward Iris.

"I reached up. I took my heavenly Father's hand and said, 'God, I'm scared. I can't see where I'm going, and I'm lost.' And inside, I could feel Him say, 'It's okay, I'm here. You don't have to worry, I know the way. You just hold my hand and take the next step into the light. Trust me, and you'll be fine.' And I did. . . And I was." Iris paused. "I took one small step into the light, then I chose to take another, and another. And I've been doing that ever since." Iris wiped a tear away as Frank watched her.

"One step at a time," Frank said.

"That's the only way I know."

"You made a good choice." Frank nodded. "More tea?"

"Yes, thanks."

Frank went to the kitchen and got the teakettle, then refilled Iris's and his teacups. He took a long look at Iris, then said, "Have you ever thought of remarrying?"

"Me? No, not really. Danny, he was it for me. You know what it's like, when you love someone like that, and you know they love you in the same way." Iris shook her head. "It's hard for someone to compete with a ghost."

"But if the right person came along, would you give him a chance?"

"It's been twenty-eight years. The right person has had plenty of time to come along. I don't think that's going to be happening now and I'm fine with it. Not to worry, I'm not lonely, I'm not sad, thinking I've missed out on life. Quite the contrary, I've lived a good, full life. I've had my share of adventures, believe me, and I plan to have a few more. I'm healthy, I have good teeth," Iris showed off her pearly whites with a playful grin. "And I have Mo. What more could a woman want?"

"What about Ben? I've noticed you two spending a lot of time together." Frank sipped his tea and eyed Iris.

Iris squinted her eyes. "Now who's the curious sort?"

"Guilty as charged. You don't have to answer that."

Frank put his teacup down.

"It's okay. Ben's a good man. I enjoy his company. Will it turn into more than that? I'm not sure, we'll see." Iris finished her tea. "All right, enough chitchat. Let's get this winterizing done."

Frank smiled and said, "Yes, boss."

CHAPTER 16

Birch

A little to the right, Eddie. There! That's perfect!" Iris watched from the ground as Eddie hung a wreath at the top of her garage.

Once Iris had completed winterizing, and had taken care of Frank's personal preparation suggestions, the rest of December crept along for her. She looked forward to this season with more than the usual anticipation because her son would be joining her.

Iris kept herself busy decorating the house inside and out and she asked Eddie to be her faithful sidekick. They strung lights outside, hung wreaths and bows, put up the Christmas tree inside, laughed a great deal, and had a wonderful time together. Eddie asked question after question about Birch and was almost as excited to meet him as Iris was to have him home.

"So, Miss Iris, how long has it been since you saw Birch?"

"We were together last fall for a few weeks. But it's been three years since we spent a Christmas together."

"Three years! That's a long time."

"Tell me about it," Iris smiled.

Due to arrive the week before Christmas, Birch planned to stay with his mother for two weeks. Iris decided to host an open house his first weekend in Eastport so her friends could meet him. She was pleased everyone accepted her invitation, even Frank.

Birch arrived the day before the party. He caught a flight into Bangor International Airport, then rented a car to make the two-hour drive to Eastport. Iris watched for him from her window and when his car pulled up, she ran out to greet him.

"Birch!" Iris wrapped her son in an embrace. She kissed him on the cheeks and the forehead, just as she had when he was a little boy.

"Hi, Mom. Good to see you." Birch picked his mother up in a hug and spun her around. They swept away the time they had been apart with their laughter.

After they went inside, Iris took her son by the arms, and held him away from her, and looked him over from head to toe. She shook her head and sighed. "Birch, you look like a man now. A fully grown, thirty-one-year-old adult *man*. How did this happen? You were just a little boy yesterday wondering where your model of the Millennium Falcon got to."

Birch was the spitting image of his father—about six feet tall with light brown hair that showed just a hint of red from his mother. A twinkle in his eyes and dimples in his cheeks added to the roguishness of his grin. Iris held his face in her hands and started to cry.

"Ah, Mom, I'm still your boy. You don't have to worry about that. Don't cry." Birch hugged his mother.

"Okay, enough tears. I'm just happy to see you." She kissed him on the cheek. "You're looking a little thin, my son. That will be my mission this holiday–put a little meat on those bones."

For the next several hours, they chatted away in front of the fireplace, catching each other up with the details of their lives. Mo made sure to take the prime spot in the room, Birch's lap.

Birch chattered away about his work in the Navy, especially about his position as a naval aviator. He filled his mother in on the training runs he'd been having with a new jet, about a few adventures he'd had at sea, and how he met a girl who had "potential".

Iris told Birch about life in Eastport. She shared

about Emma and how Mo was responsible for her meeting Ben. She warned him about Frank, and she let Birch know Eastport was a serious contender for a long-term stay. The two talked until the clock chimed twelve, then they reluctantly decided to call it a night.

The next morning, Iris called Emma. "I'm not sure about this, Em, Birch meeting Ben. Ben is the first man I've dated seriously since Danny, and I don't know how Birch is going to feel about him, about the whole situation. He's become very protective of me over the years. What if he doesn't like Ben?"

"Impossible. I understand your concern, but think about it. Can you imagine *anyone* not liking Ben?"

"Not really. It's not like we're talking about Frank. You're right, Ben is a good man and Birch, he likes everyone."

"I'm sure everything will be fine. You'll see. Relax, enjoy the day. And I'll be there for moral support, but you're not going to need it."

"Thanks. See you in a little while."

After Birch woke and dressed, Iris brought him to the inn to share breakfast with Emma. Emma was delighted to meet Iris's son. She shared stories of Eastport and how grateful she was to have gotten to know Iris and count her as a friend, all the while plying Birch with blueberry muffins, coffee, and an egg frittata.

On their way home, Birch leaned into his mother and said, "Emma is great. I'm glad you found such a good person for a friend."

"Me, too. She's the best."

The open house was to begin at four o'clock, but Ben arrived at Iris's around two. He asked to come early because he wanted the chance to meet Birch on his own, and though she had some reservations, she agreed.

Within a few minutes of their meeting, Iris could see Emma was right again. Birch and Ben hit it off well, swapping work stories as they set up tables and chairs, and making a ruckus with all their laughter while Iris finished preparations for the party.

Around four, the guests began to arrive. The Westheimers were the first to welcome Birch to the neighborhood.

"Happy to meet you, Birch. Your mother has been a wonderful addition to Eastport." Linda Westheimer said.

"Nice to meet you too. Mom's told me about your book club. She's enjoyed being a part of it."

"Well, we love having her. Say, we have a granddaughter who's considering enlisting in the Navy. Would you mind answering a few questions for us?"

"Sure. What would you like to know?"

For the next several minutes, the Westheimer's fired questions at Birch. He answered them all with a smile, and even offered to meet their granddaughter if she would like.

Soon after, Eddie arrived with his parents. "Eddie, Kevin, Charlotte, this is my son, Birch," Iris said.

"Nice to meet you, Birch." Kevin shook Birch's hand. Eddie stood next to his father, staring at Birch.

"Eddie, you want to say hello?" Kevin prompted.

"Hello."

"Hi, Eddie. I'm excited to meet you. My mom has told me how helpful you've been to her. Thanks. It's nice to know there's someone here looking out for her."

Eddie grinned. "You're welcome. Miss Iris is great."

"Hey, you want to come with me and get something to drink? I'm dying of thirst."

"Sure, me too." Eddie walked off with Birch.

"Look at that," Charlotte said. She, Iris, and Kevin watched the two young men go off together. "Your son is a charmer, Iris."

"He certainly is."

Later in the evening, Frank arrived. As was becoming his custom, he came bearing gifts of jams and preserves. Iris brought Frank over to Birch and said, "Birch, this is my landlord, and neighbor, Frank."

Frank reached out his hand. "It's a pleasure to meet

you, young man. Thank you for your service."

Birch gave Frank a firm handshake and smiled, "It's nice to meet you, sir. I've heard a lot about you."

"Not all of it good, I'm sure," Frank laughed.

"Well, we all have our moments."

"Are you going into the diplomatic corps? Seems like you'd be an excellent fit." The two men chatted for a moment, then Frank excused himself so Birch could greet other guests.

"So, that's Frank Happy," Birch watched Frank as he left the conversation.

"Yep, that's him. Don't judge him too harshly tonight. Frank may seem all brusque and bristly on the outside, but there's a lot happening on the inside."

"Hmmm." Birch watched his mother watching Frank.

The party started wrapping up at nine, and Ben was the last to leave at ten. Iris walked him out to his truck, kissed him goodnight, then returned to Birch. She joined him on the sofa, and they relaxed side-by-side, putting their stocking feet up on the coffee table.

"Mom, can I ask you something?"

"Anything but how much I weigh, son," Iris said with a grin.

"Are you serious about Ben?"

"I like Ben. He's a good man. We're still getting to know each other."

"But are you serious about him? Have you considered marrying him?"

"That's a pretty personal question, Birch Hornbeam." Iris sat up straight.

"I get that from you, Mom. I'm asking because I can see Ben is serious about you. He's got that look."

"That look? What are you talking about?" Iris gave her son a sideways glance.

"Aw, I've seen it dozens of times. My shipmates, every time one of them gets serious about a girl, they get that look. It's a cross between pain and delight. It's like they don't know which way to feel."

Iris laughed. "It's because love can feel exactly like that—a combination of pain and delight. Have you had that look with your girl?" Iris said, changing the direction of the conversation.

"Maybe . . ." Birch grinned.

"I see. Well, I hope I get to meet her before too long." Iris pushed Birch's foot with her own.

"I'll see what I can do." Birch stood up and stretched his arms toward the ceiling. "I'm beat. Think I'll head up to bed."

"Sounds like a plan. I'll be right behind you," Iris

yawned. Mo jumped down from the sofa and headed for Iris's bedroom. "Looks like we all have the same idea."

In the early morning, the raspy sound of a shovel scraping the sidewalk outside Iris's front door awakened the house. Iris assumed it was Eddie hard at work, but when she looked out the window, she was surprised to see Frank shoveling her walkway. A snowstorm had passed through Eastport overnight, blanketing the area with four inches of Christmas joy. Birch came downstairs shortly thereafter. "I'm going to go give him a hand, Mom." He put on his coat and headed out the door.

While Frank and Birch shoveled, Iris went to work making them a man-sized breakfast. By the time the shoveling was complete, breakfast was almost finished as well. She invited Frank to join her and Birch, and she was pleased it required little persuasion for him to agree.

"Hang your wet things in the utility room, then go sit by the fire," Iris instructed Birch and Frank. The two men complied, and once they were seated, Iris brought them each a cup of hot coffee. "Now, relax, get warm, and I'll finish up breakfast." She patted Birch on the back and smiled at Frank.

Iris went back to the kitchen and as she worked, she watched the two men talking as if they'd known each other for ages. A tear made its way down her cheek. She brushed it away, then set the table and called them over.

"This is some breakfast, Iris," Frank said, impressed by the spread Iris had prepared. He smiled when he noticed his blueberry preserves next to homemade biscuits.

"Well, you two were working so hard, and besides, Birch is a growing boy. Gotta keep him fed." Iris smiled at her son. "It was nice of you both to shovel out the Westheimer's place, too. I'm sure they'll appreciate it."

"Ah, it was no trouble," Birch said. He looked over the meal his mother prepared. "This looks awesome, Mom. Thanks. I know you wanted to put meat on my bones, but much more of this, and I won't be able to fit in the pilot's seat!"

"It's not every day I get to spoil my son. Let me have this pleasure."

Birch went to Iris and gave her a hug and a kiss on the cheek. "Love you, Mom."

"Love you too, son." Iris caught a wistful look in Frank's eyes as he smiled at her and Birch. She turned Birch around and led him to the table by the shoulders. "All right you two, sit down and dig in before everything gets cold."

Iris went to sit down, but before she could pull the chair out, Frank put his hand next to hers and pulled the chair out for her. She sat, said thank you, then watched as Frank took the chair to her right, and Birch took the seat across from him. Mo would not be left out, so he took turns winding himself between Iris's, Frank's, and Birch's legs.

"Birch, would you say grace, please?"

"Sure. Let's pray." The three held hands and bowed their heads. "Lord, thank you for bringing my mother to this beautiful place and for the friends she has made here. Thank you for healthy bodies that allow us to shovel snow and for the chance to serve each other. I thank you for this food and for the hands that prepared it. And I'm especially grateful to you for giving me this time to spend with my mom and for watching over her while I'm away. In Jesus's name, amen."

"Amen," Frank echoed.

"That was very sweet. Thank you, Birch. Okay, you two, dig in." Iris passed Frank the eggs. "So Frank, what happened to Eddie? I thought he was on snow shoveling duty."

"He was, but Charlotte called this morning. Eddie is running a fever. He still wanted to come, but Charlotte wasn't about to let him out of the house."

"That's a good mom." Iris nodded. "I hope it's nothing serious."

"Don't think so. I'm sure it's just a bad cold. You know how teenagers are, he'll be up raising Cain before you know it." Frank passed the eggs to Birch.

"I hope so," Iris said with a frown. "You know it is flu season."

"You're such a mom," Birch said as he filled his plate.

"True, and it's my favorite thing to be." She patted Birch's hand. "I'll give Charlotte a call later and check on him."

Frank glanced at Iris then said, "Birch, tell me more about being a pilot. How'd you get involved with that?" Birch explained his interest in flying, why he enlisted in the Navy, and how he ended up on the flight crew. From there they talked about places where he'd been stationed, how long he thought he'd remain in the Navy, and what he'd like to do when his service was over.

Iris smiled as she listened to Birch shift the discussion to Frank and his work as a geoscientist.

He's his mother's son. He asks almost as many questions as I do. I hope Frank is up for an inquisition.

Iris watched for signs she may have to intervene, but Frank didn't seem to mind Birch's inquiries. Frank explained his love of the outdoors and how that led to his career, and he seemed pleased to find out Birch had an interest in geology.

Birch and Frank continued to talk shop while they finished their meal. They were still talking as Iris cleared the dishes, filled their coffee mugs, and went into the living room to sit by the fire with Mo. She listened as they discussed everything from forensic geology to how the Navy is addressing greenhouse gas emissions. When they both realized she left the conversation some time ago, they got up, apologized, and went to meet her.

"It's okay, boys, you two are fascinating. I enjoyed listening," she said as she petted Mo.

"Well, I should be going. I think I've intruded on your time together enough. Thanks for breakfast, Iris. It was delicious and hit the spot today. Birch, nice talking to you." Frank extended his hand to Birch. "And thanks for the help with the shoveling."

"Happy to help, Frank. Nice talking to you too. Hope we can speak again before I leave." Birch gave Frank a firm handshake. Frank nodded, and Iris walked him to the front door.

"Frank is an interesting guy." Birch took a seat on the sofa.

"You could say that." Iris closed the door. "You could also say he's infuriatingly stubborn, quick-tempered, and inflexible."

Birch looked at his mother, then stared at his coffee. Iris watched him for a moment. "Birch, what are you thinking?"

"I don't know. It's just . . . never mind."

"Go ahead, you can tell me. I can see you've been noodling on something all morning." Iris took a seat next to him.

"All right. Mom, whenever you look at Ben, you look at him like he's a good, kind man."

"Well, he is." Iris shrugged her shoulders.

"I can see that, but when you look at Frank," Birch hesitated.

"What? When I look at Frank what?"

"You've got that look of pain and delight." Birch tilted his head and raised his eyebrows at his mother.

"It's mostly pain, I'm sure. Frank has a dozen ways he can aggravate me, and he uses them all."

Birch shook his head at her.

"Let's not waste any more time talking about the men in my life, unless we're talking about you."

CHAPTER 17

Merry Christmas

The week of Christmas went much too fast for Iris. Despite the snowy weather, she enjoyed showing Eastport off to Birch and he enjoyed getting a sense of the place and the people.

"I'm sorry there hasn't been much time to spend with Ben," Iris said one afternoon.

"That's okay, Mom. He's on duty. I get it."

"Sometimes he reminds me of your father. You were too young to remember this, but your dad had a habit of volunteering to take extra duty over the holidays so that people with families could spend more time at home. Ben does the same thing."

"That's nice of him. Will he have Christmas with us?"

"No, he'll be working. We decided to wait and do our

Christmas together after you go back on active duty, which will be too soon for me." Birch gave his mother a hug.

Ben did have a free evening during the week, and he asked Iris and Birch to join him for dinner with his parents in Perry, which they were happy to do.

Ben's parents were as impressed with Birch as everyone else had been. Birch enjoyed getting to meet Ben's father, Phil, especially after finding out he had served in the Navy.

"Listen to the two of them in there," Iris said to Ben as they cleared the table after dinner. "Swapping tall tales. I don't know who to believe less!"

Ben laughed. "I wouldn't bet against my father. And wait till Birch finds out that my mother was a pilot in the Air Force during World War II."

"What? I didn't know that."

"Yep. She was a shuttle pilot. She flew newly built airplanes across the country delivering them to different bases."

"Elsie did that? I knew I liked your mother."

After some prompting from Iris, Elsie told her and Birch of her time in the service. Birch sat entranced by her stories. A few hours later, it was time to wrap up the evening.

"It was nice to meet you both. Thanks for having us

for dinner." Birch shook Phil's hand.

"It was our pleasure," Elsie gave Birch a kiss on the cheek. "You are a delightful boy and have the most adorable dimples. You are going to make some woman very happy."

"Hope I can find someone like you, Mrs. Hudson." Birch hugged her. "Next time I'm in town, I'll be sure to stop by and we can swap some more stories."

"We'll look forward to it." Phil patted Birch on the back.

On Christmas Eve, Birch, Iris, and Emma went to the Eastport Community Church together for the candlelight service. Iris had been attending services at the church with Emma since Emma had invited her not long after her move to Eastport. Iris was excited to share her new church home with Birch, especially for the Christmas service.

Not long after they arrived, Iris spotted Frank walking into the sanctuary. When she motioned for him to join her, he smiled and walked her way.

"Good evening, everyone, and Merry Christmas." Frank came into the pew.

"Nice to see you again, Frank." Birch leaned over his

mother and shook Frank's hand.

"Good to see you too, Birch. Hope you've been having a pleasant visit."

"It's been awesome. Sorry it'll be ending soon though." Birch glanced at Iris. She looked at him and sighed.

"Surprised to see you here," Iris teased Frank.

"Never miss a Christmas or Easter service, Iris. I'm what they call a two-timer." He grinned.

With that, the service began. The traditional carols were sung, and the Christmas story read. A children's choir came to the front, dressed as angels. They began singing an enthusiastic rendition of "Go Tell It on the Mountain", complete with hand motions.

"There's an escapee," Birch whispered to Iris midway through the song. He pointed. "Look."

The littlest angel on the end wondered off the stage and down the center aisle in search of her mother. When she got to Iris's pew, she stopped and looked up at Frank.

"Santa?" Her eyes grew wide as she stared at Frank.

"No, honey, but I'm his helper. May I help you?"

The little girl nodded, and Frank offered her his hand. She accepted it, then he stood, picked her up and looked around the congregation. Her mother was on the other side of the room, making her way over. Frank met her in the back of the sanctuary and returned the littlest angel to where she belonged.

Frank slid back into the pew.

"Santa's helper?" Iris said.

Frank shrugged. "You never know about a person."

"No, you never do." Iris smiled.

Pastor Steve came to the front and opened his bible. "Seven hundred years before Jesus's birth, Isaiah prophesied that Jesus would be born of a virgin and that His name would be called *Emmanuel*, which means *God with us*. God has always been with His people. He walked with Adam and Eve in the garden of Eden, He instructed Noah to build an ark. He appeared as a cloud by day and a pillar of fire by night to the Israelites in the desert. He has been present in dreams, and in visions. He has come in a still, small voice, in the sound of blaring trumpets, and in the flight of a dove. But He has never been as fully present with us as He was that night in Bethlehem. The night when He laid aside His kingly crown and allowed Himself to be cradled in his mother's arms. The Word became flesh and dwelt among us. *God with us.*

"From Bethlehem, Jesus began a journey of thirty-three years to the cross of Calvary where He would be present as our Redeemer, our Reconciler, our Savior. And because of what Jesus did on the cross, we no longer have to experience God as a presence outside of ourselves. If we believe in Him, if we accept Him as our Lord and Savior, He promises that He will be present *in us* in the form of the Holy Spirit. He truly is God with us.

"That night in Bethlehem, when the shepherds arrived at the stable, they were in the presence of God. Later, when the wise men came to the house where Jesus lived, they too were in the presence of God. Though these two groups couldn't have been more different, their response to meeting Jesus was the same: worship.

"This evening, as we encounter Jesus, whether it's our first time, or whether we've known Him all our lives, our response should be the same as the shepherds and wise men: worship. So, stand with me now, take the person's hand next to you and let's offer God our worship together by singing *Silent Night*."

Iris stood and grasped Birch's hand with her left hand, then looked at Frank, who was standing to her right. Frank smiled, then held out his hand. Iris smiled shyly, then slipped her hand in his, then the two looked awkwardly toward the front, and joined in the singing. At the end of the song, the congregation turned toward each other and many wishes of "Merry Christmas" were shared. Birch hugged Emma and wished her a merry Christmas.

Frank turned to Iris. "Merry Christmas. Enjoy this

time with Birch. He's a fine man. You've raised him well."

Iris looked at her son. "That he is. Thank you." She turned back to Frank.

I should hug him. Should I? It's Christmas. I should hug him. Oh, just do it.

Before she could change her mind, Iris gave Frank a hug and said, "Merry Christmas, Frank."

Frank held her in return and the strength of his embrace was unexpected, as was the briefness. Afterward, he smiled and said, "Good night, Iris." He wished Emma and Birch a merry Christmas, then he was on his way. Iris watched him leave, then gave a sigh. Birch and Emma watched Iris, then nodded to each other.

Christmas morning was a slow rise for both Iris and Birch, the week's activities having caught up with them. Mo would not be put off, however. He walked over Iris's face to wake her up at the usual time. She was sure he knew Santa Paws had left a little catnip for him in his stocking.

Iris got up, put the coffee on, fed Mo, then got showered and dressed. Soon thereafter, Birch joined her for a light breakfast and their Christmas morning tradition—watching *It's a Wonderful Life*.

When the movie ended, Iris kissed her son on the cheek. "I love you, Birch. I'm so glad we've had this Christmas together. Best one I can remember in a long time."

"Love you too, Mom, and yeah, this has been awesome. Eastport's a great town. I can see why you like it. I think you can be happy here. So, do you think you'll stay?"

"Undecided, but this much I can say, it'll be difficult to leave."

"Wow, I can't remember you saying that about any place we've lived. Eastport, I'm impressed," Birch said to the town, lifting his coffee mug in a toast.

Iris tapped her son on the leg. "Time for presents!" She and Birch spent the next hour exchanging gifts, reminiscing about past Christmases together, and enjoying each other's company. As the conversation dwindled, Birch noticed two gifts under the tree.

"You forget some, Mom?" Birch asked, pointing to the gifts.

"No, one of those is for Ben. And that one . . ." She pointed to a small, rectangular box. "That one's for Frank," She wrinkled her forehead. "I haven't figured out when to give it to him."

Birch smiled at his mother. "Well, it *is* Christmas Day. Now might be a good time to do it."

"Now? Like *now*?" Iris scrunched her face.

"Why not?" Birch went to the window and looked out on the street. "There aren't any extra cars, doesn't look like he's got company. Why don't you walk over there and give it to him?"

"I don't know. I don't want to bother him on Christmas Day." Iris waved Birch's suggestion off with her hand.

"Mom, trust me on this, a gift from you on Christmas will not be a bother."

"Don't start," Iris lowered her chin and eyed Birch. Birch met his mother's gaze. Iris rolled her eyes. "Fine, I'll go." She went to get her coat. "But if he gives me a hard time, it's on your head."

Birch laughed, helped Iris on with her coat, handed her the gift, then took her by the shoulders and walked her to the front door. As he opened it, he said, "Good luck, soldier." Iris saluted, shook her head, and went on her way.

Once more, Iris found herself staring at Frank's front door. She hesitated to knock.

You're being foolish, Iris. Knock on the door.

She took a deep breath, and with some trepidation, she tapped on it.

In a moment, Frank answered, and instead of his usual glare, he greeted Iris with a warm smile and a, "Well,

Merry Christmas, Iris. I'm surprised to see you here. Come in, it's freezing out there."

Iris looked over toward her house and could see Birch watching from the front door, beaming at her. She shrugged her shoulders at him, then walked inside Frank's home.

"Let me take your coat," Frank said, leading Iris into the living room. She looked over the room.

Well, it's no accident my home is so well appointed. He really does have an eye for color and design. Masculine, simple, surprisingly refined. This house is just like him.

A manger scene on the mantle and a small, live tree in the room's corner spoke a quiet message of Christmas. Iris noticed one package still under the tree.

"I hope you don't mind me stopping by, but I wanted to give you this," Iris handed Frank her gift. "Merry Christmas, Frank."

Frank took the gift, looked at it for a moment, then looked at Iris, "This is very nice, thank you. And I have something for you, too." Frank placed Iris's gift on an end table, then moved to his Christmas tree, picked up the present beneath it, and brought it back to Iris. "I've been wanting to give this to you, but I wasn't sure when . . . I, uh, I didn't want to interrupt," Frank said with an uneasy smile.

Iris let out a small laugh. "I know exactly how you feel."

"Well, sit, sit." Frank motioned to the sofa. "Would you like some tea or coffee?"

"No, thank you. I'm fine."

Frank, hospitable? Who knew?

Frank placed the present next to Iris, then took a seat in the chair next to her. Iris asked, "Would you like to open your gift now?"

"Ladies first." Frank motioned to Iris with his hand.

"All right."

Why am I so nervous? It's just Frank.

She picked up the gift, a large square box, and placed it on her lap. Frank had wrapped it so Iris could simply remove the lid, which she did. She folded back the tissue paper inside and revealed a black trapper-style hat. She removed the hat, and felt the warm, shearling interior and soft sheepskin outer covering. "Frank, this feels amazing!" She held the shearling against her cheek. "Thank you so much."

"I know it isn't exactly New York fashion, but it'll keep you warm."

"I'm sure, and it's incredibly soft, inside and out," Iris said, continuing to hold the hat against her cheek.

"But wait, there's more," Frank said with a smile.

Iris tilted her head at Frank. She looked in the box and pulled back another layer of tissue. There she found a forest green and black plaid cashmere scarf and a pair of black waterproof gloves. Iris gasped, then looked at Frank, who smiled at her. She took them out of the box and wrapped the scarf around her neck.

So soft and warm, this is perfect. How'd he do this? Practical and beautiful.

She tried the gloves on. "Frank, these gloves are amazing. And they fit perfectly. When you said I should have waterproof gloves, I thought you meant those awful, bulky skiing things, but these . . ." Iris admired the snug fit of the gloves and the soft, thermal fleece lining. "I didn't even know they made something like this."

"Well, you're not from around here." Frank nodded toward the box one more time.

"More?" Iris raised her eyebrows. Frank smiled. "Frank."

"Go ahead, take a look."

He's up to something. I can see it.

Iris looked in the box, carefully removed one more layer of tissue, then burst into laughter. There at the bottom of the box was a pair of bright red Long Johns and a red handkerchief. "Frank, you're ridiculous, but I love them."

She removed the gloves and scarf and tucked them back into the box. "Thank you so much. This was very thoughtful, and I appreciate you looking out for me. You're a wonderful gift-giver." Frank nodded and looked toward the floor.

I've embarrassed him. Keep things moving, Iris.

"Okay, your turn." She handed Frank his gift again.

Frank took the gift from her and stared at it for a moment.

"Please, open it. It's okay, I promise, it won't explode."

He smiled, then unwrapped the gift, as Iris bit her lip.

Please like it.

Inside was a box and when Frank lifted the lid, he blinked a few times, then carefully took out the contents— a fiftieth anniversary edition of *The Lord of the Rings*. Gilded edges framed the book and an extraordinary deerskin leather cover with a leather strap safeguarded the pages. Frank held the book, his brow furrowed as he examined it. His large, rough hands caressed the cover as gently as if it were a newborn babe. He turned the book over several times, shaking his head as he did. He looked up at Iris and continued to shake his head.

"Do you like it?" Iris held her breath.

Please say yes.

Frank nodded. "Yes."

Is that a tear I see sneaking in the corner of your eye?

"Thank you, Iris. This is . . . remarkable."

Iris sighed in relief and smiled. "Well, I guess I should be going. I don't want to interrupt your day any more than I already have." Iris stood up. "Are you having company or are you going somewhere?"

"No, I'm not." Frank stood with her.

"Neither? You're going to be alone on Christmas Day?"

"Not completely. I'm planning to spend some quality time with a few football teams. Should be a nice day. Go, enjoy your son." Frank said with a smile as he got her coat.

"Get your coat on, Frank."

"Excuse me?" Frank held Iris's coat for her.

"We're not going to discuss this. You're coming with me, and you're going to spend the rest of the day with me and Birch. And we're not going to waste time arguing about it because you know, in the end, I will win. I will not have you spending Christmas Day alone. That's the end of it. So, go get your coat." Iris said this in a tone and with a look that let Frank know it was indeed useless to argue, so he shook his head, got his coat, and walked Iris home.

CHAPTER 18

The Visit

The new year would bring the end of Birch's visit, so during this last week of his time in Eastport, along with spending time with Iris, he met with Frank often, discussing geoscience and career possibilities, and he met with Ben several times as well. As best he could, he wanted to get to know these men who'd become so important to his mother. In the end, he decided they were both fine men, and he was confident they would look out for his mother while he was away. He had his opinion of who he thought was best suited for her, but he kept his opinion to himself.

On New Year's Eve, Iris and Birch decided to join in a quirky Eastport tradition. They bundled themselves up and walked to the Tides Institute and Museum of Art, just across the street from the WaCo Diner, for the Great Sardine and Maple Leaf Drop, a double ringing in of the new year. At 11:00pm EST/12:00am AST, a large wooden maple leaf, lit with dozens of twinkle lights, dropped from the top of the museum along suspended wires to the street below, marking the start of Canada's new year. A rousing cheer and the impromptu singing of "Oh, Canada" followed.

"To the diner!" Iris said, grabbing Birch's arm. Mother and son marched across the street with other celebrants to stay warm and wait for the next part of the celebration.

Ben joined them around 11:45 when they went outside for the final countdown. At midnight, in homage to the industry that was prevalent in Eastport for so many years, an eight-foot sardine followed the path laid out earlier by the maple leaf. This set off another round of cheers and the singing of Auld Lang Syne.

Ben kissed Iris at the appropriate time and wrapped her in a warm embrace. "I wish I could have made this evening more romantic for you, but I'm glad we could at least have this moment together," he whispered in her ear.

"Me, too."

"Happy New Year, Birch," Ben said with a handshake.

"Happy New Year, Ben."

After additional shaking of hands and kisses on the cheeks of those surrounding them, the trio went back to Iris's to enjoy the fireworks over the water from the warmth of her living room.

Iris soaked in every moment she could with her son on New Year's Day, and when January second dawned, the day he was to leave, Iris did her best to stay composed. The last thing she wanted was Birch to see her in a puddle of tears, so she held herself together during the packing, and the breakfast, and the last goodbyes as he got into the car. As he pulled away, Iris stood on the sidewalk watching until his car was no longer in sight, then she put her head down and trudged back into her home.

Frank watched the entire scene from his living room window.

A week later, another storm passed through Eastport, leaving a quilt of snow atop the blanket that had been laid earlier. Frank was outside shoveling the walkway when a black SUV pulled up in front of Iris's house. He stopped what he was doing and watched as two uniformed men got out, put their caps on, made sure their jackets were straight, then walked with purpose to Iris's front door. One officer knocked on the door, then stepped back and waited. When Iris opened the door and saw the men, her face told the complete story of why they were there. She turned away, and the men entered the house. Frank dropped his shovel and went to her.

The front door was ajar, so he went inside, and closed the door without a sound. He came through the foyer, and into the dining area, cutting his way through the shroud of catastrophe that filled the house. Iris sat in the wingback chair in the living room, and the officers sat next to her on the sofa. They all looked up at him when he entered.

"Iris?" Frank said, looking at the officers.

"Ma'am?" the chaplain said as he looked toward Frank.

Frank stood stock still, waiting for Iris's response.

"It's all right, please go on," Iris said in a voice devoid of emotion.

Frank didn't move from his spot. He kept his eyes fixed on Iris as she listened to what the chaplain had to say. He watched her as she sat stoically with her back straight, motionless except for the folding and unfolding of her hands. As she listened to the chaplain, she closed her eyes several times, but always she kept her chin up. He watched her clench her hands together in a grip so tight it turned her knuckles white as details were revealed. She made no sound and disregarded all eye contact, choosing to stare ahead when her eyes were not closed. At last, the chaplain's story ended. They all sat in silence for a moment, then the chaplain asked, "Would you like us to leave now and come back at another time, ma'am?"

"Yes, please. Thank you. I know this was difficult for you. I appreciate you coming." Iris stood and walked them to the door. Frank stepped aside. The men left, then Iris closed the door behind them.

Iris stood motionless, staring at the door. Frank went next to her and touched her arm. "Iris?" Iris looked at Frank, then her knees buckled, and she dissolved into tears. Frank caught her, and with his arm around her, he led her to the sofa. He sat her down, and she folded herself in two and sobbed inconsolably, rocking herself back and forth. Frank sat beside her, patting her back and holding her hand. Minutes passed before Iris sat herself up, her face awash in tears. Frank asked, "What can I do?"

"Emma."

Frank stood and picked up his phone and paced as

he called the inn. "Emma, Frank here. I'm at Iris's. She's had some bad news. Can you come?" Frank paused to listen. "Yes, as fast as you can. And can you let Ben know?" He hung up the phone and took a deep breath.

God, help me.

He went back to Iris.

The next few weeks were a bleak mid-winter for Iris. Ben, Emma, and Frank did their utmost to comfort her and be a source of support. It amazed them how well Iris held herself together through all the arrangements, notifications, details of the funeral, and burial at Arlington Cemetery. Ben, Emma, and Frank all traveled with her for the burial, and while each of them shed a tear for the loss of this young man, his mother sat impassively throughout the ceremony, even as she received the folded flag from his coffin.

After the funeral, Frank, Emma, and Ben got together in the hotel café while Iris rested in her room.

"I'm so worried about her," Emma said. "Losing Birch like this. . . her only child. I'm not sure what to do."

"She's not talking, barely eating. She can't keep going like this," Ben said.

Frank remained quiet.

"Do you have any thoughts, Frank? How can we help her? I hate to bring it up, but between the three of us, you have the most experience with something like this." Emma said.

Frank nodded. "She's still in shock. She hasn't accepted it yet. It's better she's not left alone for a while. As much as we can, someone should be with her. I can cover the mornings. I know that's tough for you two. Nights can be long and terrifying. I'm sure she's not sleeping soundly and probably won't for a while. Ben, can you stay with her, in case she wakes up?

"Absolutely."

The trio continued to make plans and the next day they returned to Eastport with Iris. They brought her home and Emma unpacked Iris's things and put her to bed. Ben prepared to spend the night on the sofa.

The next morning, as Frank was getting ready to go to Iris's he got a phone call.

"Frank? It's Ben. Can you meet me at the diner in about fifteen minutes? It's important."

"Ayuh."

Frank walked to the diner and took a seat at the counter. He ordered a cup of coffee and waited for Ben. A few minutes later, Ben walked in. Frank nodded in acknowledgment as Ben sat down. Judy smiled at Ben and went to get him a cup of coffee. Frank waited for Ben to speak.

Ben avoided eye contact with Frank and held his coffee mug as if it were a suspect attempting to escape. "You know I'd do just about anything for her, right?"

"Ayuh." Frank replied, looking at his own coffee mug.

"Well, I can't do this, stay with her overnight." He looked at Frank. "I slept in the living room so I could hear her if she woke up. Last night, my radio, it must have gone off a hundred times and as sheriff, I can't turn it off."

"Understood."

"I'm amazed it didn't wake her. I guess she was too exhausted to hear anything. But one of these nights, I'm gonna get a call, and I'll have to leave. I can't do that to her. That would be the night she'd wake and need me, need someone." Ben rubbed his hand on his chin. "I hate to ask, but could you do it? I'd ask Emma, but she can't leave the inn. Could you stay with her?"

Frank continued to stare at his coffee. He nodded. "Ayuh." He took a sip, then looked at Ben. "I'll do it on one condition—you don't tell her it's me staying there."

"What? Why?" Ben narrowed his eyes.

"She'll feel better thinking it's you asleep on the

couch. If she wakes up, discovers it's me instead, fine. I'll explain. But if she doesn't, she doesn't need to know."

Ben nodded. "Agreed."

"Emma too. She can know I'm there, but don't let her tell Iris." Frank stood up. "I'll start tonight." He left a tip on the counter and walked out of the diner.

Frank took it upon himself to fix Iris a light breakfast every morning. She would wake, enter the room without a sound, wrapped in a blanket of malaise, and eat a small portion of what Frank had prepared. Her eyes never moved from a downward gaze and though Mo was her constant companion, she barely acknowledged his existence. Following breakfast, she would go back to bed. Frank would stay nearby and repeat the process at lunch, then he'd remain until Ben or Emma could come later in the afternoon or for dinner.

A few days after their return, Frank became concerned about Mo as well.

I hate cats, but that one sure is devoted to Iris. He's not looking so great.

Frank picked the cat up and placed him in his lap. "Mo, I know this is hard on you. You must be worried. We all are. But she needs you. You need to take of yourself . . . for her." Mo rubbed his head against Frank's palm. Frank petted him. "Guess I'll have to look after you, too."

Two weeks later, after breakfast, instead of returning to bed, Iris walked into the living room and took her place on the rocker by the fireplace. Frank joined her, sitting near her on the sofa. The two sat in silence until Iris turned to him.

"Frank."

"Yes?"

"Frank. My son is dead. Birch, my baby... he's gone." She wept, her mother's heart breaking with grief.

"I know. I know." Frank went to her. He knelt beside her and wrapped his arm around her. Iris crumpled over on herself and sobbed, overwhelmed by the reality of her loss. "That's it, you cry now. You go ahead and cry. He was a fine man, and he was taken from us too soon," Frank said as he patted her back. "You cry. I'm here. It's time."

Iris continued to cry, her body racked with pain. She sat up and began shaking her head. "I don't know what to do. I don't know what to do," she repeated over and over. She rubbed her hands between her cheeks and forehead, as waves of tears flooded her eyes and spilled down her face.

"Iris, look at me." Frank took her hand. "Look at me, please." It took a moment, but Iris gave Frank her attention, her face streaked with tears and her body shaking.

That's it, Iris, focus on me.

248

"You know *exactly* what to do." He maintained his gaze as she looked at him as if searching for a lifeline. "Iris, you've done it before. You can do it again." He enveloped her trembling hands in his and said once more, "You know what to do."

Iris stared at Frank, then nodded, closed her eyes, and prayed.

The next morning, Iris took a turn for the better and when she did, Mo did too. Frank was in the kitchen making breakfast. He stopped whipping eggs and smiled as Iris came out of her bedroom, having showered, dressed, and put on a little make-up.

That's a good step, Iris. You can do this. Keep taking the next step into the light, even if it's a small one.

Iris smiled, and said weakly, "Thank you, Frank, for all you've done. I appreciate it."

"No need for thanks, just being neighborly. How are you feeling today?" He searched her eyes for any positive signs.

"Better." Iris took a deep breath, and one tear made its way down her cheek. "I know my son, and he wouldn't want me sitting around in sackcloth and ashes anymore."

She wiped away the tear. "It's time I rejoined the human race."

"Welcome back," Frank said as he placed a plate of scrambled eggs on the breakfast bar.

"You know, you surprise me." She gave him a fragile smile. "You're a pretty good cook. I thought you only knew jams and jellies, but you make a mean scrambled egg."

Frank returned her smile, then poured a cup of coffee, and sat with her while she ate her breakfast, one small forkful at a time.

What a chore for you, to eat a simple meal. But you are determined, I can see that. You're a formidable woman, Iris Hornbeam.

When Iris was through, she made her way to the living room and Frank followed. "Would you like me to make you a fire?"

"Yes, please, that'd be nice." Iris sat down on the sofa and Mo followed. He walked back and forth across her lap a few times, then settled in next to her, curled up into a little black ball. Iris reached over and petted him.

Soon, Frank had a pleasant fire going. He sat in the chair next to Iris and watched her as she watched the fire. The two were silent for some time.

"Is there anything I can get you, do for you, Iris?"

She shook her head and whispered, "No, thank you."

She sat for a few moments, staring at the fire, then she turned to Frank. "Frank. I don't know if I can do this." Her eyes brimmed with tears.

Frank went over and sat beside her. "Did I ever tell you about my first encounter with a hornbeam?" Iris shook her head no. "It was early in my geoscientist career. I was doing a study on the transition from marsh to meadow in one of the state parks. I was camping in the meadow, and there was a line of hornbeams marking the end of the meadow and the beginning of the marsh. There they stood, tall, strong, like so many sentries holding the line around the meadow. I have to admit, when I first saw them, I was a bit intimidated, a little afraid even. They seemed to be like those menacing figures that were the stuff of my nightmares as a child. But over time, that changed. I came to respect and love those trees for their power, their mystery, their strength, the way their trunks entwined themselves in their own magical way, like Celtic art. Their sinewy threads weaving a meticulous and beguiling pattern. And I was lucky enough to see it, to experience it." Frank took Iris's hand. "*You* are a Hornbeam, Iris. You have that same strength in you, that same Celtic artwork. You *can* do this."

Iris closed her eyes, and she squeezed Frank's hand as another tear fell.

The next morning, Frank was ready and waiting again as Iris awakened and came out for breakfast. They chatted as she did her best to fortify herself for the day with a full meal of French toast and orange juice Frank had prepared. Following breakfast, they adjourned to the living room, where Frank had already made a pleasant fire. There, the two talked softly about nothing in particular, and when their conversation dwindled down to silence, Frank studied Iris for a few moments.

Why did this have to happen to her? Hasn't she suffered enough in her life already?

"Iris, I am so sorry. I am so very sorry. I don't know why God did this to you, but I'm sorry it happened. I wish I could change it for you."

Iris sat back and looked at Frank. "You think God did this?" She shook her head at him. "Frank, you don't know God at all. God didn't do this." She looked at the fire. "A man chose to get drunk. Then he chose to get behind the wheel of his car. He ran a red light. And he hit my son as he was on his way to serve his country." She turned to Frank and said, "That's who's responsible for this, that man, not God. Don't blame this on Him."

"But Iris, you're a Christian, a person of faith. Where was He? Where was God when this was happening to you? Happening to Birch? Where *was* He?" Frank said, with more than a hint of anger in his voice.

Iris pulled Mo to her lap. She looked at Frank for a moment. "You sat next to me in church just a few weeks ago on Christmas Eve. You sang the songs, you listened to the story, but you missed one important part, 'You shall call His name Emmanuel, God with us.' *God with us.* I'll tell you where He was Frank. God was in the front seat of my son's car, holding my baby so he wouldn't be alone when he died. He was in my living room when the chaplain came to give me the news. He stood next to me in the funeral home when I had to arrange for my only child's burial. In the cemetery, He was right beside me with His hand on my shoulder when they handed me a flag and placed my son's body in the ground. And he has been with me every single second of every day since, holding my hand, making sure I don't go crazy. That's where He's been."

Looking at the fire with tears in her eyes, Iris continued, her voice breaking, "He's been in Emma when she comes by every afternoon and sits with me and cries with me. He's been in Ben when he comes over to make sure I feel safe and cared for. He's been in Eddie when he comes to shovel the walk or do some made up chore so he can be here and give me a hug and tell me he loves me." Then turning to Frank, she said, "And he's even been in you Frank, when you come here every morning like clockwork to make me breakfast and watch me to make sure I eat something and then stay, just so there will be another living soul in the house. *God...with...us.* God has been here the whole time. I'm sorry you couldn't see Him."

Frank sat in silence. Iris wiped the tears from her cheeks and said, "I'm going to go take a nap now." She stood and started walking out of the room, Mo cradled in her arms. "Thanks for breakfast. You've been a great friend, and I appreciate everything you've done. I've put you out enough, though. You don't have to come back tomorrow. I'm going to be fine."

"I'll be by anyway, just to be sure."

Iris nodded, then made her way to her room.

Frank remained in the chair, staring at the fire.

CHAPTER 19

A Proposal

Iris continued to adjust to the loss of her son. Though it was difficult, having good friends like Emma, and Frank, and the concern and attention Ben showed her made it bearable. Every day she seemed to get stronger, and more like the Iris everyone had met the previous year, though everyone was certain she would never be completely the same.

"I'd like to take you somewhere special for Valentine's Day," Ben said a few days prior to the holiday.

"I don't know if I'm up for a crowd," Iris said, settling into her sofa.

"I know this quiet little place. Not much in the way of ambience, but it'd be just the two of us. Could you handle my house?"

Iris smiled. "That would be perfect, thank you."

On Valentine's Day, Ben brought Iris to his home and they shared the dinner he had ordered for her. They chatted over the meal and Ben even got Iris to laugh a few times. After dinner, they retreated to the living room where Ben made a lively fire, then he sat next to Iris on the couch. She leaned into him, staring at the fire, and he enveloped her in his arms.

"Iris," Ben said after a few moments. "There's something I've been wanting to talk to you about."

"Yes?" Iris sat up.

"I know this will be difficult, so I want you to hear me out. Okay?"

"All right, I'm listening." Iris felt her stomach tighten.

Please, no more bad news.

Ben took a deep breath, then clasped, and unclasped his hands together. "I'd pretty much given up hope I'd ever meet someone special. Didn't think it was in the cards for me. And then one day, I got a 911 about a panther in a tree."

Iris smiled, thinking back to the first time she met Ben.

"Didn't find the panther, but I did find a remarkable woman. We've been together almost a year now, and it seems like the wrong time to bring it up, but after Birch, well, it didn't seem like a good idea to wait either." He paused and took her hand. "Iris, I love you. You know that."

Iris nodded.

"And I know we're not on the same page yet when it comes to how we feel about each other, but I'm going to ask you something anyway."

Don't do it, Ben. Please, don't do it. I'm not ready.

"Iris, would you do me the honor of becoming my wife? Would you marry me?"

Iris's eyes got very wide, and her stomach drew even tighter. "Ben . . ."

"I know, I know. This is a lot, especially considering all that's happened. But Iris, I don't want to miss the chance to tell you how I feel, what you mean to me. I wish I could change things for you. Take away your pain. I'd do anything if I could. The only thing I can do is let you know how much I want to be here for you, how much I want to take care of you, how much I—You understand, right?"

Iris nodded. "I understand."

"Like I said, I know we're not on the same page yet, as far as how we feel, but my hope is over time, you'll come to love me in the same way I love you. I don't need your answer tonight. I just needed to tell you, to ask you. Would you think about it? Would you consider what I'm asking?"

"Of course, I'll think about it, but Ben, I'm not sure I'm good at decision making right now, especially a decision like this."

"I understand, I do. All I'm asking is for you to think about it." Ben gave Iris a gentle smile. "And so you know, I'm not going anywhere. I'll be here for you Iris, whatever you need, no matter what your answer is." He leaned over and kissed Iris's forehead, then held her.

As she held him in return, she stared at the fire.

I have no idea what I need. And I'm not sure I want to know.

CHAPTER 20

911

Three weeks later, Iris still hadn't given Ben an answer. True to his word, he was patient and didn't pressure her for a response. On an unusually temperate day, Iris went out on her back porch to clear the dregs of winter away. She looked out and saw Frank in his yard, doing the same, so she made her way over to the fence. She laid her arms on top of the gate. "Hi, Frank."

"Morning. Getting some fresh air?" Frank said, looking up at Iris.

"Yes. It's nice to have a day above freezing." Iris scanned Frank's yard. "Anything new with you?"

"No. Just getting prepped for spring. Almanac says it'll be an early one this year. Hopefully, it's correct."

Iris nodded in agreement. "Hope so." Iris paused and scanned Frank's yard again.

"Iris, something on your mind?"

"I have some news." Iris laid her chin on her arms.

"Good news, I hope." Frank walked toward her.

"I think so," she said, her forehead wrinkling. She took her chin off her arms, then held on to the top of the gate. "Ben asked me to marry him."

Frank froze.

"I haven't given him an answer yet, but I will soon. It's only fair."

"I see," Frank said, looking down. He picked his head up, and with a smile Iris thought looked forced, he said, "Well, I guess congratulations are in order?"

"Probably." She returned her own forced smile.

"Iris, you don't sound too sure. Are you really ready to marry Ben?"

"Ready as I'll ever be." She shrugged one of her shoulders. "Ben's a good man. He is. He's solid, reliable. He loves me. I'd be foolish not to marry him."

"Hmmm."

"You don't think I should?"

Frank looked down at the ground again, then he shook his head.

Please tell me the truth.

He looked up at Iris. "You're a grown woman, Iris. You've had more than your share of tragedy. If you believe

260

you can be happy with Ben, then I wish you well."

Iris stood up straight and watched Frank turn and hurry back into his home. She closed her eyes and sighed. "Guess I was wrong about you."

Iris did accept Ben's proposal, with the proviso they wouldn't rush the wedding. It was enough for Ben to hear they would get married, and while he was willing to wait, he was hopeful he wouldn't have to wait much past spring.

Iris saw little of Ben over the next few weeks. It had been an unusual winter and several early spring snowstorms passed through the area, keeping him busy with emergency management. The storms also kept everyone else inside, so she didn't see much of Frank or Emma either. She was glad to have Mo's company as she waited for spring to assert itself.

The weather broke, and the sunshine and milder temperatures made short order of the snow and ice. After a few days of warming sun, the only evidence snowstorms had visited Eastport were the melting snowmen, and mountain ridges of white stretching along the roadsides.

Iris looked forward to being outside again and preparing her garden for spring planting. She got her chance one pleasant day, early in April. She got dressed in her work clothes, pulled out her gardening tools, and headed out the backdoor with Mo tagging along. Ben called shortly after she began her work and offered to come and give her a hand. Fifteen minutes later, he arrived and pitched in. Ben and Iris chatted and worked together for about an hour, enjoying the fresh air and sunshine.

"I'm going to be sore tomorrow after not using my gardening muscles all winter. It's worth it though. What a nice day." Iris stopped. "Where's Mo?" She looked around her yard for her wayward cat.

"I don't know. Now that you mention it, he hasn't been pestering me." Ben joined her in scanning the backyard.

"Me neither. He's gone. We have to find him." Iris looked around again. "Oh, please no." Iris ran to the fence gate.

"Oh please, no, what?" Ben got to his feet and followed Iris.

"He's got this thing with Frank's garden. He's always digging over there. He'd better not be at it again now that he can get to the soil." Iris opened the gate. She looked over the garden, and sure enough, she could see where Mo had been digging, but he was nowhere in sight.

"Mo, where are you, you little ditch digger?" Iris called out. "Mo!" She hustled down Frank's garden path and when she got to the end, she looked toward the greenhouse. The door was open. A shiver slid down her spine. "Ben! Here!" She ran to the greenhouse.

She went inside. There was Frank, lying face down on the floor with Mo curled up next to him. "Frank!" Iris ran to him, knelt on the floor, and turned him over. She put her cheek next to his nose and felt a faint exhale.

He's breathing, good.

"Ben!" she called again. Ben came running in. He went straight to her. "He's burning up," Iris said, holding Frank's head in her lap with her hand on his forehead. Ben checked Frank's pulse, then called 911. He gave details to the 911 operator while Iris tended to Frank, trying to raise him to consciousness.

"Frank, please wake up."

God help him, please. This can't be happening.

The ambulance arrived without delay and the EMTs worked on Frank briefly, loaded him into the ambulance, then with sirens shrieking, they made a sharp turn out of the driveway and headed for the hospital. Ben and Iris followed in Ben's truck. When they arrived at the Emergency Room, Iris tried to follow the EMTs into the exam room with Frank, but Ben held her arm and pulled her aside.

Iris frowned at Ben. "What are you doing?"

"You're not going to be able to go in with him, Iris. You're not family. It's not allowed."

Iris looked at Ben, then looked toward the exam room. "Ben, you know everyone. I need to be in there with Frank. You need to make this happen. He has no one. I will not allow him to go through this surrounded by strangers, not after what he did for me when—" Iris stopped herself then focused on Ben, "Please. Get me in that room, Ben. Please."

Ben nodded and left to speak with the hospital staff. A few minutes later, he returned.

"You can go in with him in a bit," Ben explained. "I called in a few favors."

"Thank you." Iris hugged him.

Ben took her hands and kissed them, then looked at her. "They're getting him settled. They're going to run a few tests, give him some fluids, that type of thing. Once they've got him stable, they'll call for you."

Iris looked toward the exam room. "I understand. Is he awake yet?"

Ben followed her gaze. "No. You may have to prepare yourself—"

"Don't say it, Ben. Don't you dare say it. Frank's not going anywhere. Not yet. Not if I have anything to say about it."

Ben nodded and wrapped Iris in his arms.

Please, God, don't give him a reason to say "it".

264

Twenty minutes later, a nurse came to the waiting room and called out, "Ms. Hornbeam?"

"Here I am," Iris raised her hand.

"You can go in now. Follow me." Iris followed the nurse to Frank's room. When Iris got to the doorway, she stopped and gasped. Frank lay motionless in the bed, an oxygen mask on his face, and IV tubes attached to his arms. His ruddy complexion had turned pale, almost gray. His breathing was shallow, and the slow beeping of the heart monitor gave Iris a chill. Ben came behind Iris and walked her into the room. He pulled up a chair for her so she could sit by Frank's bed. Iris lowered herself into the chair, never taking her eyes off Frank. Ben leaned over and whispered, "I am so sorry, but I have to go. I got a call and there's been a fire in town. I need to be there."

"It's okay. You go, they need you. I'll be fine. You know where I'll be," she said, still keeping her gaze on Frank. Ben nodded and started out the door. "Ben," Iris turned toward him. "Please be careful. And thank you."

Ben came back, kissed Iris on the forehead and said, "I'll be back later." He tapped Frank on the leg and said, "Hang in there, Frank." Then he walked out the door.

Iris took Frank's hand, bowed her head, and closed her eyes. "Lord God, you know this man. I know he doesn't know you well, but please help him. You said all things are possible through you. Well, could you make this one thing possible for me, please?" Iris continued her prayer vigil silently.

Hours later, Ben returned. Iris looked up as he came in the room. "Are you okay? Is everyone okay?" She rushed to him and held him close.

"I'm fine," Ben said, welcoming Iris's embrace. "It was a house fire. The missus burnt the pork chops, and a bit of the kitchen too. Everyone got out, no one was hurt. They'll have some remodeling to do, but it could have been worse." Ben looked Frank's way, keeping his arm around Iris. "How's Frank?"

She looked at Frank and said, "Still has a fever. They've given him something for that. They say he has double pneumonia. Apparently, he's been sick for a while." Iris looked back at Ben and said, "That's why I haven't seen him. I thought it was because of the snow. I should have checked on him. I should have called him or something."

"Iris, this is not your fault. Frank could have told someone he wasn't feeling well, he could have gone to the doctor. He can be pretty stubborn."

Iris's voice trembled. "I know, but I'm his neighbor. I'm his friend. I should have checked. Ben, if he ..."

Ben wrapped Iris in his arms, and she rested her head on his chest. "You should go home. You're exhausted.

266

There's nothing else you can do here tonight. Why don't you go get some rest, and come back tomorrow?"

Iris pulled herself away and wiped her tears. "No. I'm not leaving. I won't leave him here alone. I asked Emma to bring me a few things, and she dropped them off a little while ago. I'm going to stay here till he wakes up or until— He'll wake up. I know he will, and I'll be here when he does."

"Okay, whatever you want, whatever you need to do." Ben rubbed Iris's arm. "I have to go back to the station now and it may be a late night. I'll check in on you tomorrow. But if you need me, you call me, and I'll come right away."

"Thank you, Ben. Thanks for understanding." Ben nodded, kissed Iris, and left once more. Iris walked back to Frank's bedside and sat down. She turned her eyes upon his still body.

How different you look. Hard to believe you're the same man I first did battle with a year ago.

Iris leaned over and whispered in his ear. "You listen to me. Don't you get any ideas of leaving here. You hear me? I know you can be difficult, but you wouldn't be that mean to me."

Iris held Frank's hand and continued to talk to him. "I have so many more questions for you. Like, what the heck are torrefied pellets? Someone told me yesterday I should use them. And how do I take care of the sea roses? Should I be trimming them now or do I wait till after they bloom? There's so much more I need to know, about the flowers, about Eastport. There's so much more I need to know about you. Don't you dare give up. Don't you do it." She squeezed Frank's hand, then whispered more prayers for him.

Iris fell asleep in the chair next to Frank and stayed put through the night. The next morning, Frank was transferred to an ICU room in the main hospital. Emma relieved Iris so she could go home, take a shower, and pick up a few more things to prepare for a longer stay. When she returned, there had been no change in Frank.

Iris took her position in the chair next to him, held his hand for a moment and said a prayer, then she pulled a book out from the things she had brought and began to read aloud. "Book One, The Fellowship of the Ring."

Iris continued to read throughout the day, hoping to see a change in Frank, but there was none. Nor was there any change the next day, nor the next, nor for the rest of the week. On the fifth day, Frank's fever broke, but he remained unconscious.

As she had done for five days prior, Iris began her visit on the sixth day by holding Frank's hand and saying a prayer. Afterward, she pulled out the third book for the week. "Here we go, Frank, Book Three, The Return of the King." She read of the hobbits' continued journey, and the battles fought for Middle Earth. She read of narrow escapes and impending doom. She read of Frodo's choice: does he reach for Samwise's hand and life, or does he follow Gollum toward death? She stopped reading and gazed at Frank, his body lying placidly in the bed. She leaned over and brushed the hair from his forehead with her fingertips then continued to stroke his hair.

Those lines around your forehead and eyes that get so deep when we argue, they're relaxed and smooth now. You seem so peaceful lying there. Too peaceful.

She swept away a tear, then bent down and whispered in his ear. "Frank, choose life. Please. Frodo is going home, home to the shire. It's time for you to come home, too. Please, Frank. Wake up."

Iris returned for the seventh day, and continued to read to Frank throughout the morning, taking a break here and there to hold his hand and pray. Just before lunch, she finished the story, closed the book, and placed it on her lap. She sat in silence, her hands folded on top of the book and heart heavy with worry. As had happened so many times before when life was difficult and she couldn't see a way through, a song she learned as a child began to play in her mind. She closed her eyes and listened, as tears dropped like rain upon the book on her lap. Without being aware, she began to sing, "Jesus loves me, this I know, for the Bible tells me so. Little ones to Him belong, they are weak, but He is strong. Yes, Jesus loves me. Yes, Jesus loves me. Yes, Jesus loves me. The-"

"The Bible tells me so." Frank sang the last line of the song, his head facing the ceiling. Iris gasped and her eyes grew large as she stared at Frank, hoping, but uncertain he really was awake. Frank took a deep breath, looked around the room, then turned toward Iris. He looked at her, as if trying to understand what he was seeing. "Iris?"

"Yes, I'm here." Iris took his hand. "You're awake. Thank God."

Frank looked toward Iris, his crystal blue eyes piercing hers. Then in a groggy voice said, "You look like hell."

Iris laughed out loud, then said, "It's good to see you too, Frank." She wiped the tears from her eyes.

"What am I doing here?" He looked at all the tubes entering his body. "What's all this?"

"I found you passed out in the greenhouse. You were burning up with fever. Do you remember being there?"

Frank paused for a moment, then nodded.

270

"What were you doing in there?"

"It was Sunday."

Iris smiled and nodded.

"What day is it now?" Frank asked.

"Monday."

"I've been here all night?" Frank's eyes darted about the room.

"No." Iris paused. "You've been here all week."

"All week? I've been in this bed for a week? I've gotta go. I gotta get home and take care of things." He threw the blanket off himself.

Iris jumped to her feet and held his arms down to keep him from getting up. "No, you need to stay put and let the doctors check you out. You've been very sick, Frank. You've had pneumonia—double pneumonia, as a matter of fact. I don't know how long you were passed out in the greenhouse, but you've been unconscious and in this hospital for a week. You're not going anywhere until the doctors say you can." Iris gave Frank a stern look. "Now sit back." Frank obeyed.

Iris placed the blanket back on Frank and tucked it in. "You don't have to worry. I've been taking care of things at your home. Everything's fine. I've been picking up your mail, I took out your trash. I've even been watering the plants. Heck, I've watered those orchids every day. What a chore!" Iris said, feigning exhaustion.

"Every day! Iris, you'll kill them!"

"Calm down, Frank. I was just checking to see if you were really back with us." Iris gave Frank a cheeky smile. "I haven't touched the orchids other than to give them each an ice cube yesterday—Sunday. It's all good."

Frank shook his head and said, "Iris, sometimes you can be a real pain in the—"

"I know, but you love me anyway," Iris interrupted. She patted him on the arm, then said, "Now that you're awake, I'm going to go home and get a shower and take care of a couple of things. I'll let the nurses know you're up and back to your charming self. Take it easy on them. They've been working hard to keep you alive. I'll be back in a little while."

Frank watched Iris pack up her things and when she stood to leave, he said, "You don't have to come back. I'll be fine. I don't need you to be here."

Iris stopped, turned back, and walked toward the bed. She placed her things down on the chair, lowered her chin and said, "Frank, you scared me, and I don't like to be scared. Now you have to pay the price. I'm going home, and then I *will* come back, and you're going to let me. You're going to let me stay here and keep you company until the doctors release you, *then* you're going to let me take you home. And once you're home? You're going to let me check in on you. You're going to let me bring you meals, and make sure you take your meds, and you drink enough fluids, and get enough rest."

Iris clenched and unclenched her hands. Frank noticed and closed his eyes. Her voice trembled as she continued. "You're going to let me do all of that, and you're not going to give me a hard time about it. *Do you understand me?*" Iris fought back the tears welling up in her eyes.

Frank nodded.

"Good. Now, here's an ice cube for you." Iris leaned over and kissed Frank on the forehead. Then, looking into his eyes, she said, "Call me if you want me to bring you anything. I'll be back in a few hours." She stood upright, gathered her things, and left.

Standing outside of Frank's room, she allowed tears of relief to flow for a moment, then she brushed them away, took a deep breath, and left for home.

CHAPTER 21

David

Iris returned in less than a few hours and seeing Frank sitting up in bed, the tubes removed from his body assured her of his recovery. He was eating apple sauce with an undisguised expression of disgust.

"Well, you're looking better." Iris smiled as she entered the room. "Got a little color in your cheeks. You're almost back to your somewhat handsome self."

"Now, don't go getting mushy on me." Frank glared.

"Would I do that?" Iris laughed. "Seriously, how do you feel?"

"I feel like I need to get out of this bed." Frank shifted his blankets.

"What did the doctor say?"

"He said if I can get solid food down and have a— well, you know, I can go home tomorrow."

"You shouldn't have any problems with *well, you know*. We all know you're full of it, Frank."

Frank laughed. "I don't know why I put up with you, woman."

Iris nodded, took Frank's hand, and squeezed it. "I missed you too."

Iris kept Frank company for the afternoon, filling him in on the latest gossip of the neighborhood and making him laugh so much the nurse came in to check on him. Iris apologized for the commotion, but her apology was half-hearted. It had been a welcome change for her for with each bout of laughter, she could feel another knot in her stomach untie itself and her body settle into something she hadn't experienced since Birch's death—peace.

After the two shared dinner together, Iris watched Frank as he put his head back and rested.

It's time to tell him. No more putting it off. Get ready, Iris. He's not going to like this.

"Frank," she patted him on the arm. "Tell me what happened with your son."

"Not much to tell." Frank sat up. "We had an argument. He stopped talking to me."

"What was the argument about?"

"I'm not even sure now." Frank pushed his food table away.

"Frank." Iris gave him the look every woman knows to give a man when she wants the truth.

"Eh, I said something stupid. David got mad."

"*You* said something stupid? Shocker." Iris gave Frank a wry smile. "What did you say? Just tell me. You know I won't leave this alone."

Frank took a deep breath and stared at Iris. He shifted in the bed. "David wanted to start his own business. He wanted to leave the solid, well-paying job he had, and he wanted to go out on his own. I thought he was being reckless. He had a wife, she's a wonderful girl, and he was hoping to have children soon. Starting your own business is risky. He could lose everything he'd built up—his savings, his home. I couldn't understand why he'd want to take such a foolish chance, and I told him so." Frank tried to adjust the pillows behind his back.

"Guess he didn't think it was foolish." Iris stood and moved the pillows into place.

"No, he didn't. We argued about it, and it got pretty heated. In the end, David said if I couldn't support him, I should go, so I did." Frank shook his head at the memory. "Turns out, he was right. Told you I was an idiot. I've been watching and his business has become very successful. I'm sure he's making more now than he ever did working for someone else. And I can see he loves what he's doing. I'm very proud of him."

"Have you told him that?"

"No. Haven't had the chance. He's still mad at me." Frank pulled up his blankets.

"How do you know? If you haven't talked to him, how do you know he's still mad?"

Frank looked down at his blankets and mumbled, "'Cause I'd still be mad and he's a lot like me."

"I see." Iris studied Frank. "Well, it all makes sense now."

"What makes sense?"

"Why you asked Eddie to come and take over the plowing and the shoveling when I know you prefer doing it yourself. And why you offered to lend him some of your equipment. I couldn't figure it out. Now I understand, you're trying to give him a good start in his business."

"Eddie's a good kid and I didn't want to make the same mistake twice."

Iris sat up straight in her chair. "Frank, you need to make this right."

Frank shook his head no. "I think it's too late for that."

"How can you say that? To me? How can you even say that?" Iris's green eyes flashed. "David is your son, your only son. As long as the two of you still have breath in your lungs, it's not too late."

Frank looked down at the foot of his bed. He furrowed his brow and avoiding eye contact with Iris he said, "I'm sorry. That was thoughtless of me."

Iris calmed herself. "Frank, do you really want the last words you've spoken to your son to be angry ones? I know you don't. Look at me." Frank turned toward Iris and she locked her eyes on his. "You need to make this right, not just for you, but for David. Don't let him go through another year thinking his dad doesn't love him enough to fight for him."

Frank sighed. "Iris, I don't even know how to start."

"It's simple." Iris patted Frank's arm. "You just did it. You start with those two words: 'I'm sorry.' That's it, Frank, two little words. Trust me, the rest will follow."

"I don't know. Meb-be," Frank paused for a moment. "Between you and me, I'll have to work up the nerve." He looked at the end of his bed again, stretching his feet up and down.

"Well, you'd better work it up fast."

She scrunched up her face.

Here it comes.

"David's here."

"Here? David's here? How? Where?" Frank looked toward the door.

"He's not here, here. He's home, at my house. I called him."

"You called him?" Frank said, his mouth agape.

"Yes." Iris sat up straight. "After we brought you in and saw how bad it was, I called him. Honestly, we didn't know if you were going to make it." Iris paused. "I called him to let him know. I thought he'd want the chance to see his father."

"How'd you find him?" He looked at Iris sideways. "Did you go through my things?"

"Eww, no," Iris made another face. "Frank, there aren't many David Happys who live in Perry. He was not difficult to find, and he came right away. He's been here all week, but he didn't want to come to the hospital. He wasn't sure how you'd feel if you woke and saw him here. He didn't want to upset you."

Frank stared at his blankets for a few moments. "He's been here all week?"

"Yes. All week. He's been staying at my house, working remotely. He wanted to stay nearby just in case—" Iris paused, not wanting to finish her sentence. "I didn't want him rattling around in your house alone, so I convinced him to stay with me. Mo's been keeping him company while I'm with you." She placed her hand on Frank's arm and said, "David's a great guy and he loves you."

Frank looked up at Iris. "When do you think I could see him?"

"Whenever you want. Just takes a phone call." She squeezed his arm.

"I guess you can call him and tell him it's okay."

"No." Iris stood up, then retrieved Frank's phone from the bedside table drawer and handed it to him. "You call him."

Frank took the phone and stared at it for a few moments, then handed it back to Iris.

"Seriously, Frank? You need to do this. Don't be so stubborn."

"Could you dial it for me? I'm having trouble seeing the numbers."

Iris smiled. "My bad. Sorry. Of course." She dialed the number and handed the phone back to Frank.

Frank held the phone close to his ear and listened as the number connected. "David? It's Dad." He paused. "I'm feeling fine, Dave." Frank took a big breath, looked at Iris, then said, "Listen, son. . .I'm sorry."

Iris watched Frank's eyes well up. She patted him on the shoulder, then left for home.

CHAPTER 22

Home Again

The next morning, Frank was scheduled to be released from the hospital, and David joined Iris to bring him home. Frank hadn't regained his strength, so David helped him get back into the house and settled.

"Okay, it looks like you two have all you need for now," Iris said, bringing in Frank's things. "I'm going to head home, but I'll be back later with dinner for you both."

"You don't have to do that," David said. "I can whip something up."

"I insist. Now, I should go and give you two some private time."

"But you'll be back?" Frank asked.

"I'll be back. I promise."

Several hours later, Iris returned to Frank's home with dinner and an extra visitor.

"Mo? You brought Mo here?" Frank said, sitting up in his chair.

"Frank, there's something you should know," Iris said, as Mo jumped onto Frank's lap. "The day you collapsed, Mo was with you. He'd been with me and Ben while we were working in the yard, and at one point, he disappeared. We went searching for him. I thought he hopped the fence again and was in your garden, so I came around looking for him. I saw a hole where it looked like he had been digging, but he was nowhere around. I kept looking and found him in the greenhouse, curled up next to you. I'm not sure what would have happened if Mo hadn't done that."

Frank looked down at Mo, who had been making himself comfortable in Frank's lap. "The entire time you were in the hospital, Mo has been pacing and looking over here. I'm sure he knew something was wrong. I needed to bring him tonight so he could see for himself that you're okay. You don't mind, really, do you?"

"No. No, I don't mind at all." Frank began to pet Mo. Iris smiled.

David watched the interaction between Iris and Frank, then said, "Iris, please stay for dinner."

"No, thank you. I don't want to interrupt."

"You couldn't do that. Stay." Frank said. "Please?"

Iris took a quick breath.

He wants me to stay. What a switch from our early days.

 "All right." Then she gave Frank a devilish smile and said, "But I'm taking control of the CD player."

Iris spent the rest of the evening getting to know David, harassing Frank, and laughing more than she had in ages. Mo did not leave Frank's side for a moment. If he wasn't in Frank's lap, he was weaving himself between his legs or sleeping on his feet.

As Iris cleared the dishes after dinner, she caught sight of David helping his father into a chair in the living room and while she knew Frank was annoyed at needing assistance, she could see how much it meant to him to have his son's arms wrapped around him, keeping him steady.

"You okay, Iris?" Frank asked.

"I'm fine. Got a little soap in my eyes, that's all," Iris wiped away a few tears and then dried her hands on the dish towel. She laid the towel down and put on a smile. "All right, you two gents have a good evening. Mo and I are going home. I picked up your meds from the pharmacy and I stocked your refrigerator earlier, Frank, so you should have everything you need. Call me if I forgot anything. I'll check in on you tomorrow." She walked toward the two men to say her goodbyes.

"You sure you can't stay a little while longer?" Frank asked.

Iris smiled. "I'm tired, it's been a long day. Besides, you two can use the alone time. You have a lot of catching up to do." She patted Frank on the shoulder and picked up Mo.

David stood. "I'm going to head home tomorrow after Dad's up and has breakfast. That is, as long as he's doing okay. I'll be back for the weekend." The two walked together to the front door.

"Thank you for calling, Iris. This has meant the world to me. I'm grateful. And thanks for being willing to check in on him. I hope it won't be too much of an inconvenience."

"It's not a problem. I know your dad can be difficult at times, but he's almost tolerable on occasion." Iris grinned.

"What do you mean I'm almost tolerable? I'm a peach," Frank yelled from the living room.

"Nothing wrong with his hearing." Iris shook her head.

"I heard that."

David and Iris looked at each other and said in

unison, "He's *ba-ck*".

"I'll keep an eye on him, don't you worry. He doesn't scare me," Iris said with a wink. She hugged David, then she and Mo left for home.

The following day, Iris returned to Frank's, making sure he ate lunch and took his medication. Much like they had done after she lost Birch, Iris and Frank fell into a routine, but at different houses. This time, Iris would come to Frank's home to be sure he was the one eating and doing all the things he should to regain his strength and get healthy.

Ben was on night shift, so Iris's evenings were free, and she spent them with Frank. They talked about books they loved, and continued their argument over which jazz saxophonist was better by taking turns playing CDs and pointing out reasons why they were right. Frank pulled out his copy of *Summary Effects of Precipitation, Erosion, and Deposition on Landforms* to prove to Iris he wasn't kidding when he said he referred to it often.

Iris held the book in her hands.

I guess I shouldn't be surprised. Frank doesn't usually stretch the truth. Look how worn it is, and he's kept it all these years.

In the mornings, Iris would spend time with Ben. He'd stop by on his way home from work and they'd catch up with each other. Iris would make dinner for him, and breakfast for her, then she'd fill him in on Frank's recovery, and he'd share about the latest arrest, or the bar fight he had to break up, or a new trend coming to law enforcement, or family news. After breakfast, Ben would leave to get some rest, and Iris would take care of a few things at home, then head back to Frank's.

When David returned on Saturday, he was shocked to see how much his father had improved, and he credited Iris for the change. David did not come alone for the weekend. He brought his wife, Violet, who was four months pregnant. Frank glowed when David told him the news, and once more, Iris found herself with soap in her eyes.

CHAPTER 23

The Big Dig

Frank continued to improve and by the time May arrived, he was back to his old self. Iris smiled whenever she saw him outside digging and hoeing, preparing his garden beds for spring planting, relieved she was spared from having to grieve once more.

Winter had passed and Iris wanted to rid herself of the gray pall it had left behind. She busied herself with her own spring planting. She filled the window boxes with pansies, their clownish faces bringing a smile to her own. She went to the backyard and decided to add some pansies to the garden as well, hoping they would encourage the other flowers to work their way out of the soil sooner.

She pressed her spade into the soil, then closed her eyes and inhaled the earthy aroma. "Isn't that the best smell, Mo?" Iris opened her eyes expecting to see Mo nearby, but all she saw was an empty yard. Mo was gone— again.

Iris called for her capricious cat, then realized where he most likely had gone. She went through the gate to Frank's yard, and sure enough, there was Mo, digging in Frank's garden bed. "Mo! Not again. What is it with you, cat?"

Frank came out of the house and hurried toward Mo. "Mo, you leave my garden alone."

"I'm sorry, Frank," Iris said, as Mo hopped the fence. "I don't know why he does this. I've known Mo for eleven years now, and he's never bothered with gardens or dirt or any of it before. He seems obsessed with yours." Then Iris tilted her head and stared at the spot where Mo was digging. "Or at least, obsessed with this spot."

She walked over to the small hole Mo had begun. "Frank, isn't this the same spot Mo was digging up last year?"

"Ayuh, sure looks like it." Frank examined the spot. "You're right, that is strange."

"Do you think, I know this is odd, but do you think there's something there? Something that's attracting him?"

"No, unless he likes azalea roots or peonies."

Mo hopped up on the top of the fence and paced as

Frank and Iris watched him.

"I wonder." Iris stooped down to the dirt and moved some dirt with her hand. She realized what she was doing, stopped, and looked at Frank. "May I?"

Frank nodded.

Iris picked up a nearby trowel and started excavating a larger hole. As she dug, she examined each trowel full of dirt as if she were an archaeologist.

I have no idea what I'm looking for, but maybe we can finally get to the bottom of why Mo does this.

Eight inches down into the earth, Iris gasped and sat back on her heels. She looked up at Frank.

"What is it?" He tried to peer over her shoulder.

Iris looked back in the hole. She reached down and pulled something out. She held it in her closed hand for a moment, then she raised her arm toward Frank and opened her hand to reveal a man's gold wedding band.

Frank stood still, staring at what Iris held in her hand, then his own hands shook, and his face flushed. He walked past Iris and knelt in the garden bed, staring at the hole and the plants surrounding it. He started puffing like a caged bull, then with a violent move, he wrenched out the plant closest to him, then another, and another.

"No, Frank!" Iris held his arm, trying to stop him.

"Get back, Iris." Frank yelled, jerking his arm away

from her. He pulled and tugged and heaved plant after plant.

Iris stood frozen.

What is he doing? Has he lost his mind?

She approached him again as he stood and tried to man-handle an azalea bush. He lost his grip and caught Iris full in the face with the back of his fist. She flew backward and landed on the ground, looking up at the sky, then all went black.

"Iris! Iris!" Frank yelled.

Iris lay motionless on the ground. Frank fell to his knees beside her and rested her head in the crook of his arm. "Please, God, no," Frank murmured as he stroked her hair. Mo jumped down from the fence and circled the two, then he sidled up to Iris's face and nuzzled his face against hers.

After a moment, Iris stirred, then she opened one eye, then the other. She smiled at Mo, then looked at Frank and said, "That's some punch you got there, Frank."

"Iris, I am so sorry." He sat her up, then clutched her to himself, repeating over and over again, "I'm sorry."

Iris patted Frank's back. "I'm okay. It's all right, it's all right." Iris remained in Frank's arms until she felt he was calm, then she held him by the shoulders, and looked into his eyes. "Lucy, you have some 'splaining to do."

Frank, with moist eyes, smiled in relief and stood. "Let's get you in the house and get some ice on that first." He held out his hand to help Iris up. Taking it, she stood, her legs a little shaky. Frank put his arm around her waist to keep her steady as they walked back to her home with Mo following closely behind.

Once inside, Frank guided Iris to the sofa and had her lie down. He made an ice pack for her, brought it to her with some ibuprofen and water, then started a kettle for tea. While waiting for the water to boil, Frank made a fire and when it was rolling, so was the water, so he went back to the kitchen and finished the tea. He brought Iris a cup and set it down on the coffee table, then put a pillow behind her back as she sat up. Iris smiled. "Thank you. You've done enough. Now have a seat."

"You sure you don't need anything else?" Lines of worry filled Frank's forehead.

"Not a thing. Please, sit."

Frank went and sat at Iris's feet at the end of the sofa and Mo tucked himself in beside Frank. Frank stared at the floor while Iris took a few sips of tea. She put the cup down, replaced the ice pack over her swollen eye, and looked at Frank. "Speak."

"I'm sorry, Iris."

"I know that, Frank. I'm not upset with you. I'm not,

truly. I know you can be cranky with me, but I also know you would never intentionally hurt me. This was an accident."

"I would never hurt you, Iris. Never."

Poor man. Looks like he'd rather have punched himself, or worse.

"I know. It's all right. Now, tell me what all this was about. Why were you destroying your lovely garden? Was that your ring?"

"Yes. It was mine, is mine. It's my wedding ring. I lost it years ago." Frank hung his head.

"Were you gardening and it came off? Is that why you were so upset with your plants?"

Frank shook his head no. "I took it off after a fight I had with Claire. I took it off and threw it in the yard. Never thought I'd see it again."

"You had a fight with Claire?" Iris raised her eyebrows.

"I know, hard to believe, right? Claire was perfect, and I picked a fight with her." Frank went back to staring at the floor.

Iris looked at Frank with her one good eye. "I don't believe you, Frank."

"What?" He looked up at her.

"I said, I don't believe you." Iris shook her head. "No

one's perfect, not even Claire, not even Danny. As much as I loved him, we had our war of the words too. Now, why don't you tell me what really happened."

"You're not going to want to hear this, Iris." Frank shifted in his seat.

"Probably not, but tell me anyway." She pulled the throw blanket over her legs, adjusted the ice pack, and settled herself in.

Frank stared at the floor for a while. Mo stood, then moved to Frank's lap. Frank smiled at him. "Thanks, buddy." He gave Mo a pat, then took a breath. "Claire and I had been married for about two years. They were good years, but we were still getting used to each other, still finding our way as a married couple. Claire had started a new position at the hospital, and as the newbie, she had to pull the worst shifts. There were months at a time when we'd just pass each other in the hall, one of us getting up and the other one going to bed. It was difficult."

Iris nodded.

I remember what that was like.

"I wish I could say I handled it better, but I didn't. I put pressure on Claire to do something, anything to change her schedule. I didn't mean she had to give up nursing, but I thought maybe she could work for a doctor's office or a school, anything that would give her more normal hours.

Her heart was set on the hospital, though.

"All I wanted was for us to be together. I married her because I loved her, and I wanted us to be together. It seemed to me we didn't want the same thing. I gave her a rough time of it, and she shared her problems with her friends at work. And one of those friends . . . was Ben."

"What?" Iris removed the ice pack from her eye.

"Yes, Ben." Frank nodded. "Claire and Ben met as kids when Ben's family came to Eastport on vacation. They even dated for a few summers when they were in high school. One year when he was in college, Ben came for the entire summer, and he and Claire became the 'it' couple. Most people thought they'd end up getting married."

Iris got a chill. Ben did say he'd gotten close to marriage once. That was Claire?

"But they broke up. Ben intended to go back to Boston to become a police officer. Claire didn't think she could marry a cop. She'd didn't think she could handle it. She'd be too worried. She thought if she married him, she wouldn't have a minute of peace. And she was probably right, she was a worrier.

"Anyway, years later, Ben became sheriff here, and he bumped into Claire at the hospital. They renewed their friendship."

"Frank." Iris paused.

Do I really want to ask this? Yes, I need to know.

"Frank, did Ben and Claire have an affair?"

"No, no, they didn't. Had things not changed, though?" Frank paused and took a sip of his tea. "I overheard Claire talking to Ben on the phone one night. She was telling him how unhappy she was. I didn't handle that well either."

"Did you, did you get violent?" Iris pulled her legs up to her chest.

Please say no.

"No, absolutely not." Frank looked Iris in the eye. "After today, I can understand why you'd ask, but Iris, I swear, I have never hit *anyone* in my life, much less a woman. Until today."

"You didn't hit me on purpose."

"I know, but you're still going to have a black eye." Frank clasped his hands together. "I know people think I've been in fights because of my nose, and how gruff I can be, but I've never fought anyone, not once." He looked back at Iris. "My nose? I've broken it twice, once when I was ten and fell off my bike, the second time, well, that doesn't matter."

Iris smiled and said, "Some tough guy you are."

"Yeah." Frank shook his head. "I might not have hit Claire with my fist, but I hit her with my words. I told her if she was so unhappy, she didn't have to stay married to me. I'd *release* her. Then I took off my wedding ring and threw it out the door and into the yard."

"What did she do?" Iris stretched her legs out again and leaned toward Frank.

"At first, nothing. She stood there and stared at me. To this day, I'm not sure what she was thinking. Maybe she was trying to decide whether or not to take me up on my offer. When she finally spoke, she was very quiet and very calm. She said, 'Frank, I'm not leaving you. I chose you. You're my husband. I'm sorry I forgot that for a little while. It won't ever happen again.' Then she turned and went upstairs."

"Did you follow her?"

"No." Frank shook his head. "I was still too angry, and I didn't want to take the chance I'd say something I couldn't take back. So, I slept on the sofa. But first I went out to the yard with a flashlight and tried to find that ring." Frank pointed to the ring Iris had placed on the end table. "Of course, I couldn't. I gave up and hoped I'd be able to find it in the morning. I went back in the house and laid down on the sofa and started thinking about the past year. I realized how selfish I'd been. How could I ask the woman I love to give up the one thing she'd been wanting to do her entire life?" His eyebrows formed a "V," and he shook his head at himself.

"The next morning, Claire had the day off from work, so I took the day off too. When she got up, I apologized. You may not believe this, but I actually said, 'I'm sorry', no buts. We talked it out. I told her I didn't want her to leave the hospital if that's the place that made her happy and I'd try my best to make it work with her, and not be so selfish.

"For her part, she said she'd no longer talk to Ben or anyone else about our marriage. If there was a problem, she'd talk to me, and we'd work it out. She was sorry too, and she wanted our relationship to work, so she planned to talk to her supervisor about improving her hours.

"We spent the rest of the day together, hashing it out, talking about all the things we should have talked about well before then. By the end of the day, we were back on solid ground. We never had another day like it.

"I've been looking for that ring every spring since. I have tilled, and raked, and hoed, and nothing. I don't know how Mo did it, but I think he knew it was there. I owe him an apology, too."

"I think he's already forgiven you," Iris nodded toward Mo, who was curled up on Frank's lap, purring.

"You're all right, Mo, for a cat." Frank petted him, and Mo nuzzled his head into Frank's hand.

"So, that's why you've been working on the garden all these years?"

Frank nodded.

"Well, you made something beautiful out of all that pain. Well done."

Iris stared at her tea for a few moments. *Now I understand. This whole summer, all those invitations...*

"Ben, is he why you wouldn't come to my housewarming, or the picnics, or the barbeques? Is that why I had to practically coerce you to come to Thanksgiving dinner, because Ben would be there?"

Frank looked down at the floor in reply.

"I see." Iris nodded.

"Iris, you know Ben and I, we aren't exactly friends, but we were young, all of us. We were just beginning to find our way in this world, and we got a little lost. You've told me a number of times Ben's a good man. Well, you're right, he is."

Iris looked at Frank. *I'm amazed you would admit that.*

"After we reconciled everything, Claire explained to Ben they couldn't be friends, and he never approached her again. He let us be. He's been a good sheriff. He's been good for the town. I have to give him that. What happened was a lot of years ago and while I might not like Ben, and it may pain me to say it, I respect him. And I'm sorry, I shouldn't have let my feelings about him interfere with being a good neighbor to you, or a good friend."

Iris put the ice pack back on her eye and contemplated everything Frank had told her. She watched him as he pet Mo, his face still pained by what he had done to her.

"Frank," Iris paused.

"Yes?" Frank looked back at her, his eyes filled with regret.

"I forgive you."

Frank closed his eyes.

"It's going to be okay. *We're* going to be okay." Iris nodded. "It's all done now. I understand and I forgive you."

Frank put his head down and stroked Mo.

A faint smile drew across Iris's lips. "So, how do we fix that garden?"

Frank looked up at her and smiled.

CHAPTER 24

Fisticuffs

What in the world happened? Are you okay?" Ben took one look at Iris's swollen eye, grasped her by the hand and rushed into her home. He led her to the sofa and sat her down. "When you said you weren't feeling well, I figured I should stop by and check on you."

"You didn't have to do that. I'm fine."

"You don't look fine. Did you faint? This looks serious, Iris." Ben felt her forehead. "I think I should take you to the ER."

"No. I didn't faint, and I'll be fine." Iris took his hand from her head.

"What happened?"

Iris looked down.

"Iris?"

Iris remained quiet.

Let it go, Ben.

Ben lowered his voice and studied Iris. "Did someone do this to you, Iris?"

"It was an accident," Iris said, looking up at Ben.

"Accident? What happened? Tell me." Iris looked away. Ben took her hand. "Tell me now, please."

"It was Frank." Before she could say another word, Ben was on his feet.

"Frank did this to you?"

"Sit down, Ben. It was an accident. Let me explain. Please." Iris patted the sofa next to her. He stared at her for a moment, then sat down beside her.

"Frank was working in his garden, he was pulling out some plants, and I came up behind him. He didn't know I was there. His hand slipped from the plant and caught me in the eye."

"Slipped? Really? I'm gonna kill him." Ben stood up and marched toward the backdoor.

Iris intercepted him and stood in front of the door. "No, you will not."

"You're right. I won't kill him. I'll just give him a black eye like the one he gave you. Move, Iris." Ben's face flushed.

"No, Ben, you'll do no such thing. You will not touch

him."

"Why are you defending him?" He leaned into her.

"Because I told you, this was an accident. It was my fault. I got too close to Frank."

"Yes, yes, you did. You are definitely too close to Frank," Ben said through gritted teeth, then turning his back on Iris, he walked away.

"What do you mean by that?" She matched his anger, and followed him, her hackles up.

Ben turned back toward Iris. "I mean, you're supposed to be marrying me. When's that going to happen, Iris? Is it going to happen? Lately, it's hard to tell who you're engaged to—me or Frank."

"Don't be ridiculous," Iris spat out her words.

"Am I? Am I being ridiculous when you spend as much time as you can with that man? Bringing him meals, making sure he has whatever he needs?" Ben said, pointing to Frank's house.

"You know why I do that. Frank is alone. I know what that's like. He was there for me in the worst days of my life. I owe him. I will not apologize for trying to pay back a debt." She crossed her arms.

"You've paid that debt, many times over. Frank is well. And he's not alone. He has a son. He doesn't need you babysitting him or coddling him. Do you tuck him in at night while I'm at work?"

You did not say that to me.

Iris's eyes turned to midnight green. She lowered her chin and took a step toward Ben. "Of all people, you're questioning my integrity. You?"

Ben looked at Iris. She drew herself up and did not release her stare. Ben closed his eyes. "No. I'm not. I'm sorry. That was a stupid thing to say. I know you wouldn't— You don't have it in you to betray me like that."

"No. No, I don't. I would never do that to you, Ben." She looked him up and down, then asked in a quiet, terse tone, "Would you do that to me? Would you talk to another man's wife? Would you gain her confidence and make her feel like she'd made a mistake, that she should have been with you instead?"

Ben tilted his head at Iris.

Ah, there it is. You know I know about you, Claire, and Frank now, don't you? Now what do you have to say?

Ben drew himself back. "What did Frank tell you?"

"Not much. He told me you and Claire had dated when you were younger. You wanted to marry her, but in the end, the two of you broke up. When you came on as sheriff, you became friends again. I can fill in the blanks. I am a writer, after all."

"It's not what you think, Iris." Ben shook his head.

"Really? Why don't you explain to me what I think, Ben? And then you can explain to me how I'm wrong." Iris re-crossed her arms and continued her stare.

Ben looked at Iris for a moment, then nodded, and walked away. He took a seat on the sofa in the living room. Iris followed him, eyebrows furrowed, arms wrapped tightly around her body. Mo began pacing back and forth on the back of the sofa. "Have a seat, Iris."

Iris remained standing, still glaring at Ben.

"Please," Ben motioned to the sofa.

Iris remained still for a moment, then walked to the cushions farthest away from him and lowered herself on the sofa. Ben nodded at her, then took a deep breath. "I met Claire when my family would come up here for the summers. I was nine or ten when we first met. I made friends with her brothers. At first, I only wanted to hang out with the boys. She was just the pesky little sister, but somewhere along the line, that changed. By the time I was in high school, I couldn't wait to get to Eastport and see her each summer. Her parents wouldn't let her date until she was sixteen, and so I waited. When she was eligible, we began dating. I was seventeen.

"We'd write each other when I went back to Boston, and I hoped sometime in the future she'd be allowed to visit. That never happened. But we kept in touch, and we saw each other over the summers. I was convinced she was the one for me. I pursued her all during high school, and before I went off to college, we made a lot of those promises to each other you do when you're stupid kids in love.

"After my junior year at UMass, I spent the entire summer up here. She had finished her sophomore year in nursing school. We saw each other almost every day. I couldn't imagine my life without her, so I asked her to marry me. She thought about it for a week, then she turned me down." Ben stared at the floor.

Iris's mood softened as she listened to Ben. "That must have been difficult to hear."

"Yeah, well, she knew I wanted to go into police work. It was all I ever talked about, besides my band," he said with a smile. Iris returned his smile, but her brow remained furrowed. "She couldn't see herself living that life, always worrying whether I'd return at the end of the day. As she put it, 'I can't kiss you goodbye in the morning and not know if I'm going to kiss you again that night.'"

"I understand," Iris whispered.

"I didn't, although I should have. Claire was the sensitive type. I thought about everything she said, and then figured we were too young to be making that kind of decision. Denial is a powerful thing. So I went back to Boston, threw myself into my studies, finished college, then went on to the Police Academy. I'd always hoped once I graduated, things would change, that somehow, I would find a way for us to be together. And then it happened, I got the sheriff's job. I was here just a few weeks when I ran into her at the hospital."

"Was that the first you saw her since you broke up?"

"No. I came up every break I could during college. Then after I graduated from the Academy, I kept coming up on any vacation time I could get. I hoped she'd change her mind, but she never did. She wouldn't even go on a date with me. She told me once she didn't want to give me false hope. If Claire was nothing else, she was consistent. Once she graduated, she became a traveling nurse. It was difficult to catch up with her, but I still had hope, false or not.

"By the time I became sheriff, it had been a few years since we'd seen each other, and when we met that day in the hospital, I couldn't believe she'd gotten married. I didn't know Frank, but I didn't like him. I wouldn't have liked anybody Claire was with.

"She looked the same, except she looked sad. Tired and sad. I asked her about it, and it didn't take much for her to share what was going on. Frank was pressuring her to change jobs. I felt bad for her. Claire was born to be a nurse, and she wanted to work in the hospital. It was all she ever wanted. I wanted to help her."

"Did you now?" Iris leaned back on the sofa.

"Yes, I wanted to help her. I will admit if things didn't work out between her and Frank, I would have been waiting in the wings, but I wasn't about to break up her marriage. On my life, Iris, I would not have done that," Ben said, looking straight into Iris's eyes. "I was there to listen, to give her support. I knew that was my role. Claire and I had been friends since we were kids and I cared about her. I still loved her. I wasn't going to abandon her."

"No, you wouldn't. That would be against your nature. You're always taking care of people, no matter what it costs you. If I'm honest, that's one of the things I like best about you."

Ben rubbed his hands together. "When she told me later she and Frank had patched things up and we shouldn't continue our friendship, I accepted it. I left her alone, and we never talked again." He paused. "Last time I spoke to her was at her funeral when I said goodbye."

Iris closed her eyes. The anger she felt receded like the evening tide and compassion took its place. She looked at Ben and saw tears forming in his eyes. He shook them off. She felt a catch in her throat.

"I suppose Frank gave you a different version of the events."

"Actually, he told me the same story. He also told me you're a good man. He said you're a good sheriff and that you've done a lot for Eastport and while he might not like you, he respects you." Iris paused. "Does that sound like someone who deserves a black eye?"

Ben rubbed his face. He looked up at Iris. "No, I guess not. Well, that's a surprise."

"It happens. Especially with Frank."

"I'm sorry, Iris. I'm sorry I lost my temper and I'm sorry for what I said to you. I shouldn't have reacted that way. You didn't deserve that."

Iris could see the tension still in his jaw, and the pain reflected in his eyes.

"I loved Claire. I wanted to marry her. I would have married her. I was convinced she was the one for me, but I was not the one for her. I thought all this was buried a long time ago, but I guess I should have told you. I'm sorry about that too. Can you forgive me?" He turned toward Iris. "Will you forgive me?"

Iris went and sat beside Ben. She took his hand in hers, then looked up at him. "Of course. I think all this is buried now, Ben, if you'll let it be. Frank is my friend, but you are the man I've chosen to marry. I'm sorry I've made you feel otherwise."

Ben nodded and hugged Iris. "I love you, Iris."

"I know you do." She patted his back.

This was hard for him. Can't you see he was heartbroken? He's carried this all these years. And now you're friends with his nemesis? And he's never asked you not to be. Even now. Iris, he *is* a good man. What are you waiting for? *What is wrong with you?* Stop torturing him and tell him what he needs to hear.

She took Ben's hand again and looked up at him. "Ben, I know I can be headstrong and a bit of a challenge, but if you still want to marry me, knowing how I feel, I'm ready to marry you." She smiled. "I'd just like to wait a few weeks until the swelling goes down."

"Of course, I still want to marry you." Ben kissed Iris's hand. "More than anything. Tell you what, let's set a date. It'll give us something to look forward to and help put all this behind us."

"Okay, how about June 17th? That will get us through Memorial Day and the lupines should be blooming by then. They would make for some nice pictures."

"June 17th it is." Ben kissed Iris and Mo curled up between them.

CHAPTER 25

Spring Planting

Iris placed a bucket of supplies on the floor. Mo sauntered over and examined the bucket. "Time for spring cleaning, Mo." She started with the windows in the dining room and when she got to the glass doors, she noticed Frank in her yard, digging a large hole. Next to him was a young tree. She went out to investigate.

"Frank, *chupta*?" Iris peered into the hole.

"*Chupta*, huh?"

Iris blushed. "Well, I figure if I'm going to live here for a while, I'd better start using some of the lingo."

"Good for you." Frank continued to dig. "And, so you know *what I'm up to*, is I'm planting a tree."

"I can see that. But why? Why here?"

"It's for you, Iris. I wanted to do it sooner, but the ground wasn't ready yet. It's warmed enough now though.

If I plant it here, you can see it from anywhere in the back of your house and it doesn't block the view of the bay."

"Well, that's nice, but I'm still not sure why you're planting a tree for me. What kind of tree is it?" She looked at the tree and held one branch in bud in her hand.

Frank paused and looked at the hole. He looked up at Iris, his forehead wrinkled. "I thought you already knew." He nodded toward the tree. "It's a birch tree."

Iris took a quick breath. "I see." Her eyes welled up with unexpected tears.

"I thought it would be a nice remembrance for you." Iris nodded. Frank went back to the tree, loosened the roots, then slid it into the hole. He filled the dirt in around the roots and as he did, he said, "Your husband named your son right."

"Why do you say that?"

"Don't you know, Iris? About birch trees?"

Iris shook her head no.

Frank smiled at her, then looked at the tree. "Birch trees and hornbeams, they're from the same family. They're both hardwoods." He looked back at Iris. "Birch trees don't grow tall, but they grow strong and fast. They're a useful tree. Natives used to make canoes out of them, so they're perfect for the Navy."

Iris grinned.

314

Frank patted down the soil, then stood next to Iris and pointed to the tree. "White birches, like this one, they can be short-lived, some only live twenty, thirty years." Then he looked back at her. "But they sure make an impact while they're here."

"Yes, they do," Iris managed to say as a tear found its way down her cheek.

"I'm sorry. I didn't mean to upset you. I can take it away."

"No, no, don't do that. And don't be sorry. This was very kind, very thoughtful. It's a good thing. Thank you." She turned away from the tree, squeezed Frank's arm, and walked back to her house.

CHAPTER 26

Mo

S omething's wrong with Mo," Iris cried into the
phone.

"I'll be right there."

In a moment, Iris could hear Frank come in through
her backdoor.

"Iris?"

"Here, in the bedroom."

Iris sat on the floor, holding Mo. She looked up as
Frank came into the room. "What's happening, Frank?"

"I don't know." He knelt, petted Mo, and felt for his
heartbeat.

"He's been acting strangely all week. He hasn't been
eating well. I thought he was being finicky. He does that
sometimes. And he's seemed more lethargic than usual.
Frank, what is it?" Iris's voice quivered.

"We need to get him to the vet. I'll drive."

Iris nodded. She found Mo's favorite blanket, wrapped it around him, then cradled him in her arms, and rushed out with Frank.

On the way to the vet, she sent a text to Emma and Ben to let them know and to ask for their prayers. When she and Frank arrived, the attendant took one look at Mo and showed Iris into an exam room straight away. The vet came in shortly thereafter.

Frank remained in the waiting area, pacing. Ten minutes after Iris and Mo went to the exam room, Emma arrived. Ben followed five minutes later. Frank filled them in, and they waited in tense silence.

Soon after, Iris appeared without Mo. She went over to the trio. "They're running some tests." Emma stood and hugged Iris. Ben put his hands on Iris's shoulders, and she turned and fell into his embrace. Frank put his hands in his pockets and walked outside.

A few minutes later, Iris excused herself from Ben and Emma. "Would you mind waiting for word? I could use some air."

Ben held her hand. "Want me to come?"

"No, thanks. I just need a minute to catch my breath." Ben nodded and sat with Emma.

Iris stood on the steps of the vet's office for a few

moments, taking a few deep breaths. She saw Frank sitting on a nearby bench, walked over to him, and sat beside him. Neither spoke, they kept their eyes forward and stared at the traffic passing by.

After losing count of the number of cars that had driven past, Iris looked at Frank. "You okay?"

"Me? Iris, don't give me a thought. You concentrate on Mo." Frank shook his head. "I'm sorry this is happening to you. You'd think God would give you a break. I am so angry. So angry at Him. First your husband, then your son, and now your cat? Why is He picking on you? What did you ever do to Him? What's He got against you?"

Iris looked at Frank.

I have no idea what to say to you.

"I don't know how you're not angry. I'd be shaking my fist at God about now, asking Him, 'Why me?'"

Iris watched another car go by. "You know, that question has never made sense to me." She paused and looked back at the vet's office, then returned her gaze to Frank. "Of course, I get angry, Frank. I'm human. But I don't ever remember asking, 'Why me, Lord?' when something good happened in my life. Why should I ask that when something bad happens? I mean, what is so extraordinarily special about me that I should be excluded from the bad things in life? I have lived on four continents, and I've seen bad things happen all the time—to good people, to bad people, all the time. Why should I be exempt from that?

"I grew up with two parents who loved me. I had a dad who showed me what it meant to work hard, to stick with something to the end, and to be generous, and loyal. I had a mom who loved me unconditionally, taught me patience, and how to hold my tongue." Frank looked at her side-eyed. "I know. I still have to work on that one. Even so, I never asked, 'God, why did you give me such incredible parents?'

"I have been loved by a wonderful man and I loved him in return. We grew into somewhat responsible adults. We had adventures all over the world. We had a son together, and we shared heartaches and joys together. I loved that man and I cherish every second I spent with him. I never asked, 'Why me? Why did you give me such an amazing husband, Lord?'"

Tears were poised in Iris's eyes again. "Mo showed up at a crossroads in my life. He's brought me more happiness than I ever thought possible from an animal, much less a cat. He's kept me company, entertained me, and while at times he irritates the heck out of me, he's been a wonderful companion. And I never asked, 'Why did you send me Mo, God? Why me?' Not once.

"Yes, I get frustrated. Yes, I get angry. There have been times when I'm in so much pain that I can hardly breathe, but it never occurs to me to ask, 'Why me, Lord?'"

"Iris." A voice called from behind her.

Iris looked up to see Emma at the door of the vet's office. It was time to go back. Iris patted Frank on the knee. "You're asking the wrong question, Frank." She stood, wiped her tears away, and went back inside.

The vet asked Iris to join her in her office, and Iris asked Ben to come as well. They were gone for only a few minutes, and when they re-emerged, Ben carried Mo in his arms as Iris cried beside them.

"Mo's on his way home," Ben said. "He's not in any pain, so Iris would like to take him back and stay with him till—. It shouldn't be too long."

Emma came and wrapped her arm around Iris's shoulders and walked her to Ben's truck.

Everyone made their way back to Iris's and, as they had done so many evenings before, Iris sat in the rocking chair with Mo on her lap. Ben made a fire, Emma made tea. Frank watched, standing in the corner of the room. After they'd been home for about an hour, Ben got a call.

"There's an emergency in town. I should be there."

"It's fine. You should go where you're needed. Emma and Frank are here. I'll be fine."

"Okay, if you're sure. I hate to leave you."

"I'm sure."

Ben kissed her on the head, then he knelt and gave Mo a pat. "See ya, buddy." He took Iris's hand. "I'll be back as soon as I can. I promise."

Frank watched as Ben left, then went outside and sat on Iris's porch in one of the rockers.

Iris continued to sit and caress Mo. His breathing shallow, but steady.

I'm glad you seem at peace, Mo. Iris looked outside. Wish I could say the same about Frank. He and that temper, I'm sure he feels badly.

"Emma, could you keep watch for a few minutes? I'd like to go outside."

"Of course, take your time. I'll call if there's a change." Emma patted Iris's hand and switched places with her. Iris went to the porch and sat in the rocker next to Frank.

They rocked in silence, then Frank looked at her. "I'm sorry, Iris."

"I know," she said, looking out at the birch tree.

"I shouldn't have said those things. I'm an idiot. I'm sorry I upset you earlier."

"It's okay. I understand. And I want *you* to understand. Just because I don't go around bitter and angry, doesn't mean I don't feel that way sometimes. I have hard feelings, I do, but I choose not to be ruled by them. I choose to remember I have faith."

Frank turned toward her. "I have faith, Iris."

"Do you? Good. But you know, Frank, faith is more than simply believing God exists. It's more than believing He's able to do whatever needs to be done. Faith is trusting God knows what's best for me, whether He does what I want Him to do or not. In these awful, awful moments of life, I choose to remember it's not my place to demand from God. My place is to walk beside Him, to put my hand in His, to grab on to Him as tightly as I can, and to believe and trust in the fact that no matter what, God loves me, He wants what's best for me, and He is with me. Always."

"Iris, you said I've been asking the wrong question. What should I be asking?"

"I'm going to let you think on that. In the meantime, I'm gonna go back and take care of my cat." She stood, patted Frank on the shoulder, and went back inside.

An hour later, Mo was gone.

CHAPTER 27

Time to Say Goodbye

Frank sat at his kitchen table, having a morning cup of coffee when there was a knock on his back door. He went and opened it. "Iris?"

Iris stood alone on his back porch. Her eyes showed the strain of her most recent loss.

"I have a favor to ask." Her voice broke. "I was thinking. I was wondering. Would you mind." She stopped, unable to get the words out. She looked down, gasping for air, and Frank could see her clenching her hands into fists once again.

Frank wrapped her hands in his. "What is it you need, Iris? Tell me, I'll take care of it."

Iris stared at him, the signs of grief etched in her face. "Would you mind terribly if I buried Mo under the birch tree?"

"No, of course not. I wouldn't mind at all. I think that's a perfect idea."

Once again, you amaze me, Iris.

"May I borrow a shovel?"

"Come with me." Frank took Iris by the hand. He brought her to the shed where he pulled out the tools that were needed and then he took her back to her yard. "You stand here." Frank placed Iris off to the side. "I'll do it."

Frank determined the best spot for Mo's final resting place, then he dug the hole. When he finished, he nodded to Iris. She went back into her house, then brought out Mo, wrapped in his favorite blanket. Iris kissed the blanket once before laying Mo's body in the ground. She stood for a moment, then bent over, picked up a handful of dirt and sprinkled it over him.

Another loss. How much can one woman take?

"You go on in, Iris. I'll finish."

"No, I want to stay." Iris raised her chin in the same manner he had seen her do when she received the news of Birch.

"Okay, whatever you need to do."

You are one strong woman, Iris Hornbeam. You do your name proud.

Frank took the shovel and filled in the hole, then patted it down. When he was through, he stood beside Iris and the two looked at the birch tree and the filled hole in silence. As tears flowed from Iris's heart, she continued to stare at the fresh grave. "You know, I hate cats," then she turned toward Frank and said, "but I loved Mo."

Frank nodded and wiped the mist from his own eyes "Me, too." Iris reached for Frank's hand, and as they clasped their hands together, Iris bowed her head and said a quiet prayer.

CHAPTER 28

Frankly, David

A new and welcome tradition began not long after Frank returned from the hospital and continued for weeks to follow. Frank's son David and his wife, Violet, became frequent visitors to Frank's home, dropping by almost every Sunday afternoon. On one such Sunday, David came alone. The two men sat on the back porch when David stood up and began to pace.

Frank watched his son move back and forth like a pendulum. "Something bothering you, David?"

David stopped and turned toward his father. "Dad, what's with you and Iris?"

"What do you mean?" Frank tilted his head at David.

"Excuse me for being blunt, but why haven't you asked her to marry you yet?"

Frank sat up straight. "David, why would I do that?"

"Really, Dad?" David raised his eyebrows. "Because you're in love with her."

"David, Iris is going to marry Ben, soon."

"Is she now?" David crossed his arms and leaned back on the railing.

Frank snapped back, "Of course she is. Why wouldn't she? They've been seeing each other practically since the day she arrived. Seems pretty settled to me."

"Is that so?"

"Why are you sticking your nose in this, David?" Frank frowned at his son. "Iris is a good woman, and she deserves a good man. She believes she's found one in Ben. Why are you trying to interfere?"

"Dad, while you were in the hospital, Iris and I spent a lot of time together, and we'd talk. You're right, she is a good woman, a very good woman. She's smart, she has a kind heart, and she's very compassionate. I assured her I would be here for you, even if I wasn't actually in the hospital, and I tried to convince her she didn't have to stay with you every day, but she wouldn't hear of leaving you alone in there. She told me you came to her home every day for two weeks straight, and took care of her when her son passed away, and she owed you. Honestly, Dad, I don't think her son had anything to do with it." David looked his father in the eyes. "Iris loves you."

Frank sat back in his chair and stared at his garden.

Change the subject, David. I don't want to talk about this.

David leaned toward his father. "Did you hear me? I said Iris loves *you*, so why are you going to let her marry Ben?"

"What choice do I have, David?" Frank whipped his head toward his son. "You're asking me to break up a couple that has been together almost a full year. I won't do that." Frank's face burned red. "Besides, it's complicated."

"Because of Mom?"

"You're treading on thin ice now, son."

David nodded. "I know." He sat down next to his father. "Dad, there's something I need to tell you. You're not going to want to hear it, but I promised Mom, so like it or not, you're going to listen."

"What did you promise?"

"Mom knew you like a book."

"Yes, she did, and she read me well."

"When she was sick, when she knew what was coming, she pulled me aside one day and gave me a lesson on what it means to love someone." David stood up again and went to the railing. He looked out at the garden, then turned toward Frank. "She told me she loved you, more than anything, then she said, as much as she loved you—

because she loved you, she hoped someday you'd find someone, someone who you could love, and someone who would love you. She wanted that for you, Dad. She didn't want you to live the rest of your life alone in perpetual mourning."

David sat next to his father. "She said you love hard, that you'd need a strong woman. If you ever found one, I was to tell you she'd be happy for you, that she'd want this for you. She knew. She knew you'd hesitate, that you'd be reluctant to move on because of her. She made me promise."

Frank stared at his son, his throat tightening.

David continued. "She said, 'Davy, before I go, I want you to promise to tell your father when the day comes that he has my blessing.'" David swallowed hard and whispered, "I promised."

He reached out to his father and placed his hand on his arm. "I believe she's happy for you, or at least wants to be happy for you, Dad. I think she'd like Iris. I know I do."

Frank looked down at the floor, clenching his jaw. *Claire, I miss you. How can I even think of—*

"Dad, just because you love someone else, doesn't mean you love Mom less. She knew that. I know that. You should know it too."

Frank looked at David and shook his head slightly.

332

I can't do it. No.

"Let me ask you something. How are you going to feel when Iris walks down that aisle and the man she's walking toward isn't you?"

Frank stood up. "I think we're finished with this discussion, David." He left his son and went inside.

CHAPTER 29

Wedding Bells

While there had been thoughts of postponement following the loss of Mo, Ben and Iris decided to move forward with getting married. Ben thought it may help Iris through her grief to begin a new chapter in her life, and she agreed. So, over coffee and blueberry muffins at the WaCo Diner on a Saturday afternoon, they moved the date up to the coming Friday, Ben's next day off, May 13th. They would go to the courthouse and take their vows before the judge, keeping things simple. They intended not to tell anyone until after the ceremony, but Iris couldn't keep the secret from her best friend. When Emma came to Iris's home for lunch on Thursday, Iris filled her in.

"I'm pleased for you, Iris," Emma said, stirring her coffee. "It's time you find some happiness."

"I hear a 'but' in there, Emma. What is it?"

Emma continued to stir her coffee. She tapped her spoon on the rim of her cup, laid it down on her saucer, then she looked up at Iris. "Are you sure? Are you sure about Ben?"

"Yes, again, I'm sure."

How many times am I going to have to answer this question?

"Ben is a good man. He's kind, he's thoughtful. We can be happy together."

"Iris," Emma sighed.

"What, Emma? Go ahead, say it. You'll implode if you don't."

"I've never once heard you say you love Ben. Not once the whole time you've been together." Emma shook her head. "You talk about how he's a good man, how he's a kind man, but what about love, Iris? What about how you *feel* about him? I know he loves you, but do you love him? Has that changed for you?"

"I love Ben, I do." She looked into her coffee cup. "But I'm not *in love* with him."

"Then for heaven's sake, why are you going to marry the man?" Emma asked, leaning back.

"I never thought I'd be with anyone ever again after Danny. Never wanted to be. Now here I am, about to marry a good man, a handsome man, who loves me, and wants to care for me. Someone I can care for and care about. That's more than I ever thought possible."

"But Iris, what about Frank?"

"Ugh. What is it with Frank?" Iris smacked her forehead. "Frank and I, well, there is no Frank and I. I am with Ben. I've been with Ben for a year. Frank, he's, he's a friend, a very good and trusted friend."

"Iris, what aren't you telling me? I know there's more to this."

Iris closed her eyes. Do I tell her? She's your best friend. Tell her.

She opened her eyes and looked at Emma and said quietly, "Frank. I don't think he feels that way about me. I gave him a chance when Ben first asked to marry me. He didn't give me a reason why I shouldn't. And even if he did—"

"Iris, there's something I should tell you. I know I promised I wouldn't, but I think you need to know."

"What is it?" Iris studied the look on her friend's face.

Whatever it is, it's not good.

"Emma, what did you promise?"

Emma took a long breath and sighed. "After Birch died, we wanted to help, all of us, Ben, Frank, me, but Ben and I, we didn't know what to do. We didn't know how to help, but Frank did. He knew. He understood because he's lived it."

"Wait, you understand, Emma. You lost your husband not that long ago. You know what it's like."

"No. No, I don't. It wasn't the same." Emma shook her head. "My husband, he was sick for a very long time, years. He had ALS and died one of those slow, agonizing deaths. When God called him home, it was sad, but it was relief. He was ready to go. And when the time came, I knew he wasn't in pain anymore and he was in a much better place. I took comfort in all of that. It hurt, but it wasn't the same."

"I see." Iris nodded. "So what did Frank say?"

"He suggested things we could do to help you and one thing he said was it was important you not be alone, especially after the funeral. He'd been watching you holding yourself together. We all had. He knew there'd come a point when the reality of what happened would sink in. He didn't think it would be good for you to be alone when it did. He volunteered to come by every morning and make you breakfast and stay with you until Ben or I could come. It was difficult for us to get away in the morning, but Frank assured us, he'd be here. And he thought it best someone stay overnight with you in case you woke up. He thought you might be afraid, and someone should be with you. He remembered nights were the worst, and I agreed with him. I had more than one nightmare after Harry died. Frank thought Ben should be the one to stay. Ben agreed it was a good idea, and he tried to be here."

"He tried?" Iris leaned in.

"Yes, *he tried*. He came the first night and slept on your sofa, but his police radio kept going off and he was afraid you would hear it and it would wake you," Emma said, taking Iris back to those early days.

"I did. I did hear it. After we all got back from Arlington, and you all told me to go to bed, and you'd lock up, I went and lay down. I didn't even take my clothes off. I just lay down and went to sleep right away. But I woke up a few hours later, and I was lying there, not knowing what to do, and then the radio went off. And I thought, 'Good, Ben's here. Someone who loves me is in this house and I'm not alone. It'll be okay.' And I went back to sleep," Iris said through tears.

Emma nodded. "Well, that was true the first night, but not for the rest." Emma paused and took a sip of her coffee.

Iris waited on tenterhooks for Emma to continue her story.

"Ben was worried work would interrupt and one

night he would have to leave you alone, so he asked Frank to come and take his place. Frank agreed on one condition, no one tell you it was him, not Ben, who was staying."

"What? Frank? That was *Frank*? Emma, that first night when I woke up, I was terrified. Of my grief, I was terrified. But hearing the radio let me know I wasn't alone. And the next night, I woke up again, and I listened, and I heard a man breathing, sleeping soundly in the living room. And I thought, 'Good, someone who loves me is in this house and I'm not alone. It'll be okay.' I did that every night for two weeks straight. And now you're telling me, you're telling me the *someone* was Frank?"

"Yes. It was." Emma's eyes glistened.

"He was staying with me every night and he never said a word. Why? Why didn't he tell me? Why didn't *you* tell me?" Iris stood and walked behind her chair, then paced the room.

I can't believe this. Why would they keep this from me?

"I couldn't. I promised him. He didn't want you to know. He only wanted to take care of you. He wasn't interested in credit." Emma wiped away a tear. "Honestly, I don't think he wanted to interfere with you and Ben. But, Iris, if he could have, if it was possible, I think that man would have placed you on his back and carried you through your grief."

"Samwise Gamgee," Iris whispered. She paced to the other side of the room. "Why are you telling me this now, Emma." Iris stopped pacing and closed her eyes. "Of all times, why now?"

"Because Frank does love you."

Iris made a sharp turn toward Emma. "Did he tell you that?"

"Iris, he didn't have to. Everything he has done for you over these past months screams it."

Iris sighed and sat down. "I wish," Iris held her face in her hands, then she held her temples. "I wish. Well, it doesn't matter what I wish. This doesn't change a thing. I'm marrying Ben." Iris brushed away her tears.

"What? After all I've told you, you would do that? *Why*?"

"I could never be with Frank, even if he does love me, even if I—I could never be with him."

"Why not? Iris, please, tell me." Emma took Iris's hand. "Why not?"

Iris paused. "Emma, can you imagine what it would do to Ben to lose two women he loved to the same man? First Claire, now me. I can't do that to him. I won't do that to him. He doesn't deserve it." Iris sat herself straighter in her chair.

"So, you'll live a loveless marriage instead. Iris, you and I both know marriage is hard enough when two people love each other. Don't do this. Don't do this to you and don't do this to Ben. Please."

"I'm doing this *for* Ben. Emma, I like him. I enjoy his company. He's a wonderful friend, and I do care about him. I can be there for him, and I know he'll be there for me. I know it won't be the same as with Danny, but I can do this. I will do this."

"Does Ben know how you feel about him?"

"Yes, we've talked about it many times," Iris said with a sigh. "We even talked about it the day he proposed. He said he knew we weren't on the same page as far as how we felt about each other, but he hoped given time, I would come to love him in the same way he loves me. That's my hope too."

"I hope you're right. I hope you're both right."

Emma and Iris sat in silence for a few moments, then Emma stood and walked behind Iris, bent down, and wrapped her arms around Iris's shoulders, giving her a hug. Leaning her head beside Iris's, she said, "I hope you're making the right choice. I wish you the best, Iris, I sincerely do."

"Thanks, Em. You're the best friend I ever had, truly." Iris patted Emma on the hand, "And I love you."

"Right back atcha," Emma gave her friend a squeeze and a kiss on the head. "But, Iris, Friday the thirteenth? Really?"

Iris laughed, with a tear still in her eyes. "Good thing I'm not superstitious."

The next day, Friday, the thirteenth, Frank stopped by the inn. Emma had asked him for a jar of his blueberry preserves to serve at a special brunch she was hosting.

"Mornin', Mary." Frank said.

"I suppose." Mary kept her eyes on the computer. "She's coming."

Emma walked into the lobby from the Morning Room. "Good morning, Frank."

"Good morning. Lobby looks like spring, Emma." Frank sniffed the air. "And it smells great."

"Thanks." Emma had a watering can with her and began watering the plants in the foyer. "Been working hard on the brunch. That's homemade scones you're smelling. You're welcome to stop by later and join in. I appreciate you bringing the preserves." Emma smiled as she went to the next plant. "They're a hit with my guests."

"Is that Eddie?" Frank asked, noticing a young man

bringing chairs to the Morning Room.

"Yes, I've been hiring him every now and again when I need an extra set of hands. Glad he was available today, especially since Iris—."

"Since Iris what?" Frank asked, still looking at Eddie.

"Since Iris, since Iris is busy today." Emma returned to her watering.

Frank watched Emma.

Her hands are shaking. Something's up. Why are you so nervous, Emma?

"What is Iris so busy with that she can't help you?"

"I, um, I'm not sure." Emma shifted her eyes away from Frank and moved to the next plant.

Frank's suspicions fermented to concern. "Emma, where's Iris?"

Emma ignored him.

"Look at me, Emma," Frank walked toward her. Emma bent closer to the plant, examining its leaves. Frank bent down and put his head near Emma's and whispered in her ear. "Where. Is. Iris?"

Emma stood straight, but remained silent. Frank stared at her. "Something's wrong. I can see it in your eyes. You're not going to tell me?"

Emma closed her eyes.

Frank turned to the little woman behind the front desk. "Mary?"

"I ain't sayin' nothin'." Mary kept her head down and continued her work.

"Fine. I'll call her and find out myself." Frank pulled out his phone. Emma put her hand over it to stop him from dialing.

"Don't call now, Frank. She's unavailable."

"What do you mean, Emma? What's going on? Is there something wrong? *Is there something wrong with Iris?*"

"Not wrong, exactly."

"Emma, please." Frank bored his eyes into Emma's.

"Iris and Ben are getting married today. At the courthouse in about thirty minutes."

Frank kept his eyes on Emma, his jaw clenched and twitching. He nodded, then turned, and ran out the door. Frank's mind raced with images of Iris over the past year, and while he didn't know what he was going to do once he arrived, he knew he had to get to the courthouse as fast as his sixty-three-year-old body would take him. He arrived at the courthouse steps in just a few minutes. He hustled up the stairs, through the front doors, then dashed down the hallway toward the Justice of the Peace. As he turned the last corner, he barreled into Iris.

"Frank?" Iris grabbed on to him and stopped his forward progress. "Good grief, one black eye was enough, thank you. What are you doing here?" She looked at him for a moment. "Are you all right?"

Frank put his hands on his knees as he tried to catch his breath. "I've come to stop you from making the biggest mistake of my life."

"Your life?" Iris bent her head over to see his face.

Frank looked down and shook his head at his slip of the tongue, then looked back up at her. "*Your* life, Iris. I- I've come to stop you from making a mistake. Don't marry him. Don't marry Ben."

"And how exactly are you planning to stop me? With a jar of blueberry preserves?" Iris arched her eyebrow and pointed at the jar in Frank's hand.

Frank stood straight and looked down at his hand.

Good move, Frank.

"This was for Emma. I was in a hurry. I guess I forgot to leave it. I ran over here as soon as she told me what you were about to do. Don't do it. Don't marry him."

Iris shook her head. "Frank, why are you doing this?"

"I've been thinking about what you said to me, about asking the wrong question. I've been racking my brain over it all week. Couldn't sleep, I was thinking about it so much.

346

Iris, you can be a real pain, you know that?"

"Yes, I know." She rubbed her forehead.

"Well, last night, I woke up at about two in the morning. I knew I wasn't going back to sleep, so I got up, paced around the house for a while, then I went for a walk and ended up by the church. The cross that stands out front was lit, and I stood and stared at it for the longest time.

"I started thinking about the real cross, the one that was rough and unforgiving. The one meant for thieves, and murderers, and liars, and cheats. And I thought about the innocent man who was nailed to it. He didn't ask for any of the things that happened to Him. He didn't ask to come to this world, to walk through those last years of His life teaching people, healing people, dealing with a lot of people who only wanted something from Him. He didn't ask to be lied about, or to be beaten, or made fun of. Didn't ask to die. He didn't ask for any of it. Yet, it all happened. And He never once asked, '*Why me?*'. If ever there was someone who could have posed that question, it was Him, but He didn't. Made me feel ashamed." Frank paused.

"Then I thought about what you said about faith—it wasn't enough to just believe God exists. It's about believing God is with us, no matter what. I didn't think that was true, that God loves us and wants what's best for us. That He's *with* us. Didn't think it was true at all. Then I remembered."

"Remembered what?"

"I remembered those awful nights with Claire when she was so sick she could hardly raise her head, and I needed strength to help her, and I prayed, and the strength came. God was with me. And the day she died, she'd been asleep for almost a week, but she woke up and looked at me. She was saying goodbye, and she was smiling. She was so peaceful." A tear made its way down Frank's cheek. "I needed to see that. *God was with me.* I thought of so many other times when I didn't realize God was right there, in the middle of my life. *He was there.* I just didn't see Him. You were right, Iris.

"I knelt in front of that cross. I knelt and I prayed, first real prayer in forever. I think I finally asked the right question. I looked up at the cross and said, 'Jesus, will you forgive me?'"

Iris smiled and nodded as tears made their way down her own cheeks.

"I guess I've been angry at God for so long, I never thought to look at things from His perspective—what it meant for Him to lose His son, someone He loved, or what it meant for Jesus to give up everything, even His own life so I could be an idiot and ignore Him. I made peace with Him last night and I'd like to make peace with you too."

Frank moved closer to Iris. "You were wrong about one thing, Iris. I wasn't just asking the wrong question. I wasn't asking enough questions." Frank put the jar of preserves down on a nearby bench, then took Iris's hand, and looked her in the eyes. "How are you doing? How can I help you? What do *you* need?"

With each question, the tears flowed harder down Iris's cheeks.

"I'm sorry. I should have been asking you all those questions since the first day we met. I'm selfish. I'm grumpy. I'm self-centered and I have a quick temper."

"All that's true." Iris took her hand away and pulled a tissue from her pocket to dab away her tears.

Frank smiled. She's an honest woman. Blunt, but honest.

"Iris, will *you* forgive me?" He paused a moment, then added, "Will you be my friend?"

Iris tilted her head at Frank, sighed. "Of course, Frank, of course I'll be your—we are friends and I've already forgiven you, you know that."

Frank took Iris's hand again. "Iris, don't marry him. Do not marry Ben."

Iris jerked her hand away. "And what business is it of yours who I marry?" She gave him a sharp look. "Or is it whom?" She looked toward the side, thinking.

"*Whom.* And none, I suppose, but he is not the right man for you."

"Ben is a good man," Iris insisted for the thousandth time.

"Yes, he is. He is a good man. But Iris, you have more spunk in your little finger than Ben does in his entire body. There are so many things you love: history, art, poetry, music, science, nature, literature. Your mind is full of these things. What's Ben's mind full of? His work. That's what he loves."

"That's not all he loves. Ben loves his family. And me." Iris stood a little taller.

"Yes, I'm sure he does. I'm sure he loves his family. And you." Frank said, conceding the point. "I mean no disrespect to Ben. But will that be enough for you? Every evening he comes home and tells you about the latest bar fight he broke up and every weekend you get to have dinner with the in-laws. Is that the life you were looking for? Is that the next adventure for you?"

Iris paused, looked at the floor for a few moments, then raised her head and looked away from Frank. "Well, you don't have to worry. There's not going to be a wedding today." Then she looked back at Frank. "Ben called it off."

"*He* called it off? Odious fool."

"Frank, two minutes ago you were going to stop this

wedding with a jar of preserves, and now you're mad at Ben because he called it off?"

"You've got a point there." His look softened. "What happened? Why didn't he go through with it?"

"Because," Iris paused, "he said generally, it's not a good idea to marry someone . . . when you're in love with someone else."

"Ben's in love with someone else?"

"Oh, Frank, you are an idiot," Iris rolled her eyes at him.

"I know, Iris. I know." A slight grin made its way across Frank's face.

God, I love this woman.

He took her hand once more. "Marry me."

Iris retrieved her hand, took a step back, and let out a small laugh. "Now why would I want to go and do a thing like that? Why would I want to marry a grumpy old man who pretends he hates cats and everyone else?"

Frank took a step toward Iris. "Because you know the truth."

"That I do," she said, nodding. "But no. I don't think so, Frank." She took another step back.

"Iris, marry me."

Iris stood straight. "No."

Frank exhaled and kept his eyes steady on her.

"Now, Iris, you can say no, but I'm going to continue to ask you this. Every. Single. Day. Probably several a times a day. I'm going to bother you about this every time I see you, *every time*. My voice will be the last thing you hear in your head before laying down on your pillow each night. I will visit you in your dreams and haunt you in your nightmares. When you wake up in the morning, your tea kettle will whistle, 'Marry Frank'. Your microwave? It'll beep in agreement." He took her hand once more. *"I will not leave you alone, Iris. That's a guarantee."* Frank stopped, Iris stared, then Frank continued. "So, why don't we skip all that and go right to the part where you say, 'Thank you, Frank. I'd love to marry you.'"

Iris sighed, and a tear rolled down her cheek, but she shook her head no.

Frank held Iris's cheek in his hand and wiped away the tear with his thumb. He wrapped his arms around her waist and drew her close. As they had done from the very first day they met, they locked eyes. "Marry me."

Iris's breath quickened as Frank leaned in and brushed his lips against hers. He touched his forehead to Iris's and whispered, "Iris, please, marry me." With their foreheads still touching, Frank could feel Iris's body trembling, yet she shook her head once more and whispered, "No, I can't."

Frank lifted his head. "Iris."

Iris met Frank's gaze. She stepped away, still shaking her head. Frank watched her as she wrestled with herself.

God, I know she wants this. I know I want this. But I guess that doesn't matter. What matters is if You want this for us. If You do, please, shine a bit more light on her next step.

Iris closed her eyes for a few moments, then she turned back toward Frank, and fixed her eyes softly on him. "Can we get a cat?"

Frank smiled. "We can get whatever you want."

Iris's eyes brimmed with tears. "I want you, Frank. I want you."

Frank took a step closer to her and held out his hand. "Then will you please marry me?" Iris took his hand and entwined her fingers with his then took the last step toward him. She reached up and wiped a tear from his cheek. She placed her hands on his chest, lifted her chin, and caressed his lips with her own.

They parted and Frank wrapped one of her curls around his finger. "Can I take that as a 'yes'?"

"Yes." Iris smiled, her body relaxing. "Thank you, Frank. I would love to marry you."

Frank let out a sigh of relief, releasing the tension

that had been in his own body for months. He smiled at Iris, then took her soundly in his arms, and kissed her in a way that a year ago, he didn't think possible.

They separated, and looked at each other, then Iris said, "You know, Frank, you can be a real pain."

"I know, but you love me anyway."

"Ayuh," Iris nodded her head.

Frank held out his hand, and Iris placed her hand in his. "I love you, Iris."

Iris took Frank's other hand and said, "And I love you." There they stood together as the easternmost contented couple in the United States.

Three weeks later, on a Thursday afternoon, Iris and Frank stood before the pastor at Eastport Community Church with Emma, David, and Violet at their sides. Here they exchanged vows neither thought they'd ever want to say again. With the giving and receiving of rings, and a kiss to seal their promises, Iris and Frank truly became Mr. and Mrs. Happy.

A month passed and Mrs. Happy sat at her desk and looked out the window of their cottage, watching her newly minted husband working to create a garden that would include a hornbeam tree planted near the birch tree. At her feet, Mosey, their adopted baby girl, wound herself in and out of Iris's legs, tripping over herself as she went.

Iris picked up the little white snowball, laid her in her lap, then pulled out her laptop. She opened it, brought up a blank page, and stared. She stroked Mosey and the kitten in turn, tried to nibble Iris's fingers. Iris smiled at the tiny bundle of fur, turned her attention back to the blank page, took a deep breath, then placing her fingers on the keyboard, she typed: *"That looks like about ten miles of bad road, let's take it!"*

A Note from the Author

Eastport, Maine, is a real place. It truly is the easternmost city in the United States, situated on the easternmost portion of Moose Island, Maine. My family visited Eastport and the surrounding area for ten days in 2011 and we had a fantastic time. We walked the path by the bay in downtown Eastport, we went on a whale watching tour, we visited Campobello Island and the Roosevelt estate. We drove through Perry and found the 45th parallel marker. We explored Machias and saw the Bad Little Falls, and we spent time in Lubec, at the West Quoddy Head Lighthouse where my children each took turns being the easternmost person in the United States. And we got terribly muddy walking on the bottom of the ocean at low tide in the Bay of Fundy.

When I began writing *Iris and Mo*, I needed a setting. Eastport immediately came to mind. I remembered it being a quirky little place, and I thought this easternmost city in the U.S., along with the surrounding areas, would provide me with ample material to explore. I didn't know how true that would turn out to be.

Almost all the locations mentioned in the book are real. To get into the town, you *can* make a left at Raye's

Mustard Mill and Museum which sits just behind the IGA. You can then follow Washington Street and make a right on Water Street. You can stop to pay respects to the Mermaid Statue overlooking the harbor, and the Fisherman Statue. You can have breakfast, lunch, or the occasional dinner at the WaCo Diner (and it really is pronounced 'whack-o'). You can visit the Tides Institute and Art Museum, or any number of galleries or shops. You can stroll along the path by the bay, and you can visit almost any of the other locales mentioned in the book.

If you time your trip well, you can also take part in one of the numerous festivals occurring during the year. Every festival or fair mentioned in the book is an actual event you can attend, although don't try to enter anything into the Machias Blueberry Festival jam and jelly contest. That was a total figment of my imagination.

While there are many things mentioned in the book that you *can* do, there are a few things you cannot. You cannot visit the Sunrise Inn, the Eastport Community Church or Eastport High School. These places are all fictitious. You also can't visit Iris's or Frank's homes, although, if you pay attention to the description in the book, you can figure out where their homes and the Sunrise Inn would be located if they did exist.

My husband and I returned to Eastport in August

2023. I called our trip my non-book-tour tour. I wanted to revisit all the book locations and see how they've changed over the years. Water Street bubbled with tourists and the fisherman statue still stood tall by the park. The mermaid statue, a beautiful addition to the harbor, arrived several years after our first visit and she looked lovely. The West Quoddy Head Lighthouse was undergoing some needed maintenance and repairs, and the globe that stood outside of the 45th Parallel Gift Shop (now closed) looked the worse for wear. The whale watching tour was a blast (we saw a minke whale, plenty of seals, a few porpoises, and a bald eagle), and even though it drizzled all day, we enjoyed the Machias Blueberry Festival and a visit to a working blueberry farm.

Many of the gardens that I'd remembered so fondly from my first visit no longer existed. A local told us the increasing deer population had decimated many of the community's patches of paradise, so most people had given up gardening as a hobby.

We breakfasted one morning at the WaCo Diner, and I must admit, I half expected Ben to walk in and call out his order to our server. Alas, he didn't, but we were treated to some locals and their colorful accents and stories.

While we were in the area, I scoped out other

locations for the next book in the Eastport Series, *A Good Place to Turn Around, Ben's story*. I hope you'll return to Eastport with me and find out what's next for Ben.

If you'd like to know more about Eastport, especially as represented in *Iris and Mo*, visit my website www.kidspitpub.com. There you'll find a photo gallery of the cast of characters for the entire Eastport Series. There are also photo galleries of the locations mentioned in the books, bonus chapters, other writings, links to places of interest in Eastport, and additional locations in Maine.

Thank you for spending some time with Iris and her friends. I hope you'll have the opportunity to visit Maine in the future. If you stop by Eastport, give the seals a wave from me and if you see Frank and Iris, tell them I said hello.

A Glossary of Maine Slang

Apiece – A measure of distance. How much distance? Hard tellin' not knowin'.

Ayuh – A simple yes

Chupta – "What are you up to?"

Cunnin' – Cute, mostly reserved for young ones

Dubber – One who is none too smart

Finest kind – The best or excellent

Flatlander – Tourists or anyone not from Maine

From away – A non-Mainer, very much like a flatlander. If you don't go back more than three generations of Mainers, you're still from away.

Gawmy - Clumsy

Hard tellin' not knowin' – I have no idea. Actually, I do. It means I have no idea.

Lobstah – Don't be a lunkhead. Say it out loud and you'll get it. Singular or plural, it's pronounced the same.

Lunkhead – Someone who is dull-witted or foolish, similar to a dubber

Right out straight – Busy, busy, busy

Stove up – To damage

Waggy – *Tired*

Wicked – An emphatic "very" or "extremely", as in this is wicked good lobstah, or it's wicked awful weather

Yessuh – Said in agreement. "He's a good one, yessuh."

362

About the Author

Marilyn K Blair is a wife, mother, teacher, businesswoman, musician, enthusiastic Philadelphia sports fan, and devoted woman of faith. An avid RV-er along with her husband, Jim, Maine has become their favorite place to visit since honeymooning there almost forty years ago. She is a lifelong resident of Pennsylvania and currently resides in the beautiful farm country of Lancaster County.

For bonus chapters, photos, and information about
the Eastport Series,
as well as other stories and devotions
visit www.kidspitpub.com

Contact Marilyn K Blair at KidSpitPub@gmail.com

Support your favorite authors – Tell a friend, spread the word,
and leave a review.